Nobody But Us

Nobody But Us

LAURE VAN RENSBURG

GRAND CENTRAL
PUBLISHING

NEW YORK   BOSTON

Copyright © 2022 by Laure Van Rensburg

Cover design by Sarah Congdon. Cover images from Stocksy and Shutterstock. Cover copyright © 2022 by Hachette Book Group, Inc.

Grand Central Publishing
Hachette Book Group
1290 Avenue of the Americas, New York, NY 10104
grandcentralpublishing.com
twitter.com/grandcentralpub

First published in 2022 in Great Britain by Michael Joseph, a division of Penguin Random House UK
First Grand Central Publishing edition: April 2022

Grand Central Publishing is a division of Hachette Book Group, Inc. The Grand Central Publishing name and logo is a trademark of Hachette Book Group, Inc.

The publisher is not responsible for websites (or their content) that are not owned by the publisher.

The Hachette Speakers Bureau provides a wide range of authors for speaking events. To find out more, go to www.hachettespeakersbureau .com or call (866) 376-6591.

LCCN: 2021952440

ISBNs: 9781538720462 (hardcover), 9781538720448 (ebook)

Printed in Canada

MRQ-T

10 9 8 7 6 5 4 3 2 1

To my mother, who always thought I would be a published author. Sorry it took so long.

"I desire the things that will destroy me in the end."
Sylvia Plath

The house will tell them what happened. Everything here tells a story. The truth will set you free, they say.

They're wrong.

It begins with the silent heartbeat of blue lights pulsing through the windows, before the outside world invades the space with thuds and footsteps. Through the open front door cold sneaks in and rushes up the stairs. The house shudders and comes to life.

It spreads with voices, which shatter the silence further. Gradually, a few words rise through the pandemonium of noises—*victim, unresponsive, Jesus Christ.* They belong to a police officer with a Burt Reynolds mustache. A shiny badge reads "Deputy Wilcox"—black letters etched on brass, the O almost scratched into another C. His eyes are full of questions as he tries to take in what happened here. He smells of coffee, the foam of it hemming the bristles of his mustache. Yellow teeth in need of cleaning peek from under his chapped lips. Palming his chin, he takes in a scene rarely witnessed in those quiet parts of the county. A car wreck, maybe, the odd wood-chopping accident. But this? This is what animals do to each other—and in the bowels of the forest, not in some fancy house. What's happened here stains the carpet and the walls with red and reeks. He closes his eyes, but the images cling to him, trapped behind his lids. They follow him as he heads back downstairs. All around, the house unfolds like a scene in a pulp novel.

On the third step lies a discarded heart on a broken chain.

A present to a girl who no longer exists. One of Wilcox's colleagues collects it, dropping it inside a little plastic bag where the romantic token becomes another clue to the gruesome events that have unfolded here. Once sealed, the bag joins others, mostly pregnant with what looks like shredded clothing. One of them holds the broken pieces of a mug.

On the first floor, there are more officers dotted around, more eyes asking questions, more chaos. An explosion of camera flashes; the static fuzz from police radios; the smack of latex gloves; a persistent smell which gets worse down here and forces Deputy Wilcox to breathe through his mouth. The stench of death and body fluids seeping out. Blood streaks the door frames and walls; the kitchen counter is smeared with it—riddles staining plaster and wood, written in cast-offs and spatters left to be deciphered. In the living room a wheelchair lies on its side like some wounded animal, while the charred remains of a bag smolder in the fireplace.

Everything here tells a story.

Leaving the mayhem behind, Deputy Wilcox shuffles toward the gaping mouth of the front door.

Outside, the sharp bite of cold air stings. Sunlight stains the horizon with pale yellow and orange, leading the way for a new day. No more overbearing clouds stretching over; blue has reclaimed the sky, where seagulls scream at the intruders disturbing the peace and quiet of the coast.

The snow out front is peppered with a trail of blood; at the end of it a gloved hand excavates a knife from its icy tomb. In the distance, the double doors of the garage yawn open and another officer on his haunches inspects the deep gashes in the flat front tire. Nobody was getting out.

Amid the askew police cars, there's an ambulance waiting. Behind its bulky shape and flashing lights, the woods have stopped being an ominous presence; trees have disentangled themselves from the darkness. Everything is different under the light of day. But even if the snow is shimmering now with beauty, beneath it the ground is still dead.

Two paramedics jump from the back of the ambulance. The air inside is flavored with the strong smell of ammonia. The mattress on the stretcher is thin and squeaks with every move.

"Where to, guys?" asks the deputy.

"Mercy General Hospital," replies the medic with blond hair in a low ponytail. He looks too young to be responsible for someone's life.

After the ambulance's doors slam shut, one word hangs in the air, acrid like sulfur from a lit match, one word that doesn't belong in this place.

Mercy.

Day One

One need not be a chamber to be haunted,
One need not be a house;
The brain has corridors surpassing
Material place.

Emily Dickinson

1. Ellie

If I'm not careful I could get hurt. Badly. Breathing evenly, I advance on a sidewalk encased in a sheet of ice where every step challenges my relationship with gravity. The big weekender bag in my hand and the heavy tote sitting on my shoulder threaten to tip me off balance. Enough packed for three days. But first, we need to get out of the city.

The car is only a yard away, but one step is all it takes—my right foot escapes my control, sliding sideways. Grabbing me by the arm, Steven breaks my fall before I end up an embarrassment on the sidewalk. My hip still aches from my previous fall a couple of days ago. Luckily, he wasn't there to witness that. My body sprawled on the snow after running out of the subway and slipping on the last step, the innards from my bag skidding across the ice. Me on all fours corralling my belongings, an additional obstacle for busy commuters with much better balance than me.

"Careful there, you don't want the trip to be over before it starts," he jokes, offering me one of his most charming smiles.

I need him for stability. Only once my balance is fully restored does he relieve me of the bag in my hand and drop it in the open trunk of the Lexus. Despite wearing dress shoes, he doesn't slip once.

"Sorry."

The apology burns my cheek a deep crimson, and I hastily stuff my body inside the car before I can humiliate myself further. I drop onto the passenger seat in a bundle of wool—layers of sweater, coat, gloves, a long navy scarf coiled around my neck and a sloppy beanie on my head. With a sharp shrug of his shoulders, Steven's coat slides down his arms. He folds it before laying it on the back seat, then he slips into the driver's seat in one swift, controlled move. On the other side of the gearbox, I wiggle in my seat, fighting to untangle myself from my clothes.

I'm in a deadlock with my coat when the air is stirred with the low humming of the phone vibrating on the dashboard. Before I can glance at the screen, the phone is in his hand. He smiles at whatever he reads before frowning.

"Is everything OK?" I ask, but he doesn't hear me, his attention firmly on his phone. "Is everything all right?" I repeat.

"Yes, sorry, it's fine, just work."

His expression worries me. "Do you have to go in?" One word from him and it could all be ruined. It's happened before. Just a couple of weeks ago, his text canceling our dinner at Nessia's came only a couple of hours before we were supposed to meet. The idea that our anniversary trip could be called off at such short notice finds its way under my skin and draws a shudder out of me. I fight the helpless panic, and the seat belt, which doesn't want to budge. The harder I tug, the less it moves. This can't be happening right now. His face doesn't give me any clue as to what his decision will be.

"Whatever they need, they can do without me. I'm all yours for the next three days," he says, his eyes locked with mine. And I believe him.

I sink into my seat and finally click my seat belt into place, ready for our first weekend away. Leaving work behind, he slips his phone in the slot next to the handbrake. The dying light of the screen winks, and it dawns on me: I haven't called

8

Connor back. His name flashed up on my phone while I packed, and my silent promise to call as soon as I'd finished was forgotten somewhere in the numerous back-and-forth trips between the bathroom and bedroom.

It's too late now.

The car silently drags away from the curb, tires biting on to the grit littering the road. As we trundle into the afternoon traffic, Steven's eyes flick to his rearview mirror, but they don't flick straight back to the road ahead. His gaze has snagged on something that doesn't want to let go and deepens the line between his brow. I squirm in my seat, but—as we round the corner—all I catch through the misted rear window is the smudge of a fuchsia coat and a shock of blonde curls.

"First trip of 2015, then," Steven says before I can ask the question shaping at the back of my throat.

"First trip together."

"First six-month anniversary."

Bumper to bumper, we crawl out of Manhattan under a cloudy sky painted orange, an unmistakable sign that it's about to snow again. Flakes have been piling up for days now, cluttering sidewalks and driveways and accounting for an increase in broken limbs and mild concussions. The conditions are unavoidable: the forecast is similar down Chesapeake Bay.

The traffic improves after we leave Newark in the rearview mirror. Steven knows where we're going, but the GPS feeds him hints on how to get there. Relaxing in the passenger seat, I imagine us at our destination, the weekend unfolding in my mind perfectly.

With still over an hour left before we get there, the fuel needle indicates we have roughly a quarter tank left, and Steven steers the car into the next exit, leading to a gas station.

"Can you get me a bag of Hershey's Kisses?" I ask as I leave him to fill up the car.

In the meantime, I get the bathroom key from the station attendant—a young girl with bright cobalt hair, wearing a polyester uniform and a look of boredom on her face. The ground is slippery with slushy snow; I allow the wall to guide me around to the back of the building.

The crisp January air bites the skin exposed above my scarf wrapped around my neck. I bury my nose deeper in, breathing through the soft cashmere. A gift from Steven. I don't even want to think how much it costs, but he knows I hate the cold. I am not built for it. Still, I would take cold over damp. Cold only gets beneath the layers of your clothes; damp will insinuate itself beneath your skin and not let go. I shiver.

Inside the windowless room, the air is soured by the acrid smell of urine and cheap bleach. Breathing through my mouth, I hover above the bowl, trying to pee as quickly as possible, ignoring the free literature of profound one-liners and questionable art scribbled on the wall.

Only a hundred miles separate us from our final destination, and then: nobody else but us, for three days. Three days. Seventy-two hours, 4,320 minutes of us with nowhere to hide from each other. I hope I don't mess this up. Apparently, you don't really know someone until you've gone away with them. Where did I read that? What will I learn about Steven this weekend that I don't already know? I shrug and finish, before deciding against washing my hands in a basin that seems to be growing new forms of life.

Deep breath in. Outside, the air is heavy with gas fumes. I walk back to the main store just in time to see the attendant blushing at whatever Steven has said to her. She fiddles with the army of bracelets snaked around her wrist, looking down as she smiles and replies. Their exchange grounds me to my spot by the door, the steam of my breath making my face wet beneath the layers of my scarf. Frozen, I watch his lips move, imagining what words might be crossing their threshold. The artificial light catches in the silver threading the hair at his temple, adding a glow to his regal profile.

"Sorry."

The word jolts me out of my trance, and I sidestep to let a middle-aged woman with oversized glasses and a kind face open the door. As I follow her in, the bathroom key weighs heavy in my hand.

Inside, the scene has changed; Steven swipes his black AMEX and receipt from the counter as cashier girl offers me a professional smile. Once they're finished, I hand her the key. Steven wraps his arm around my waist, and I nestle into his embrace.

"They didn't have any Hershey's Kisses, but I got you a bag of Reese's Peanut Butter Cups," Steven says as we walk away, leaving the blue-haired girl behind.

"Thank you." Reese's are his favorites, not mine; the over-abundance of peanut butter always makes me feel sick. Before I can add anything, he hands me his credit card receipt.

The car beeps open in an invitation for us to get out of the cold. Flakes have just started falling again, finding their way in the gap between the scarf and my skin—little pinpricks of cold which send a shiver across my shoulders. On the other side of the car, Steven cracks his neck.

"I can drive the rest of the way if you want," I offer, making small folds in the receipt from the girl with blue hair.

"No, I'm fine."

"Are you sure? It's a long drive, I don't mind."

"It's OK. I don't want you to have to worry with all that snow on the road."

"You know I'm a good driver."

"Of course you are. But you just relax and we'll be there soon," he says as he slips into the driver's seat.

Back on the freeway, the air inside the car is thick with the growing reality of this weekend. As the heat spills out of the air vents, I glance at Steven's profile illuminated intermittently by the artificial glow of highway lights and passing cars. Light and shadows travel across his face like fleeting thoughts.

My eyes keep flitting between the constellation of brake lights ahead and his face, but they settle on him—the lines of his straight nose, high forehead, the curve of his bottom lip. A swarm of feelings swells up inside my chest, so strong they threaten to spill out into the car. My nails dig into the fleshy part between my thumb and index finger until the pain overshadows everything else. I can't believe we've made it to six months—so much has stood in the way lately—but we've left all that in the city, and all that remains is us. *Nobody but us.*

As we cross state lines, the droning rhythm of the highway settles heavy on my lids. Tilting the back of the seat a little further, I unfurl, settling in for the rest of the drive down to Chesapeake Bay. My feet fight with my tote bag on the floor for the space I need.

"Why don't you drop it on the back seat?"

"No, it's OK." Leaning over, I push the bag against the bottom of my seat so I can finally stretch my legs into the footwell.

"That thing always looks like it's about to explode." His laugh billows inside the confined space of the car. Unzipping the bag, I stuff the unopened packet of Reese's Cups in.

"What have you got in there?" he asks, throwing a side

glance only to see me lean further and close it back. "Hiding a present for me?"

"No." I definitely don't want him to see what I've got for him, at least not now. "Just the usual. Wallet, toiletries, books, stuff. You know."

"Books? You brought homework on our weekend?"

"Yes. No. Just research, not homework. I've got this essay on Dostoevsky coming up. Maybe I can do some reading."

His eyes leave the ribbon of asphalt unearthed by headlights to glance at me before they return to the road.

"Still working on that? Which one is it? *The Idiot*?"

"No, *The Devils*."

He laughs again. "That's great. You're telling me that you've brought along a bunch of Russian philanderers and murderers on our weekend away."

"Well, *professor*, I thought you could do with some competition for my attention. Plus, you can always help me discuss 'pride and guilt in *The Devils*' if we run out of things to say."

"Hopefully, I can keep you busy enough so we don't have to talk about Dostoevsky," he says, his hand leaving the grooves of the steering wheel to stroke my cheek.

"Well, we'll see," I reply.

His hand on the back of my neck, he pulls me toward him for a quick kiss.

2. Steven

Steven cuts off the engine. His phone has been vibrating on and off for the last forty-five minutes, and the buzzing seems unusually loud in the confined space of the car. Next to him, Ellie is still asleep in the passenger seat. Twisting the ring on his little finger, he reads the string of messages which have been demanding his attention, threatening to wake up Ellie.

Miss U xxx.

Need 2 talk xxx.

Why R U not answering?

I know about her. Know U R with her.

The last one pulls his brow together, not at the explicit assertion of knowledge but at what is implied, the power derived from knowing, of how it could be used.

He hasn't seen J. since he made the decision to focus on Ellie, though it's fair to say the relationship had run its course anyway. Despite her constant messages, he hasn't called J. back, and the few times he's seen her loitering out-side Richmond Prep, he's been deep in conversation with a colleague and slipped away before she could approach him. Her clinginess has left a sour taste in the back of his throat; such childish behavior. She really doesn't compare to Ellie. The timing of this trip couldn't have been better.

He stares at the pallid glow of the screen, formulating an answer. He types the starts of sentences that convey too much or too little, deleting them until his steadfast fingers produce a simple answer, one that will buy him time.

Bad reception here. Will call as soon as I can.

He slides his phone back into his breast pocket, determined not to let what might be unfolding in New York spoil his weekend. Not with what he has planned. On the dashboard, the receipt Ellie's fingers have folded into a tiny crane stares back at him.

He shifts in his seat for a better view of Ellie. She sleeps, still restrained by the zigzag of her seat belt, curled into a ball under a caramel rainbow of hair: strands of butterscotch entwined with fudge and deeper burnt toffee. Fingers curled, the end loop of her infinity tattoo—with its top part that doesn't fully touch—peers from under her sleeve. He grimaces at the sight. Others he's sure wouldn't. He imagines boys kissing the inked symbol as they worked their way up her arm. But she's his. Casting them out of his mind, he brushes the hair from her face, revealing lips swollen with sleep, puckering as if sucking on an invisible thumb.

Before she fell asleep, civilization disappeared around them in layers. They had joked about it, waving it goodbye as they traded the bright lights of the freeway for the darkness of countryside roads. First to go, the bright built-up areas, the sprawling suburbs, then the odd retail parks hemming the edges of towns, the isolated motels. Finally, the other cars on the asphalt of the freeway, leaving just his car against the black canvas of the forest except for a pair of headlights that gleamed faintly in his rearview mirror until they turned off the main road, the lonesome lights behind them an almost fateful distraction. He'd nearly missed the dirt track that served as private entrance from the main road—a small dark mouth amid the tree line.

"Ellie, wake up. We're here."

Ellie stirs, blinking at him, and the urge to kiss her is

back. She rises, looking ahead, and they both stare at the outline of the house caught in the car's headlights. Even though it's only two stories high, it towers over them; he has to crane over the steering wheel to take in the whole structure, which seems made of contradictions: wood and glass, shapes that blend into the landscape as much as they stand out from its background. The lights of the SUV reflecting in the oversized windows give the building a glaring look. He feels oddly observed and judged, as if the house is silently deciding whether he's good enough to spend three days within its walls. At ground level, beyond the beams of the car headlights, the world disappears under an opaque darkness from which escapes the whisper of waves lapping the shore—a hint of the ocean that exists somewhere inside the void.

"We're here," Ellie repeats, as if she's addressing the house on the other side of the windshield, and her words break the spell it has on him. "It's so dark."

"Well, let's go in and change that, shall we?"

Sliding out of the driver's seat and into the freezing air, he rushes to the trunk and picks up their luggage while Ellie retrieves the keys from a lock box by the front steps. Bags in hand, he fights against a sudden gust of wind that lifts fresh snow off the ground and swirls it about before he climbs up the porch's steps. Above his head a jagged line of icicles hems the porch roof, their tapered edges glinting under some unseen light. He stops behind her as she struggles to work the keys into the lock with—for her only light—the pallid glow from her phone screen.

"Hurry up, I'm freezing here," he tells her, stomping his feet, head retracted into his shoulders.

"Sorry. I'm trying."

She drops the keys, and the cursing that comes under her

steamy breath draws a smile to his face. Finally, one of the keys slots into place.

"It just needs a little jiggle," she says, followed by the welcomed clicks of the moving lock.

They enter, before he closes the door with his foot. As they step further in, the slight echo of his shoes on the tiles hints at the size of the space. His eyes haven't adjusted, and Ellie has disappeared inside the darkness of the entrance hall. As Steven drops their suitcases, she shrieks at the unexpected thud, and he moves deeper inside toward her voice.

"Shit, what was that?" he asks as something catches his feet.

"That's my bag. I think some light would be a good idea, professor."

Following her instructions, he backtracks to the front door, feeling his way up and down the wall until he recognizes the smooth plastic curve of a light switch.

With a flick, light floods the room to reveal Ellie in its center, squinting and disoriented. She's lost in the middle of the space, and he smiles to think of them in this big house, in the middle of nowhere. In front of him, she stands, a lonely piece on the checkered floor of the spacious lobby—a white queen alone on the chessboard. She smiles at him. The opposing king, ready to conquer her.

Every time she blinks those big doe eyes at him, a tightness spreads in his groin. Now that they are finally here, the time ahead takes on a more defined shape. Three days of cozy dinners, exploring the coast, enjoying each other's company, each other's bodies. And no distractions, no lectures, no assignment deadlines. No being reasonable; no one else around to share her with. Out here, he will have her undivided attention. The things they could do out here, no-body to see them, not having to worry about what the neigh-bors might hear. This place offers no restraints.

He had his doubts at first, as it was all so last-minute. But going away together might turn out to be a fantastic idea.

3. Steven

After kissing him, Ellie volunteers to head back out to pick up the groceries they left in the car. Steven watches her as she opens the front door and is swallowed by a swirl of snowflakes.

"The master is right at the top of the stairs," she calls over her shoulder and smiles, blinking away the flakes caught in the comma of her lashes before disappearing completely into the night.

He grabs their bags, and his strides swallow the steps of the impressive glass, metal, and wood staircase two at a time in search of the bedroom—a place where Ellie's eagerness to please can always be put to good use. At the top of the stairs, a series of doors litters the walls on either side. He heads right, leaving the exploration for later.

The master bedroom, like the rest of the house so far, commands his attention. He hesitates, lingering in the doorway, taking in the dramatic almost floor-to-ceiling windows sprawling in front of him and the wall of trees hemming the other side. A slight unease spreads inside him at the tall, dark shadows swaying in the wind.

Dropping the bags on the emperor-size bed, he carefully takes out his folded clothes one at a time. Sliding a shirt over a hanger, he smooths out the creases from the fabric before hanging it in the walk-in closet. Next to his lies Ellie's bag, bulging with whatever clothes she has jammed in there. Her mess and scattiness have always driven him crazy—from her inability to hang her coat, instead opting to fling it on the back of chair or the arm of his sofa, to whatever junk she stuffs in and lugs around in that big shoulder bag of hers. He had to draw the line at her dog-earing books. The first time she folded the corner of a page in front of him, he jumped off the sofa and snatched the book right out of her hands before she could inflict any further damage. He had laughed to soothe the startled expression on her face before giving her a bookmark. She had teased him, called him old-fashioned. But she never folded a corner again.

Standing at the window, he searches for her silhouette by the car down below, but all he can make out are the footprints she has left behind mingled with his before the floodlight cuts out. Listening to the silence, he slowly carves out noises through the open bedroom door: Ellie moving about downstairs. He imagines her in the vast space of the ground floor, spinning around looking for the right cupboard, disoriented by her new surroundings—he knows unfamiliar environments often overwhelm her. Like they did at Jeffrey's party.

The first time he took her to a function was only a month after they started seeing each other. She had wrapped herself around his arm, waiting for him to introduce her to his friends and colleagues. She tried to act confident, but he felt a slight pressure of her fingers on his bicep every time someone seemed to approach them.

"Good evening, Jeffrey."

"Steven, so glad you could make it. How's your father?" Jeffrey shook his hand, and Steven squeezed his too hard.

"He's good, out and about promoting his new book."

Whenever in academic circles, it was always the same. People wanting to know how his father was, and what he was up to, leaving Steven perpetually living in the shadow of the great man. Hopefully not for much longer; the dean of Columbia had been casually talking to him about a position in their Literature Department, taking over the "Intro to Literature" module—a position his old man held himself thirty-odd years ago—finally earning Steven the coveted title of professor at an Ivy League institution and the first step on the tenure-track there. Taking his position at Barnard College three years ago had finally paid off. Soon he could say goodbye to the small campus and his two days a week at Richmond Prep, giving AP English Literature classes to the privileged youth of the Upper East Side. He was on the cusp of great things, and soon he would be known for more than just being Professor Stewart Harding's son.

"And who is this?" Jeffrey asked, studying the company wrapped around Steven's arm. Steven followed his gaze. Damn, she looked amazing in that strapless dress. He was so right for suggesting to her she should wear it.

"This is Ellie Masterson. Ellie, this is Jeffrey Kirkland. He works in the Mathematics Department at NYU."

"Hello, Jeffrey."

"Please call me Jeff. Only this old fart and my mother call me Jeffrey." He laughed as he lightly kissed the hand she offered him. "Nice to meet you, Ellie."

Steven smiled, proud of his standards and his ability not to compromise them. He hated nicknames or diminutives, especially for men—so tacky and demeaning, like being turned into a cheaper version of oneself. He had been worried when Ellie first introduced herself to him. *And that's short for?* Ellie, she'd replied. Just plain, simple Ellie. Although there's nothing plain about her.

Leaving them to their conversation, he headed for the bar, where he ordered a bourbon. He lingered, observing at a distance Ellie listening to Jeffrey telling her God only knew what old stories about their time at Princeton. She nodded, tucking her hair behind her ears at regular intervals, otherwise keeping her arms crossed just under her breasts.

He wasn't the only one watching her. On the other side of the bar, a small group of professors' wives—Jeffrey's included—were talking in hushed tones, glancing toward Ellie. Steven raised his glass when they noticed him, acknowledging their presence and open disapproval of the age gap between him and his date. Male eyes lingered over Ellie too. He didn't mind those. On the contrary, they could covet and flirt all they wanted; she was still going home with him tonight. Turning away, he motioned to the barman for a refill.

"Hey." Ellie's hand settled on his forearm.

"Missing me already?"

"I don't really know any of those people. All those academics, it's intimidating." She smiled at the professors' wives before dropping her voice. "Plus, I'm sure those women think I should be in their homes babysitting their kids rather than being here as someone who's seventeen years my senior's date."

"Twenty-three is a bit old for a babysitter."

"You know what I mean."

"Come with me." He laced his fingers with hers as he led her toward the upstairs bathroom. The party had enough guests for their twenty-minute absence to go unnoticed.

"Steven!"

His name slices through the air like an arrow. Rushing out of the bedroom, he barrels down the stairs, adrenaline pumping. Something about this house unnerves him—though he can't work out what exactly. He shouldn't have left her alone.

When he arrives in the lobby, the air is still.

"Ellie?"

Maybe it's the modern structure setting him on edge, the coldness of the glass, the impersonal straight lines and sharp edges. He trusts older buildings, those with history, stones that have stood through decades or centuries of rough weather, floorboards that don't line up from warping under the passage of a hundred feet.

"In here," her disembodied voice calls from the room on the right, which turns out to be a spacious living/dining room.

The panoramic view through the glass wall leaves him speechless and bewildered. Now, all is in darkness, but Steven knows that the forest sprawls toward the house until it meets the ocean, crashing waves still audible despite the thick glazing. Nature invading the modern setting of the room.

"Look at this," Ellie says, her attention on the opposite side.

Turning around, he is met by a wall lined in its height and width with books.

"How many do you think there are?" she asks, her head still tilted up.

Running his hand down his face, he frowns at her. "Christ, Ellie, I thought something had happened to you."

Any other time, he would have loved to lose himself in such an impressive mini-library, unearthing whatever literary treasures hid among those shelves: a first edition, an unusual dedication. But this isn't what this weekend is about, being lost with Ellie in the middle of Chesapeake Bay.

"Sorry, I just had to show you this." The excitement fizzles out of her voice.

"I know, thanks. I'm just beat from night driving. Let's have a look tomorrow." His smile coaxes her out of hiding.

"Right behind you."

He climbs the stairs as Ellie lags behind.

"Oh, crap." She is still standing in the entrance hall.

"What is it now?"

"There's no cell reception here," she replies, staring at her phone.

"Are you sure? I just…"

He pulls out his phone, and the two bars he had back in the car have vanished. He saunters up and down a few steps, but the screen doesn't change. It looks like they will have to deal with temperamental cell reception during their stay on top of the temperamental weather. At least this drastically reduces the chances of J. getting hold of him and spoiling his time with Ellie.

"Come on," Steven says, slipping his phone back in his pocket. "I'm sure you can survive without your phone for the next three days."

4

August 28

Yesterday you held the door open at the end of the day. When I crossed the threshold, your hand rested on the small of my back, guiding me through with the slightest pressure from your fingertips. I stiffened at the unexpected touch. I searched your face, but you gave no indication of whether your gesture had a purpose or was merely a reflex.

You're opening up to me. Kindred spirits who have found each other in this place, this maze of hallways and rooms, this sea of anonymous faces. You're like me, you don't have anyone here. This is new for you too.

Twisting that ring on your little finger, you said, "It's nice to speak to someone who understands."

Today, I caught you looking at me. At first, I dismissed it as a coincidence. I just happened to look up at the time your eyes, sweeping the space, landed on me. Why would you be looking at me on purpose? I'm just a nobody. Not that interesting. But when I dared look again, your eyes were waiting for me. And they had brought your smile along too.

5. Ellie

The condensation from the mirror disintegrates under my hand to reveal a blurry version of my face with the ensuite in the background. I wasn't sure we would make it here. He's been distracted, his gaze unfocused. I thought I was losing him. I've had doubts too. The latest one—glimpsed through a misted rear window—wore a blurred fuchsia coat and a mane of blonde curls. He's been distant, and then that awful argument at the gallery...how close it all got to falling apart. Just to think of it wakes up the dread in the pit of my stomach. Now it all hinges on this anniversary weekend unfolding perfectly. But I can make it work.

The clammy air of the bathroom fills me with expectation. I sit on the toilet, curved spine, elbows resting on my knees. This is happening, I'm here with him. Me and Steven, away and alone together. The thought prickles down my spine. As I stand, the towel around my body drops to the floor, and I get dressed, fumbling with the buttons of my pajama top—Steven's Christmas gift to me even though we had promised not to buy each other anything.

One of those nights when we stayed up late drinking wine, I confessed I've had a thing about wearing men's sleepwear ever since I watched *Roman Holiday* as a kid. Audrey Hepburn in Gregory Peck's stripy pajama set mesmerized me. He surprised me with the box a couple of days before Christmas—inside a replica of the famous pajamas. His thoughtfulness caught me unprepared. It left me speechless and a little bereft. What do you get the man who lives on Central Park

West and wears an Omega watch as an everyday accessory? Of course, as soon as I tried them on, he was only too eager to take them off. He said he loved the way they look on his bedroom floor.

The tinge of sentimentality passes, and I concentrate again as I struggle with another button that misses its eyelet. *Come on, I can do this.*

The idea of him on the other side of the wall and nobody else for miles fills me with a mix of excitement and apprehension. Hurrying out of the bathroom, I cross the bedroom under Steven's surprised gaze.

"What is it?"

"Nothing. I'm just getting a glass of water from downstairs. Do you want anything?"

"No, thanks," he answers as he slips under the cover. "I'll be waiting." The words come wrapped in one of his charming smiles which pulls me toward him, fingers losing their grip on the door handle.

"I'll just be a minute," I reply, breaking the connection before disappearing through the door.

The hallway is sunk in near darkness, but I don't bother turning the light on. The opposite wall is lined with three doors. I stare at them, almost expecting one to open with no idea of what or who would be on the other side. I have an urge to lock them even though there's nobody else here, just furniture—I imagine—in stasis, waiting for a purpose.

I grew up in so many different houses. They were just shells of plaster and wood with hollow rooms to empty our boxes into until the next move. Apart from one place, one that sneaked up on me. But that had nothing to do with the house, the town or the great weather. All those moves . . . that was one of the reasons there were so many people at Dad's funeral. Twenty-nine years of collecting friends and acquaintances from the myriad places he called home one time or another. That was Dad's talent. Me, not so much. *Just fake it 'til you make it, Bug,* he would say. The hallway blurs, and I blink away the sadness.

I leave the memories behind and make my way toward the stairs. Stopping halfway, I face the banister, hands resting on the dark mahogany. I lean forward, the wood pressing against my stomach. Fifteen feet below, the checkered floor of the foyer only exists in shades of grays. I tiptoe, edging forward, playing with gravity. Deep breaths fill me with the stillness of the night. *Nobody but us.* The heaviness of the words settles inside me, and the heels of my feet reconnect with the carpet, the faint creak from a floorboard hidden beneath.

Down in the kitchen, water gurgles as the glass fills up. Once finished, I linger, taking in the silence, the intimidating darkness. The window is a black square, cut into a shadowed wall. The quietness outside is unhinging, and I pull the glass of water tight against my chest. Manhattan is always full of noises, lights from cars or other apartments, the presence of people across the street, or in the floors above or below. Out here, who knows how many miles away the nearest person is? People are just a fading memory—like those disaster films where someone survives the apocalypse on an isolated farm and has no idea if the rest of civilization is still around.

As my eyes adjust to the darkness outside, a shadow shifts by the tree line. My body freezes. There's no noise, blocked by the double glazing insulating us. Do they have bears in Maryland? Maybe not bears...wolves? The shape moves again. I inch toward the window, drawn to the potential danger outside, needing to put a name to it. My breath comes shallow and quick. I stare at the shadow until all the rest of the world melts away, and we are the only two things left.

A sudden weight crashing on my shoulder sends an electric bolt of fear down my spine and snatches a scream out of me.

"It's only me."

"God, Steven, you made me jump."

He laughs at my skittish behavior.

"I thought I saw something." I turn back toward the window, but all that is left outside is the wind playing with the snow.

"Probably a raccoon looking for food," he replies, crossing the room to the back door. He tries the handle, which doesn't budge. Content with the result, he comes back to me and weaves his arms around my waist.

"Come to bed."

Upstairs, I pick up my book from the nightstand and settle under the duvet. Before I can find the correct page, Steven grabs it and tosses it on the floor with one debonair move. "Sorry, Dostoevsky, your presence is not requested tonight."

"That's shameful coming from a literature professor."

He kisses me, slow at first, but the longer his lips stay on mine, the hungrier his mouth becomes, straying on to my cheeks and neck. His hand finds mine under the sheets and guides it down. Like the first time we slept together. That night he guided me too, showed me his rhythm, how he liked it. I paid attention, eager to please. The body under his clothes had surprised me, not the body of a teacher, no flesh softened by hours of sitting at a desk, grading papers. I stroked taut slabs of muscles, hard and smooth like rocks polished by the sea.

His mouth and his mind are lost somewhere in the curves of my neck, his hot breath blowing in my ear, while his fingers easily free the buttons of my pajamas, confident I want this as much as he does.

For a moment as I listen to the night, my mind is distracted. On the other side of the closed curtains, the wind howls and raps against the window like an invisible madman demanding to be let in, seeking shelter from the world being ripped apart. It's fascinating how the thick glass keeps it at bay, how it also keeps things in here from getting out. As the last button pops, Steven pushes the fabric over the slopes of my shoulders. My arms freed, I throw them around him. His hand cups my cheek, fingers resting on the curve of my neck. He smiles, the gentle pressure of his fingers pushing my head down, where he wants me.

A noise wakes me up. Lifting my head off the pillow, I listen to the silence, searching for a sign of whether it came from out there or from inside my dream. As my eyes adapt to the night, doors cut themselves out from the darkness; the one to the ensuite, the walk-in closet, the one leading to the hallway.

A faint creak, and my imagination is fully awake, filling my head with words from *The Haunting of Hill House*, images from *The Shining*, convincing me that if I look up there will be someone with dislocated limbs crawling on the ceiling. Next to me, Steven breathes softly from a place of deep sleep, one arm slung over my body, his embrace of no comfort to me. I want him to wake up without having to prompt him, so he can sigh at my irrational fears before pulling me close and burying a kiss and a "get back to sleep" in my hair.

Instead, I collapse back into my pillow under the weight of my childishness. This house isn't old enough to be haunted. It's not some decrepit manor of weathered stones, peeling wallpaper and a long history of tragic deaths; it's an architect's house made of glass and steel. Although—the thought creeps in unbidden—perhaps houses could be like people. Haunted at any age.

Buried deep under the covers, I shut my eyes and will myself back to sleep. Maybe houses are not haunted regardless of how old they are; maybe we just bring our own ghosts and sometimes we leave them behind after we're gone. There is another faint creak coming from the void on the other side of my closed lids: the house telling me I might be mistaken. Warning me that this was the wrong place to come to.

6

October 17

You called me beautiful, and the compliment caught me by surprise. Smiling, you edged closer until there was no space left between us.

You said, "What you do to me…I just can't help myself."

Your lips brushed against mine, back and forth. I forgot how to breathe. Then it happened. The firm pressure of your mouth, the slow movement of your tongue.

You were kissing me.

My body froze, scared to disrupt the status quo, to give you a reason to stop. Your arms closed in an embrace, drawing me closer and sending a warm tightness between my legs. Your hands lingered in the small of my back until they latched on to the t-shirt you'd given me. You pulled it over my head, drawing the curtain on the point of no return. You filled me with possibilities, so I dared stroke the side of your face. We kissed for ages and then you guided my hand inside your boxers.

You said, "Is this OK?"

You were smooth and hard in my hand. The work of my fingers snatched a sigh from you. Your pleasure came from me. Your fingers drew moans from me, they knew things about my body that I didn't.

On top of me, the weight of your body crushed mine. Pain and pleasure strangled me. Holding on to you, my fingers dug in your damp flesh.

"OK?" you asked. With a blank mind, I nodded.

You moved, slowly at first, then more quickly. The world around me changed. You were changing me too, making me into something different, something new. You changed too, trading control for pleasure. Increased rhythm until frenzied. Eyes shut tight, I held on.

Hollow, you collapsed on top of me. I held on, never wanting to let go of you or the storm of feelings sweeping through my body. As you rolled onto your side, I was freed from your weight but not from the bond we had just created. I wanted to ask what all of this meant, who we were now, but every word I thought of died before reaching my mouth.

In the bathroom, with the water running, I stared at the image in the mirror, looking for changes in the lines or colors of my face, the shine in my eyes. Maybe they seemed a little wider. On the side of the sink your ring winked at me. I slipped it on; it felt loose and heavy on my finger. Bringing my hand to my face, I smelled you on my fingertips. I closed the tap without washing my hands and returned the ring.

You said, "What happened…" I stopped, waiting for you to crush my heart and put an end to what had barely started. "You can't tell anybody about it. People wouldn't understand, and I would get into trouble."

I woke up this morning, the warmth from yesterday still radiating south of my belly button. For once, I'm looking forward to today. Watching the others. While I sit, and eat, or walk alone. I don't care anymore. I don't feel alone any more.

They don't know what your mouth tastes like.

Stretching on my back, I smiled as my hand stroked my abdomen. As the memory of our kiss and the feel of your lips on mine filled my head, my fingers slipped below the elastic of my underwear.

7. Steven

He props himself on his elbow. Beneath him, Ellie sleeps on her side, her body curved into a question mark. Last night, she lay on her stomach, awake and biting her lower lip. He had brushed her hair off her back, kissing the knobs of her spine, following the ridge down the sunken plane of her lower back. She had followed his every move, arched into him until they had exhausted each other. The memory stirs something in him, a hunger that never seems to be fully sated. He could have her again right now just to hear how she whispers his name when he's moving inside her. There's nothing to stop him.

He meant it the other night: she stimulates him physically and intellectually. He can't believe it's been six months already. Most of his relationships fizzle out long before they reach that milestone. From the first night they slept together, she was the one who stayed. She has this inexplicable hold on him, a puzzle he cannot solve, bringing him back to her no matter how far he strays. He smiles—Ellie. The girl who stayed. That dominion worries him sometimes, that it will compromise his freedom, but recently his growing desire to explore a deeper and fuller relationship with her has surprised him. He has been reckless in the last few weeks, but no more. She's the girl for him, and the idea of her being with anybody else makes his jaw tense.

What would she do without him? Only last week, he turned up at their date to find some young, cocky wolf of Wall Street chatting her up at the bar, invading her personal space. He wasn't fooled by the polite smile plastered on her face, barely concealing how uncomfortable she was. She needed him to rescue her, which he did, slipping his arm around her waist to pull her in for a kiss. By the time he pulled away, the intruder had turned his back on them.

Instinctively, his gaze drifts toward the closet door and what hides in his bag before settling back on her. The idea of lifting her top, pressing his lips against the heat of her skin hardens inside him until the fantasy is disturbed by a soft growl from his stomach. The glowing digits on the alarm clock remind him that it's past ten, and breakfast is overdue.

He's flipping his third pancake when one of the chairs behind him scrapes against the tiles.

"You could have woken me up." Her voice croaks with crumbs of sleep still caught in her throat.

"I thought about that," he replies, smiling. "But you looked so peaceful I decided against it."

"Smells delicious."

"Bearing in mind it's almost eleven, I thought we could just do brunch."

"Great, what are we having?"

"Pancakes, bacon and eggs."

"Shouldn't I be the one making breakfast on our romantic weekend?" Turning around, he catches her smirking at him, hair piled up on her head and a rogue smudge of mascara just below her left eye. She's the only one who can make messy look attractive to him. Sitting on a high stool, she rests her chin in her hand, the lines of her body swallowed by the oversized pajamas he bought her for Christmas.

"It's 2015, not the 1950s. Haven't you heard about gender equality?"

"Try telling that to my stepmom." Ellie laughs.

The coffeemaker joins their conversation with loud splutters.

On the other side of the kitchen island, Steven drops a new lump of batter onto the pan, which responds with a hiss. The smells of a fresh brew and sweet, warm pancakes compete to fill the air with the promise of a perfect day.

"You're making me feel guilty. Let me help." She hops off the high stool, not waiting for an answer.

She pitches in, getting mugs and maple syrup from the cupboard, retrieves napkins from one of the drawers. He smiles at her and their game of playing house as he sets the tower of pancakes on the counter. Leaning over, he buries a kiss in her hair before fetching the bacon from the oven while she pours the coffee. The scene surprises him; he has never been the domesticated kind, quite the opposite. He always hated the dull repetitions of marital life. He always believed he was made for more.

"What's this?" Sitting again, she nods toward the mound in her napkin.

He smiles in response, as she retrieves the little blue box underneath. Surprise and excitement flash in her eyes; her fingers work on the white ribbon. She looks so young. He can see the little girl she was on Christmas mornings in her movements, and the creases around her eyes.

"Steven, I love it," she says, lifting the heart-shaped pendant dangling from its silver chain. "Could you?"

She hands him the necklace back, and he passes the chain around her neck before securing the clasp.

"Really, you're spoiling me. Thank you." She kisses him, and her gratitude tastes of spearmint toothpaste.

She looks at him, a faint smile on her face, her fingers resting on the silver heart, and something tightens in his throat.

"Come on, the food's getting cold."

Settling next to her, he works around his plate, slicing a

piece of egg white first, then a piece of bacon, before spearing the corner of a pancake, finally dipping the layers on his fork in the maple syrup. Next to him, Ellie dissects her food into small pieces, which she rearranges around her plate as much as she eats them. He wonders if she always fusses like that or if it's something she only does around him.

"What's your mother like?" she asks while nibbling on a strip of bacon.

The intimate nature of her question interrupts his meticulous cutting. His relationships never reach a stage that requires such openness.

"She's a very loving woman, very sweet. I think you'd like her." At the end of his fork a lone piece of pancake drowns in a puddle of maple syrup.

That's as far as he can allow himself to go. Margot Harding is a loving wife and mother. Too loving. As a child he watched her, desperate for her husband's attention, happy to accept anything from him, his numerous indiscretions included. Grateful for any scraps he would toss her way, forsaking any dignity she might have had in the process. Years later, she clung to Steven the way she had her husband—with fingers sticky with desperation. He always wondered if she clung to him or the part of him that was his father's. As a child he had relished her attention, but as a teenager her love stifled him, and he pulled away heavy with shame mixed with disgust—how could he respect her if she couldn't respect herself? Thinking of his mother for too long always brought the same anger at her weak nature.

"What should we do after this?" Ellie asks with lips wet with syrup.

"Why don't we get dressed and go for a walk in the woods? Explore our surroundings."

She glances at the window. Under a gray eiderdown of

clouds, a white sheet of snow stretches to the edge of the forest. "Are you sure? It looks really cold outside."

"Maybe, but at least it's not snowing." Instead of giving him an answer, she disappears into her mug, taking a long gulp. "Once we're back, we'll have an excuse to lounge in front of the fireplace," he adds.

They get ready, hiding their bodies under layers and thermals, while he tries to remove hers at every opportunity. She fights his hands, chastising them with playful slaps.

She finally puts an end to their campaign, imprisoning his fingers by lacing them with hers. He lets her win this round as he allows her to pull him off the bed.

"Is this what you're wearing?"

His question stops her tugging him toward the bedroom door. "Yes, why?"

"It's freezing outside. This isn't warm enough."

Before she can answer, he walks inside the closet before re-emerging with a thick cable-knit sweater. She accepts it from him before pulling it over her head. Helping her, he frees the long strands of her hair trapped under the knit, before he straightens the collar of her shirt.

"Much better. I don't want you to get cold."

His hands trail down the slopes of her shoulders, over the curves of her breasts. Her body quivers under his fingertips as they rest on her waist. Past her shoulders, the bed sprawls in an invitation to a lazy afternoon.

"Later." She laughs, pushing out of the door and into the hallway as if she's peeked inside his head.

"What's that?" he asks, nodding toward the door, smaller than the others, in the corner of the mezzanine.

"I think that's the door to the attic."

"Think?"

"It's locked."

He rattles the handle, but the door doesn't budge.

"Told you, it's locked."

"Wonder what's up there."

"Who cares, probably dusty old stuff the owners are storing. Come on, let's go."

Ellie tugs at him impatiently, but as he turns toward her, she loses her grip on his sleeve. Her hands reach out to his as her body tilts backward toward the banister. Panic widens her eyes. Time stretches like an elastic band, then snaps back as his stomach drops with fear. His arm shoots out and he grabs her sweater just before her body hits the point of no return.

"Jesus, Ellie, be careful."

"I'm…I'm sorry…" Her eyes glaze with the sheen of tears, and his heart rate begins to slow down.

"I'm sorry too. But you really scared me. I mean, falling from this height on marble floor, headfirst, you would…" The image that flashes in his mind is enough to scare the rest of the words away.

His fingers knot with hers, and he gives her hand a squeeze, which draws a smile to her face. Warmth spreads through his body, ironing out any tension left. But as they saunter down the stairs the question that's been playing on his mind remains: what would she do without him?

8. Steven

Outside, they are greeted by crisp winter air, seasoned with the brine of the ocean and the smell of rotting seaweed.

"Look at the size of those," Ellie says as he's busy with the handle, making sure the front door is locked. When he turns around her head is tilted toward the ledge of the porch decorated with a jagged garland of icicles.

"You didn't notice them last night? They're quite impressive." Reaching out, he breaks one of the smaller ones with a gloved hand, the taut leather squeaking as it strangles the ice.

"I bet it would really hurt if one of those fell on your head."

"Actually, it could be used for the perfect murder. You could stab someone," he says, re-creating the motions of that famous shower scene. "Then just let the weapon melt away, never to be found," he adds, throwing the piece of ice on the ground.

Still laughing, they decide against the beach, heading for the woods instead. Leaving the hiss of waves behind, they walk, arms locked, into the eerie silence of the forest. Once the house and the ocean are out of sight, their surroundings become a monochromatic landscape, the sky the same milky white as the ground, blurring the line of the horizon against the black bark of trees. Every step they take leaves new dents in the fresh powder.

The snow is different from the gray sludge in the city. Here, it stretches as an untouched white canvas. The overnight fall has erased the evidence of yesterday's arrival, as if they had never been here, whereas even in Central Park the snow is always marred by a thousand feet, compacted by the bustle of civilization or melted into a slush by the rising steam of human technology. The snow here is another reminder of how isolated they are.

The forest is imbued with a quiet strength that demands their attention, and they traipse silently through the trees. As they venture deeper, the snow thins out. Crusts of earth litter the forest floor like scabs on an alabaster skin.

She walks beside him, her arm entwined with his, head resting against his shoulder, eyes lost in the stack of twisted branches stretching above them.

He senses there are things she doesn't tell him, often disappearing inside her own head. What kind of world does she have in there, under the smooth arch of her skull, that is more appealing than being present with him? His curiosity to know where he fits in that world, and how great his part is, is a new feature in his relationship. He's never cared that much with the others. If only he could capture her attention, make a cage out of his fingers to keep it in.

"What are you thinking about?"

"I was thinking about Sylvia Plath's poem 'Mad Girl's Love Song.'"

There is the answer: her head is filled with the words of a poet who met a tragic end—a competition for his attention he can live with. He squeezes her arm. She smiles in response, but a gust of wind erases it quickly.

"Somehow, I've always imagined you more as a Dickinson girl, a mix of romance and Gothic."

"Don't get me wrong, Emily's great, but Sylvia's poetry speaks to me on a deeper, more personal level."

And as soon as he has captured her attention, she retreats

into her head once more. Even though they share a deep connection, they don't know much about each other's past.

But their time together? He remembers that well.

"I do seem to recall that you were reading Sylvia Plath the first time we met."

Like some kind of mystical creature or deity, she entered his life amid the fury of the elements. Oblivious to the darkening and rumbling sky, he was grading a stack of papers at his favorite café, despairing at Stuart Winthrop's essay and how the boy would never survive without his family fortune, when the front door opened, and the battering din of sheets of rain hitting the pavement grew louder.

She walked in, dripping onto the tiles, scanning the room for a friendly face—or maybe just an empty table. Hesitating, she stopped, breasts visible under her soaked dress, the skirt of it stuck to her thighs. Just below her collarbone, the shadow of a dark beauty spot peeked from under the see-through fabric. He wondered if it would feel smooth under the touch of his fingertip or like a little bump.

Her search for a table yielded no results, the other customers ignoring her presence, too busy with their own conversation as she stood there, a mixture of sexuality and fragility. Standing up, he pushed the empty chair opposite his and beckoned her to sit with him. She glanced around, and her mouth twitched before she finally accepted his invitation. Her hand dropped a sodden copy of Sylvia Plath's *Poems* to accept the towel the barista offered her. In one swift move, Steven pulled his papers out of the way.

"I'm so sorry, I'm getting those wet," she said, pale cheeks turning a lovely shade of crimson. She sat, mopping her hair, oblivious to the effect her sheer dress had on him.

"Don't worry about it."

"What are those?" She nodded toward his stack of papers.

"Essays. I'm a literature professor."

"Oh, I'm getting my master's in Comp Lit at NYU."

They talked about Plath and their mutual love of books. She listened intently to all he had to say, while her fingers folded and refolded a paper napkin. She seemed shy, with a hint of aloofness that intoxicated him. A mix of elusiveness and eagerness, which sent a thrill pulsing through his veins.

He had to see her again. He had to have her.

Now, she gazes at him with the same demure look as she did that day in the café. Sometimes he worries she has bewitched him, but his lust overshadows his concerns. Interrupting their trek, he pulls her into his arms for a kiss, her cheeks and nose frozen under his lips, before he digs out her mouth from under the layers of her scarves.

"I do remember you telling me how you hated your name," he says, breaking their embrace.

"Can you blame me?"

"What's wrong with Ellie?"

"It makes me sound like I'm twelve or something. Like a little girl, don't you think?" she says, throwing her arms around his neck.

"I don't know. I quite like it."

"That makes one of us. Anyway, I remember you saying once you weren't fond of Steven."

"You remember that?"

"I don't understand why. What's so terrible about Steven?" She laughs.

He doesn't hate his name—not intrinsically—but what it represents. Close enough to his father's name to be confused with him but always reminding him that he isn't

46

worthy enough to carry his father's full name and legacy by being denied the title of Stewart Harding Jr. His father never missed an occasion to remind him he would always stand beneath him, trapped under his shadow. Like at his parents' annual summer barbecue in his junior year. Amid the paper lanterns and the smell of cooked meat his mother proudly announced to the Millers that her son had achieved a 1,484 on his SATs. "Not bad, but not as good as his old man's 1,535 score," his father joked, his heavy hand squeezing Steven's shoulder a little too hard. "Still, we're proud of him," he added, patting his son's back. Still. The word made the compliment taste like a handout. The sting of humiliation turned into a searing burn when he had found his father at the end of the evening, cozying up to his girlfriend for a quiet chat. His father leaning intently, listening to her as he played with the signet ring on his little finger. Even after almost twenty years the sting hasn't dulled.

"You're right. Steven is still miles better." He smirks.

"Could have been worse."

"How?"

"You could have been called Junior."

He puts an end to the conversation with a kiss. One that lasts, one that explores the connection between two people. An opening making way. Tongues interlocking, inviting. Her mouth tells him how much she likes him, even loves him, although they have never said the words to each other. Under their kiss, the remoteness of their location seems sharper than ever. Only they remain in this frozen Eden, Adam and Eve—a woman who seems to have been made for him.

9

October 19

First time seeing you today, since everything changed. My heart flitted about like a nervous parakeet in its cage. I was worried you would ignore me, act like this weekend didn't happen. As everybody was hunched over, I looked up. Your eyes were waiting. Your whole face beamed as you smiled.

It was all for me.

10. Ellie

The loud crack of a branch echoes, sharp like a bone being snapped, sending a flock of birds into the sky.

"Crap, what was that?" I ask, breaking our kiss, the flap of panicked wings shattering the silence further.

"Just a deer, or a fox. Who knows?" he replies, his head buried in my neck, ignoring the new stiffness in my body.

Pushing past Steven, I scan the woods for the origin of the noise, but all I can see are black, skeletal trees, standing like extras in a horror film, the kind where the naive college girl making out with her boyfriend is the first to be slaughtered. Under this milky sky, nothing leaves a shadow, not even us.

"These woods creep me out." I shudder.

"You did choose this place."

The forest darkens around us as if the trees are huddling closer to each other. I catch a glimpse of a movement to the left. Too quick to identify, and then it's gone. Twisting and turning, the forest spins around me—bark and undergrowth stretch in all directions. I close my eyes, but the feeling of being watched doesn't lessen. A couple of deep breaths slows the drumming in my chest enough to open my eyes and paste a smile on my face.

"Well, professor, I thought it would be terribly romantic," I say, as he corrals me into his arms.

We kiss again, but something has shifted. Even though my mouth is on his, my mind is on what or who might be out there, a neighbor out on a stroll, or some other silhouette hiding behind a tree. The cold wind whips around, biting my cheeks, lifting my hair to tease the back of my neck.

"I feel like something or someone's watching us." Wriggling out of his embrace, I search our surroundings again for the presence of an intruder—my breath cold in my chest—but just find aspen trees shaped like people; the only eyes around us those etched on their bark.

"You're being ridiculous," he sighs. "There's nobody here."

Last night's shadow shifting at the edge of the forest comes back to me, how swiftly it moved against the darkness, how it could still linger somewhere close. The wind picks up, and the forest whispers around us. I wait for that crunch again, like the arm twisted too far.

"Can we go to the beach, please?"

He shoots at me a wry smile. The look an adult gives to a child being unreasonable over some silliness. Flattened against him, I lay my palms flat on to his padded Gore-Tex chest and stretch my lips into a smile.

"I just need some open space."

He indulges me in my request, and we trudge our way through the woods, the undergrowth of scoliotic twigs catching the fabric of our trousers. I glance at dark places between the trees until we break free of them and onto the narrow ribbon of snowy sand that serves as a beach. The ocean stretches dark as liquid flint, scarred with drifting ice floes. I welcome the freedom, swallowing a big gulp of salty air. We walk along the shore, where the water licks the snow—melting away flakes to reveal the sand underneath.

Ahead, dark, pot-bellied clouds gather over the ocean. The wind plucks at my hair, strands lashing across my face. Its iciness laced with the brine of the ocean stings my eyes, and I mop up the tears pooling at the edge of my lids with my glove.

"What's wrong?" Steven asks.

"Nothing."

"I don't believe that for a moment."

"This place. That beach just reminds me of someone." I mop a little harder. "Stupid wind." With a gloved thumb he wipes one of my tears. The soft smile he offers me makes me forget for a moment.

"Why is it sad?" Steven says, squeezing my hand.

"We fell out. A long time ago."

"What happen—"

"Actually, I'd rather not... Can we talk about something else?"

Glove off, he hooks his fingers to pull away a rogue strand across my face. His palm burns against my frozen cheek, the pad of his thumb stroking the skin.

Pulling me into a hug, he says, "Of course." Face against his padded chest, I pick up the faint thud of his heartbeat.

"We're here together. Tell me about what's new with you."

His arm heavy around my shoulders, we stroll as Steven tells me about his latest essay, "Nineteen- and Twentieth-century Literature: Capturing and Creating the Modern." The rhythm of his words and the waves are a powerful analgesic, until we stumble upon a puddle and a distressed seagull, half its body imprisoned under an opaque sheet of ice. The frightened bird caws, calling for a mate or a parent, and flaps its free wing with staccato efforts, but exhaustion is clearly taking root along with the cold as its energy wanes. As we watch, the wing flops open, and the cackles die.

"Poor thing. I wonder how it got trapped." On haunches, I approach the bird with wary fingers. Suspicious of my intentions or sensing my wariness, it snipes at them, and I jerk my hand back.

Steven stoops next to me and strokes the top of the bird's

head with the back of his hand. "Looks like its wing is broken."

"What can we do?"

Stuffing his gloves in his pocket, Steven tends to the bird as I scan the ground for a pebble big enough or a rock to break the sheet of ice. His fingers run down the soft down, each stroke smoothing the fretful seagull until it has come to accept Steven's presence and his touch. Despite the ache spreading through my thighs, the scene brings a smile to my face. I imagine us bringing the bird back to the house bundled inside Steven's scarf, propped on a pillow by the fire, its wing suitably bandaged. I'm still searching for something big enough to do the trick when Steven's other hand cups the back of the bird's head.

"It's OK," he whispers to the bird, and then his voice raised, an order for me: "Just go ahead. I'll catch up with you in a second."

A couple of strides away from him, the sound of a sharp snap quickens my pace.

November 3

Do you remember when you gave me your name? Gone the formal barrier of a "Mr." Your name slid on my tongue like a new candy. I discovered its texture and its taste. I left, turning it over in my mind, looking forward to next Thursday and being able to use it again.

Not just your name, but a gift. You said, "I've got something for you," as your hand disappeared into your satchel before pulling out a book. "I thought you might enjoy it, and we could discuss it once you've finished it." I ran my fingers over the white lettering—*Jane Eyre*.

I started it that same afternoon and I loved it. You already knew me so well. But more than just a present, this book was physical evidence that you thought of me. Even when I wasn't around.

Today, we stood in the shower, the air between us so thick and heavy with moisture we had to breathe through our mouths.

Today, you gave me a new name.

Today, you called me your Darling Jane.

12. Ellie

What started as light drift morphs quickly into a heavy snowfall. Strong winds fling flakes as big as feathers across our faces, forcing us to turn back. The icy chill works its way under our clothes, melting snow dripping into the collar of our jackets. Backs hunched against the hostile weather, we huddle close amid whistling gusts. Our legs slice the snow as we carve our way back across the beach, the cold seeping through flesh down to the bones and reminding us that this postcard-perfect landscape, parading as a romantic spot, is a disguise for an environment that could easily kill us. It's the deadliest kind of danger, hidden under the deceit of its beauty. Ahead the snow blurs the edges of the world with a milky haze, until one shape detaches itself from the uniform background.

The house is waiting for us, silent and hollow. The perfect host, offering itself to be whatever its guests need, filling its space with their conversations, hanging their clothes on the back of chairs or inside its closets. It becomes whatever they need it to be: a refuge, a getaway, a temporary home…It exists only for them until they leave when it becomes a blank space once again, waiting for its next occupants. And each time, it keeps their secrets.

We forgo the front entrance in favor of the kitchen's and stumble through the back door along with a spill of snow. After we stomp our boots and shrug the fresh powder off our hair, I slip off my coat, but Steven keeps his jacket on.

"I might just go and put the car in the garage before it gets completely snowed under."

"OK. I'll make some coffee. Steven?"

"Yes?"

"Could you pick up a few extra logs from the garage to get a fire started in the main living room?"

"Sure."

"Thanks."

He closes the door, sealing me from the noise of what is turning into a blizzard. Balancing on my toes, I reach for two mugs from one of the top cupboards. The second one has been pushed so far back that my fingertips graze the handle several times. I strain the muscles in my arm. Laboriously the cup edges toward me, almost in my grasp, when a long wail tears through the silence. The mug skids across the shelf and away from my jittery hand.

"Crap!"

I flinch, anticipating the moment it will shatter on the floor. The cry seems to come from the other side of the house and dies as quickly as it's appeared. Senses bristling, I listen to the silence for a clue, but it has settled now over the house, heavy and impenetrable. Inside my chest, my heart thunders. Its impossible beat scares me. My breathing turns shallow. This is the last thing I need. Not right now.

Z...Y...X...With each letter I inhale deeply until my lungs press against my ribs. W...V...My heart slows down. Crisis averted.

Crouching down, I collect the pieces of porcelain scattered across the floor as the knots in my shoulders soften. If I hurry, I can clean it up before Steven gets back, hide my clumsiness at the bottom of the trash can. I'm still busy picking them up when a new howl rips through—long and harrowing like the twisted cry of someone going mad—slices through me, and my hand spasms around a shard.

A blood drop swells on my skin; I suck it before it can fall and stain the tiles. The howl has died, and silence reclaims the space until the outside world comes rushing behind me. The bellows of a freezing gust quickly followed by the bang of the back door against the wall jolts me.

"It's getting worse out there."

I jump again, losing my balance and falling back onto the cupboard door behind me.

Steven steps in; a fresh dusting of snow glistens on his hair, shoulders, even his lashes, a pile of logs balanced in his arms.

"What happened?" he asks, rushing to my side.

"I'm sorry. I dropped a mug." I scramble to pick up pieces, trying to hide the evidence of my clumsiness while sucking on my finger.

"Ellie." He elongates my name and makes me feel like I'm ten years old. He pitches in, collecting broken ceramic, including the shard smeared with red. "You're bleeding."

"It's nothing."

Taking my hand, he brings the injured finger up toward his face before closing his mouth around the wound. We stay crouched on the floor; the suction tugs at the skin on my fingertip. His eyes lock on mine, and the moment we share is pregnant with an intimacy we have never experienced before. Somehow this innocuous gesture stirs something—an urge to leap and kiss him, taste my blood on his tongue. But before I can move, another inhuman wail rips through the air. Shuddering, I yank my finger away and almost lose my balance again.

"It's only the wind caught in the chimney." He laughs.

A flush of embarrassment spreads through my body. I grab the remaining pieces, wishing I could stuff myself into the trash can under the sink along with them. Steven's shoulders are still shaking from laughter as he picks up the logs from the floor. This is even worse than when I slid in front of him on the sidewalk yesterday. His load back in his arms, he heads out of the kitchen.

The crackles of a newly lit fire greet me in the living room. In daylight, the space is striking. Massive floor-to-ceiling windows run along the main length of the house and the back, the glass inviting the outside in—the close-knit trees of the forest creating a wall which ends with breathtaking views of the ocean and the decking area at the back, even though the landscape is quickly disappearing under the white static of snow. The house protecting us from the storm while offering a front-row seat to the mayhem nature is unleashing.

"Impressive, isn't it?" Steven says, nodding toward the wall of pines.

"Impressive, oppressive…" I cozy up next to him on the sofa in front of the fire, tucking my legs under me before handing him his drink. The piece of architecture is far too imposing to be simply called a fireplace. The word is too mundane to do justice to the column of rough-hewn stone, slicing between the wall of glass and the smooth plastered wall, nature-made and man-made. We sit there in silence for a moment, watching the flames.

"So, what do you want to do tomorrow?"

"I don't know. I just…I keep thinking about that seagull."

"Believe me, it's better this way. Forget about it." He smiles at me, before taking a sip of his drink.

"What do *you* think we should do tomorrow?" I ask.

"We could take a drive to Stockton. Check out the antique stores, maybe have lunch on the waterfront. What do you think?"

"Sounds perfect." I smile. "If this snow ever lets up."

"Hopefully it won't last," he says while he pats the

pockets of his trousers with his free hand. "Have you seen my phone?"

"Left it in your coat as usual?"

"As usual?"

"You always ask me if I've seen your phone, and inevitably it's in your coat or jacket. Do you want me to go check?" I rise from the sofa, but his hand on my arm stops me.

"Don't worry, it's not like I need it anyway. Just stay here with me."

"OK."

Silence settles like the snow outside as we both blow on our drinks. I stare at the dark mass of the forest and the shore disappearing behind a thick curtain of flakes.

"Do you really believe what you said?" I ask, resting my head against the top of his arm.

"What?"

"About the seagull. That it's better off…"

He wraps his arm around my shoulder, pulling me close and—for his only response—buries a kiss in my hair.

The hot porcelain of the mug burns my fingertips. With each careful sip the coffee flushes my cheeks and burns a pleasant trail down my throat. The knots between my shoulders relax, until I'm mellow, leaning back against Steven's arm. But now is not the moment to fall asleep. There will be plenty of time for that later.

Leaving the comfort of the sofa, I meander around the room before stopping in front of the sound system and its shelves of CDs. My index finger drags across their plastic spines as names and titles scroll out. I can feel Steven's gaze on me. One name catches my attention. With one little push, the CD is swallowed inside the slit of the stereo.

The first twangs of guitar stream from the invisible speakers. I turn the volume up as Chris Isaak's moody voice fills the air and curls the corners of my mouth. Ignoring Steven, I drift toward the fireplace. My eyes are closed; the fire warms my back. My hips translate the music into a series of low-slung rolls, skin and body absorbing the sultry rhythm until it becomes a mood I wear, my mug cradled against my chest. In the makeshift darkness I can still feel Steven's eyes on me. Turning away from the sofa, I dance with the fire, its flames licking my legs with its warmth and making me blush.

There is a shift in the air. Chris is telling me about wicked games to play when Steven's hands cradle my hips as they sway, the pressure of his body against my back. He turns me around. My eyes still closed, he relieves me of the cup. We speak to each other in heavy breaths, and I keep dancing as he undresses me. More and more exposed skin for the fire to lick. His fingers slip in the waistband of my jeans. The button pops open. The zipper growls down. He eases my legs out of the jeans followed by my underwear.

When the first notes of "You Owe Me Some Kind of Love" start, my naked body rests inside Steven's fully clothed embrace, his hardness pressing against my inner thigh. My eyes flick open, filling my world with only him. Fingers knotted behind his neck, I pull his face toward me until my mouth finds his. I kiss him with a conviction that puts me in charge for a moment, my mouth and tongue dictating the rhythm, but he quickly takes over. A log collapses with a loud crackle; the noise startles us, and his body drags mine to the ground. Despite the rug, my shoulder slams hard against the hardwood floor—that's going to leave a mark. I alleviate the concern in his eyes by pulling him closer to me for another kiss.

His hand caresses my skin. The same hand that—not long ago—broke the delicate bones of a bird. He undresses quickly, but I'm not ready yet. I wiggle from under his weight. My hands chase his, swatting them away, building his desire like a house of cards, until he can't take it anymore and it comes crashing down, his hands shackling my wrists above my head. Smiling, I struggle, and his grip tightens. His strength closes around my bones. Until it crushes. I bear it. Until it's enough. He unleashes the full force of his kiss on my mouth. Winner plucking his reward. His whole weight flat against me. He's waiting for me to open myself to him, but my legs are still closed.

"Show me how much you want me," I whisper to him.

The boulder of his knee presses against the slit between my thighs, prying them open. I resist him until he has to push harder.

"Do it."

It burns in his eyes and curls his lips—the desire to possess me. I relent. With one hand he guides himself inside me. His hand rejoins the other one around my wrists, pressing hard in rhythm. Taking what he wants. Me. And I encourage him, with whispered words between jagged breaths.

We move in front of the swathes of glass exposed to the scrutiny of the forest. The only eyes that might be watching us those of animals.

13. Steven

They sit on the floor, Steven's back propped up against the base of the sofa, Ellie nestled against his chest. Both their bodies naked under the plaid twisted around them. The fabric itches on his bare skin, the impracticability of something for decorative purposes that should only be used to cozy under when fully clothed. The fire in the hearth casts a dim light, licking the shadows away to create a pallid glow that barely reaches them.

Darkness crept up on them while they were busy with each other's orgasms, and has stitched the trees together. Distracted, he had forgotten how quickly the day vanishes in winter. In the city, night never completely exists, true blackness kept at bay by the orange glow of streetlights, by millions of windows. Here, where nature reigns, and man is merely permitted, night lies truly. It stretches unchallenged, until the sun rises again, but until dawn they are now inside the lair of true darkness.

"I think it's getting worse."

"What's that?" Steven asks, his knuckles stroking the top of her arm.

"The snow outside."

On the other side of the window, thick and compact flakes are getting bullied by a strong wind. A flurry of white streaking a black canvas—nature's attempt at a Jackson Pollock. Only a whisper of waves crashing against the shore penetrates through the dense glazing.

"Stockton's looking less and less likely."

"I can think of other things we can do to occupy ourselves." His words brush against her ear, warm like a promise.

"But I was really looking forward to visiting it."

"It wouldn't be reasonable, driving in these conditions." She opens her mouth, but he continues. "And, as the designated driver I have final say." He playfully taps the end of her nose, putting an end to the conversation.

"I guess you're right," she says as she nestles into the crook of his shoulder.

Her skin radiates heat against his, and her cheeks still carry the flush of orgasm. He drapes his arm around her shoulders, thumb stroking her collarbone.

"So, it's just us and this big house, then," she adds.

"It's an amazing place. How did you even find it?"

"A friend told me about it."

"What friend?"

"From school. His parents' friends rented this place. Every time I see him, he can't stop raving about it." His back stiffens. She's never mentioned any male friends before. Knowing her good nature it's more likely to be some guy bothering her, and Ellie, being Ellie, just too nice to tell them off. Men have always been flocking to her, flapping around her. He has seen their leering gaze like crows setting their sight on a shiny trinket. Like that creep at Sasha's opening a few weeks earlier, the latest specimen in a long line. Ellie had sulked at his drinking and left in a huff. He had been debating—while waiting for the barman to notice him—if he should catch up to her when a guy hurried past him. Steven's attention latched on and followed the shock of auburn hair and slight beard, through the glass doors and outside, where the stranger snared Ellie's wrist with his hand. She stopped and whipped around. Steven's body tensed at the intrusion, but his mind, bogged down by five bourbons, lagged behind. Outside, the stranger spoke fast, rubbing his nose with the back of his hand—bloody cokehead, Steven had thought, the gesture both familiar and alien to him. He didn't like the idea of a druggie around her. He had seen this face before—different men but the face always the same, the looks that sliced through her clothes, the lips pinched, barely concealing their hunger, the entitlement in their leaning posture when they accosted her.

As he'd watched, Ellie's whole body had seemed to tense up, an uncomfortable look frozen on her face, her big eyes wider than usual. It had triggered Steven into action, and he'd pushed through the barrage of critics and dilettantes blocking his view and his path to Ellie. But when he finally tumbled through the glass double doors, the stranger stood alone, Ellie nowhere to be seen. At least he doesn't have to worry about others here.

Her voice slices through his thoughts. "I wonder how long someone could survive in this kind of weather without proper clothing."

"Why are you asking?"

"I don't know."

"You worry too much." Her comment and childish but endearing fear earn her another light tap on her nose, which he follows with a smirk.

"Maybe you don't worry enough. Don't you have any regrets?" she asks after a pause.

"None."

"That's a bold statement."

"Everything I've done so far has led me to sit on this floor with you. How can I regret any of it."

"You're such a sweet talker."

He winds his arm a little tighter around her, enjoying the weight of her head on his chest, her cheek clammy against his skin. He smiles. Nobody but them for miles around. Outside, the wind throws a spatter of flakes against the glass, piles the snow against the front and back doors, the storm showing no signs of easing off. The chances of them going anywhere are withering under the rough weather. There's no doubt: he has her all to himself.

14. Ellie

Everything must be perfect, even though it's going to be a late dinner. The purr of the oven fan keeps me company in the dim-lit kitchen. On the other side of the glass, the cheese bubbles under the heat. I slightly adjust the temperature. The rest of the weekend hinges on tonight. Lately, his eyes have changed. They used to crease with his smile, droop with desire. They used to undress me, study the details of my face. Now, they cannot hold the same expression for long, flickering from recognition to exasperation, sometimes to indifference. Sometimes, when I speak, his gaze fixes on a nothingness above my shoulder—or on a spot of fuchsia and blonde curls in the rearview mirror. Asking what's wrong always yields a variation of the same vague non-answers. He's been short-tempered as well, easily losing the self-control he cultivates. If all goes as intended, the form-fitting dress my body's trapped in this evening should help capture his interest.

The food ready, I move to the living room, but a low thud coming from the front door stops me. Easing the door open, I stand on the threshold between light and darkness, toasty warmth and biting cold. I listen to the silence the snow creates as it blankets the place. So thick on the ground it would cushion even the sound of boots.

"Hello?" Only the faint whistle of the wind answers.

I stare, and the shadows stare back at me. None of them move. Until...was there a rustle toward the garage, the darkness rearranging itself, or are the falling flakes playing a trick on me? Before I find an answer a gust of wind wraps its cold tendrils around my body. It snatches a shudder out of me and pushes me back into the house.

Inside the living room, I straighten cutlery by the side of plates, slide wineglasses until they rest in that elusive perfect position. The bottle of Cabernet Sauvignon presides in the middle of the table. I pick up the corkscrew before putting it down again—better to leave Steven the task of opening and tasting it. He enjoys doing that. Instead, I busy myself lighting the candles littered around the room. The heat liquifies the wax, and I dip a finger in the molten grease of one of them, burning my skin, until it solidifies again. Tugging the white crust off my fingertip, I drop it onto the surface of the candle, where it dissolves again in a puddle of heat. It reminds me of the snow all around—heat or chill, the catalysts that transform, mold water into snow or turn wax into liquid. The same element in a different form.

On the bar cart, alcohol shines behind the thick glass of bottles. I tighten the cap of the gin, wondering how much Steven will be drinking tonight. His alcohol consumption, like his gaze on me, has changed. How often I've had to repeat myself lately. I might be young, but I'm not completely naive. I know he's upset about his father's National Book Award nomination.

The worst night was about three weeks ago, at the art gallery where we had been invited for an opening—or rather, Steven had, and I had tagged along as his plus-one. I'd waited for him on the sidewalk for fifteen minutes, pacing and shifting my weight like an abandoned pet waiting for its owner. My shoulders perked up every time a tall silhouette in a well-cut coat approached, only to droop when that silhouette wasn't him. Finally, the security at the entrance took pity on me and ushered me inside so I could wait for my date in the heated room with a free bar. It was another half hour before Steven's hand rested on the small of my back as he kissed my cheek.

"Could I have a bourbon?" he asked the man behind the bar.

"Of course, sir. Ice?"

"Yes, please."

He downed his drink in one move, Adam's apple bobbing under the relief of alcohol sliding down his throat. Setting his glass down, he motioned to the barman for a refill.

"Where's Sasha? I should really go and say hello." His gaze fell over the top of my head as he looked for our host, turning me into another sculpture which adorned the floor.

"You're late."

"Yes, sorry about that." His words barely made it to me, his attention still firmly on tracking Sasha in the packed room.

"I was worried. Where were you?" I spoke in a whispered tone, as if my questioning of his whereabouts was a shameful practice.

"Please don't be that girl."

"What girl?"

"It's really not attractive, Ellie."

The accusation and the coldness of his tone disarmed me from any kind of reply. He had never been cruel before—distant or aloof, but never cruel. With nowhere to run to, I retreated inside myself. I wouldn't cause a scene here. I had just been *that girl*. I didn't want to be her, I hated her as much as he did but somehow he'd thrust me into that role and then blamed me for what he created. Why do guys do that, and worse, why do we allow them? I remained by his side, nose in my glass of white wine, absorbed in trying to make sense of the abstract whirl of gouaches on canvases.

The next forty-five minutes unfolded as a choreographed play, moving from painting to painting, scripted small talk with acquaintances and regular intermissions at the bar, until I turned, drink in hand, while Steven waited for his fifth bourbon. My fingers clenched my glass so tight it might shatter.

Connor stood by one of the central sculptures. Even with his back to me I would have recognized that shaggy mess of auburn hair and that way of rubbing the tip of his shoe on the back of his trousers anywhere. I had to get out. Fast.

I sucked the air in. "Steven, do you think that's sensible?" I nodded at the glass the barman handed him.

"What?" The word escaped loaded with alcohol vapor.

Over Steven's shoulder, Connor moved to the next set of sculptures, each step taking him on a collision course which would lead to introductions, questions, explanations.

"I think I'm gonna leave."

"You give me a hard time because I'm late and now that I'm here you want to leave?" He frowned at me.

The last thing I wanted was to seem difficult, but it was less devastating than the alternative. I could make Steven forgive me. "If that's how you're going to be, I think I'd rather go."

He shrugged in response, turning back for another drink and putting an end to the conversation. I made my way to the cloakroom and then slipped out onto the pavement slick with rain to hail a taxi.

The following morning, I read an article online about his father's nomination. Later, a peace-offering text waited for me on my phone after my last class. I didn't say anything to him about the article, but I understood.

Even though Steven buried the incident under profuse apologies, a home-cooked dinner, an extravagant bouquet of peonies and calla lilies and a night dedicated to my pleasure, none of it could completely erase the nagging earworm whispering that maybe he wasn't as committed as I thought he was. That he was slipping away from me, and our relationship now existed on borrowed time. Meanwhile, Connor was asking more questions. Every time Steven and I met, the relief that we were still together was followed by the dread that this might be our last date, the same with every call and every text, every moment, until yesterday, when the car pulled away from the curb.

I fan slices of cheese on the wooden board and arrange garlands of grapes. They remind me of those nonchalant women posing on chaises-longues for turn-of-the-century artists. The room is as ready and the setting as romantic as it will ever be. I readjust my dress one last time. The ghost of me caught in the window curls her lips. But her smile is strained.

15

December 18

Christmas break. Today was our last day together until we see each other again next year.

Your presence won't be completely gone, though. I snapped a picture of the two of us last week with my phone as you lay sleeping next to me. After I got it printed at a booth from the drugstore, I deleted it, so it couldn't be found by mistake.

You're on the other side of the country, spending the holidays with your family, and I'm left all alone. Like an Advent calendar, my head is full of memories of us to keep me company. Every day I crack a new door open. Today's led me to when you wandered into the back office as I was busy making copies. The surprise and my clumsiness knocked my bag off the copy machine, its contents spilling out on the ground. You crouched alongside me to help.

"Is this your sister?" You nodded to the picture inside my opened wallet.

We had taken the picture by the sea, the wind tangling our hair, my ginger curls streaking the dark brown of hers. We stood side by side in matching black hoodies. The similarity stops there. I envy the shape of her body, plump rounded breasts, and womanly hips. I—on the other hand—am made of too many lines and no curves.

"By the way," you said, before I could tell you about Vee and that day at the beach, "do you mind if we meet half an hour early next week? I have a...friend coming to town."

The awful dread of the word "friend"—or rather, the slight hesitation that preceded it. That pause took over my mind, and my nails didn't survive the obsession. A friend. Why did you hesitate?

Was it because it's a woman?

16. Steven

She surprised him today. She took the initiative. She usually follows his lead, bends to his needs, but not this afternoon. The memories of their time by the fire keep him company as he squirts shampoo into his hand. She possesses a rare mix of an eroticism which drives him crazy in bed, always leaving him sated yet wanting more, and an intellect that allows her to discuss such things as the relationship between narrative style and moral judgment in Joseph Conrad's *Heart of Darkness*.

On the shelf a bold miniature bottle next to others—compliments of their host—cuts against the white tiles. The vivid green calls to him, and even though he doesn't need it he flicks it open. He was right. The chemical scent of apple fills the shower cubicle.

C's hair always smelled of green apples. Lying in bed with her, he would peel away the colorful layers of her clothes to reveal soft, white flesh he liked sinking his teeth into—called her his forbidden fruit. She would laugh at that, more an "I don't know how to take a compliment" giggle. His pillows in that tiny studio always smelled of apples. It only lasted a spring, but she had made his time in Pasadena bearable, while he offered her a safe haven from her parents' messy divorce…

He opens his eyes. Enough recollection. Even if he remembers them all, none of them measure up when compared to Ellie. Not even C.

By the time he steps out of the shower and into the

steamed-up world of the bathroom, his mind's made up, and he knows what to do, but not tonight. Maybe tomorrow in Stockton when they have lunch at some picturesque waterfront café. Her face when he would ask her floated in his mind, stretching his lips into a smile, but as he wraps a towel around his waist, a low rattle catches his attention, and he can't pinpoint where it's coming from.

"Ellie?" The only response comes from the drip from the shower head.

He's about to dismiss it when he hears it again, a faint scurrying overhead, and he holds his breath at the ceiling. He shudders at the idea he might share this place with a country mouse or whatever animal is trapped up there. He will mention this on the feedback form they will send to the owners. Being used to the sight of mice and rats in the subways or back alleys in the city doesn't mean he isn't offended to stay in a building where invisible rodents might roam. Maybe he should call and let the owners know. Does Ellie have a number for them? But, he remembers, the cell signal's gone, and come to think of it he hasn't seen a landline in all the time they've been here either.

Standing dripping on the mat, he dries the body he puts a lot of effort into maintaining, pats the shoulders sculpted by a morning swim five times a week, wipes the fuzzy trail on a stomach flat from sugar abstinence. His fingers rake through the thick quiff of chestnut brown hair. The ancient Greeks had the right idea—a healthy mind inside a healthy body. Moving to the bedroom, he stands naked in front of the giant window, surveying the broken limbs of bare trees that stretch until they blur with the night sky. He puts the rodents out of his mind, instead focusing on how good his life is, how his hard work's paying off. His lovely girlfriend, whisking him away on a surprise romantic weekend, booking this wonderful place for them—he wonders how much this must have cost her, how long she's been saving for it. And the chat he had with Schumacher before they left.

Schumacher stopping for him at the teachers' lounge surprised him. Even teachers could get apprehensive when being called into the principal's office. He has been stuck at Richmond Prep for so long now. The place was intended as a stopgap, to supplement his income and experience and to make the right connections among the influential people that made up the parent population at Richmond Prep, but somehow he got stuck there for a lot longer than expected. Same as Barnard College—it was only meant as a stepping stone, to get him back to New York and closer to Columbia or Princeton. He's always wondered whether his old man had a secret hand in keeping him stuck. Wouldn't put it past the old bastard.

"Stevie, can you drop by my office before you leave for the day? It's important."

The words were leveled, and the expression on his face closed. That afternoon sped by in a blur, before Steven found himself in front of the principal's door.

"Stevie, come in. Take a seat."

Steven mentally flinched at the tacky name Schumacher always called him, but being his subordinate meant he had to bite his tongue, hide under a fake smile, and shake the hand that was offered to him. He squeezed his boss's sausage fingers, one of them strangled by the gold band of a wedding ring that had lost its sheen a long time ago.

"Thanks. So what can I do for you, Donald?" Steven asked as he settled in the chair, wiping his palm on the rough fabric before resting it on his lap.

"Is there something you would like to tell me?"

Steven stayed silent as he waited for Schumacher to show his hand. Did he really think that kind of bluff would work with him?

"Sorry, I'm not sure what you mean..."

With a deep sigh, Schumacher stood up before making his way around the desk. He sat on its corner, and Steven swore he heard the wood creak in protest. The broken veins on Schumacher's nose made him uncomfortable but not as much as the principal's lack of self-control straining against the fabric of his shirt.

"I've been hearing some rumors."

Steven's back stiffened. God, he hated that word, "rumors," just a polite way to say "people unable to mind their own business." His mind raced through to find the gesture or word that could have triggered any *rumors*, while he gave Richmond Prep's principal an evasive shrug. Schumacher leaned in close enough for Steven to notice the sweat mottling his forehead; he felt his own perspiration dampen the underarms of his shirt. Good thing he liked formality and wore his blazer to the meeting. He usually also enjoyed showing Schumacher what properly fitted clothes looked like, but that was the least of his concerns right now.

"Sorry, you'll have to enlighten me."

He followed Schumacher's gaze to his own restless fingers. The acknowledgment was enough to stop him, and he rested his hands, palms down on his lap.

"I have to say I'm disappointed, Stevie."

Shifting in his seat, Steven laced his hands together, refusing to play Schumacher's game. No point admitting to anything until the "anything" has been revealed. Late-night poker at Princeton had taught him one thing—never reveal your hand. His boss folded first.

"A little birdie told me that Columbia has been courting

you." The muscles in Steven's back relaxed. "I'm sorry if you felt you couldn't approach me with this. But, if it's true, I can imagine you won't have time for classes at our little institution anymore. Not sure what would stop you from leaving us. Apart from poaching my job." He laughed, slapping Steven's shoulder.

"Sorry, Donald, not even then. Your job's safe." He joined Schumacher with a stilted laugh.

"Congratulations, Stevie." Steven rubbed the sweat off his palm on his trousers before shaking Schumacher's hand.

Smiling at the memory and straightening his collar, he smiles. Everything is coming together. Work, his reputation. The beautiful girl waiting for him downstairs. People who say you can't have it all just don't work at it hard enough. Taking a last look in the mirror, he leaves the bedroom and heads for the stairs.

17

February 1

I saw you with her. You were walking together. Her arm was wrapped around your waist, body pressed against yours, and you were smiling. She looked needy, the way she clung to you. I should have walked away but I couldn't. I had to see. That man with her, that wasn't you. You hated public displays, soon you would have to shake her off and regain your freedom. My heart crumbled into ashes when your lips closed around hers. Your kisses are a language I speak fluently by now. That one spoke of hunger. You wanted her, and that kiss wouldn't keep you satisfied for long. You would need more. Of her.

The monster truck of a revelation hit me with full force. A hit-and-run that sent my stomach flying on a collision course with my throat. Turning around, I dry heaved, but I was empty.

She laughed, and my pain curdled into anger. As she stepped off the curb, I wished for a bus to hit her, break all the bones in her body, but not kill her instantly. Or maybe you should both be hit by lightning. I wish I could make you both sick so you can know how I feel all the time.

You opened the car door for her. As she dropped into the passenger seat, you froze, fingers curled on the handle. Through the wall of tears building in my eyes, I saw your blurry face look right at me.

You'd stopped smiling.

18. Steven

In the main room, Ellie is putting the finishing touches to the dining-room table.

"Wow," Steven says, stepping in.

One corner of it has been set for two, and every surface has been covered with lit candles, the only source of light apart from the fire going strong in the hearth. Despite the modern décor, the natural lighting gives the room a Gothic feel. Taking in the atmosphere, Steven readjusts the cuffs of his shirt a couple of times.

"You look nice."

He is wearing a pair of jeans, Oxford shirt, and navy sweater; that's as casual as he will let himself go. She moves around him in a black bandage dress—a present from him—which follows the lines of her body, hinting at the promise that she isn't wearing anything underneath. He truly knows what looks best on her; the dress is a testament to that. She had put up a feeble protest when he surprised her with it, but he simply enjoys buying things for her she couldn't afford.

"Thanks," he says, stroking her cheek. "Your skin's freezing."

"I was standing outside." He frowns at her. "I thought I heard something."

Without a word, he strides out of the living room and into the lobby. The top bolt of the front door slides into place with a low thud.

"Here," he says, turning back to her. "Nothing's getting

in now. Anyway, this looks impressive. Bit of a fire hazard, though."

"Don't you like it?" Her smile evaporates as her fingers play with the silver heart around her neck.

"I love it." Cupping her face, he presses his mouth against hers, and her smile shines once again. Something catches his attention, but he's not quite sure what it is, until the right sense sharpens and his brain kicks in. Classical music— Rachmaninoff Prelude in C Sharp Minor—streams from the wall. The idea strikes him that he can't wait for the summer, when he'll take Ellie to listen to the Philharmonic in Central Park. The two of them sitting on a plaid island amid a sea of grass, sharing cheese sandwiches and a bottle of wine while listening to the swell of violins from Beethoven's Seventh Symphony or the swarm of strings and ominous brass from Mussorgsky's *Night on Bald Mountain*.

"Smells delicious. Are we having what I think we are?"

She nodded with a smile.

"I thought you weren't too fond of eggplant?"

"But I know this is your favorite. Can you open the wine, please?"

As he uncorks it, he checks the unfamiliar label. "Did we bring this?"

"No, I found it in the pantry." His hand stops twisting the corkscrew, and he arches an eyebrow at her. "A gift from our host, I guess."

They sit, with an audience of the trees outside, barely visible under the glow of all the candles. After a dinner of stuffed eggplant, mixed salad and cheese platter which they eat with a bottle of 2007 Cabernet Sauvignon, he clears the table and stacks the dishwasher; the least he can do after the work Ellie did planning this weekend and preparing dinner. As usual, she dropped the tiniest amount of food in the center of her plate. It looked like one of those degustation dishes at a gastronomy restaurant. This time he wouldn't have any of it, and before she could protest he dropped a full slice of eggplant on her plate. She politely protested but ate it anyway—he was not going to take no for an answer.

When he comes back to the living room, she's busy mixing drinks. He opens his mouth to thank her, but before he can an unexpected perfume captures his attention. Vanilla, but not the cooking kind, subtler and laced with a flowery smell—not roses—something as delicate but warmer, maybe jasmine. The scent wakes something up, a memory in the periphery of his mind—close enough to know it's there, a meaningful blur, but too far to grasp and make sense of it. The outline of a face, a familiar gesture. He has smelled it earlier, but didn't realize it at the time. It was only a hint but now it's back stronger than before, asking him to remember.

"Steven. Steven?" Ellie's voice breaks the spell and tethers him back to the present.

"Sorry, what was that?"

"Are you OK? You looked miles away."

"It's just...Can you smell that?"

"Smell what?" she asks, after taking a deep breath in.

"Never mind."

It's still there tugging at the back of his mind, telling him it is more than room perfume. Now that it has taken hold of him, it doesn't seem to want to let him go. But now is not the time.

"You look like you've seen a ghost."

"That's not what I would call what I'm looking at," he says, unabashedly looking her up and down.

"You need a drink." With a smile, she hands him a glass, which he winces at. "I'm afraid their whiskey bottle's empty, but they have gin."

"No bourbon?"

"Sadly not."

Taking a step closer, he grabs the glass as his free hand glides over the curve of her hip. He smiles, she's not wearing anything under that dress. A night full of possibilities unspools in front of him.

"What should we drink a toast to?" she asks.

"To this weekend. The two of us alone in this big house and nobody around to interrupt our time together."

Their glasses collide in mid-air, then they each take a long mouthful of gin. Ellie looks at him with a spark in her eyes he has never witnessed before.

"Let's make tonight a night we'll never forget," she says.

Another clink of glass like an explosion of laughter, another gulp disappears down their throats. The bitter taste of the gin leaves him grimacing.

"What?" Ellie asks.

"Nothing. That's some cheap gin." He takes another sip, daring himself. Rough alcohol doesn't scare him. Nothing does.

Leaning forward, he tastes her lips, licking the salt out of them. It wakes up a new hunger, which only expands with each bite of his kiss, moving into her until he has her backed against the table.

"Slow down."

He chews on her words, snatching them from her mouth.

With his glass now abandoned on the table, both his hands cup her hips, the absence of underwear under her dress taunting him. His shallow breath surprises him. His tongue spars with hers, but she's losing the battle. He wants more. In one move he flips her around and bends her over the table. Something has taken over him, something buried under the crust of political correctness and sensible behavior, awakened by nature and isolation.

"Steven, what—"

On the other side of the swathes of glass, the forest stares back at him. Dark silhouettes of pine trees sway in the night, whispering at him to take what he wants. They come closer, looming, daring him to let go, then they blur in a moment of strange vertigo, like he's lost his footing inside his own body. He shakes it off, steadies himself with both hands flat on the table top. In front of him, Ellie's bent body, the cliff of her ass, a territory to conquer. Abandoning his manners, he pushes her dress up.

Ellie says something, but his brain can't process the message. A certain queasiness creeps at the edges of him. He tries to fight it, but the tilt of the earth has other ideas, swinging him sideways—and the floor goes missing under his feet.

19. Steven

"Steven...What...What are you doing?" Ellie asks, frantically tugging the bottom of her dress back into position, her eyes wild and wider than usual, more blue than green.

"Not sure what came over me," he replies, smoothing the perspiration out of his hair, untucked tail shirt peeking from under his sweater. "Lost my footing or something. Just give me a minute."

Picking up his drink, he takes another swig of it, but the alcohol does nothing to slow his heartbeat. He has never lost control like this before, but that feeling, the power he felt before he lost it...alone here, he could do anything he wanted. He just needs a minute to gather himself. They can try again in a moment. His mind is already plotting how he can replicate it, still high on the surge of adrenaline, pheromone or whatever his body is burning through. The flames from the candles blur into sequins of light. He shakes it off, light-headed for a moment before the flames lose their halo.

"Steven, you're OK?"

He hums in response, palming his neck, his skin clammy under his fingers.

"It's never recommended to mix alcohols," she adds.

"What do you mean?" The words stick to the roof of his mouth, and he takes another swallow of his drink.

"Mixing wine and spirits. I've seen enough students' hangovers caused by this." He snorts. His laugh echoes under the vault of his skull. "I'm no student. I just hope I'm not coming down with something." Stranded out here with no signal, the prospect of getting help if he were to be sick adds to his queasiness.

"I hope not as well."

Vanilla and jasmine. The scent is back again.

"Do you smell that?" he asks, but he doesn't listen or hear if she's answered.

Where does he know that perfume from? The face associated with this scent still eludes him. He's dismissing the thought with another sip from his drink when the fire catches his eye. Flames so bright, their yellow pulsating amid an aura of orange. The mesmerizing sight reaches an unexpected crescendo when a log collapses, sending crackling sparks up the chimney. Steven staggers back as the explosion of light blurs his vision. Ellie's face swims in and out of focus. Eyes screwed shut, he pinches the bridge of his nose. When he opens them again, the room and Ellie are back to normal.

"You really don't look well." Ellie's words sag with worry. "Are you OK? Steven? Answer me."

For a moment, he feels like the ocean has crept under the house, turning the living room into a heaving vessel on a choppy sea. The gin swirling in his glass adds to the sensation. Taking a deep breath, he waits until the feeling subsides. Dry-mouthed, he drains the rest of his drink.

Regaining his composure, he stares at the glass in his hand. "That is some seriously strong gin. Did we bring this?"

The words drag, as if his jaw has turned into concrete. The stiffness spreads to his limbs and his mind. He shakes his head but can't shed the heaviness, its hold already too strong.

"No, I found it on the cart." Ellie's voice echoes inside his head. "Maybe you should lie down. You really don't look good."

His vision splits, and two of her—slightly misaligned—look at him. He sees one through the other, as if she is standing there with her ghost.

Staggering around, he starts to laugh, but it doesn't sound like him. The room spins around, letting him know the joke's on him. His legs buckle. The rush of the fall overpowers him until his hand grips the back of the sofa. The world is sliding away.

"Steven?"

There is panic in her voice, and something else at the edge of it, but her words are distorted, as if they are traveling through a great ocean. Hooking a finger under the wool, he pulls at the neck of his sweater—but the gesture doesn't help. The air around him thickens, heavy with a new warmth that presses against his chest, lodges in his lungs, air that makes it harder to breathe. The floor sways beneath his feet. The strength in his legs weakens. The glass falls from his hand, shattering on the floor, the sound of a thousand bells ringing in his ears. With her hand under his elbow, the other on his back, she guides him to the sofa.

The room dims, and darkness creeps in at the edge, swallowing the living room until all that's left is a pinprick of light and the high-pitched gabble of Ellie's voice. The mystery perfume is stronger than ever. It is all around him, insinuating itself until it is all he's aware of. Persistent and soothing. Like a hand stroking the back of his neck.

Day Two

Ourself, behind ourself concealed,
Should startle most;
Assassin, hid in our apartment,
Be horror's least.

Emily Dickinson

20. Steven

His shoulders are killing him. Seated, chin resting on his chest, he rolls his head on each side to loosen the muscles. He wants to call out, but his mouth is so dry, and his tongue is stuck to the roof of his mouth. Slowly, he runs it over his teeth a couple of times, but he still can't form words. His eyelids weigh a ton. He concentrates on lifting them, and the darkness is replaced by a blinding whiteness. As it recedes, fuzzy shapes emerge, the outline of a sofa and blurry smudges of yellows and reds dancing inside a dark frame—the fireplace. He's in the living room.

The room is darker than before, and he is stuck in front of a giant untuned TV screen, just showing static. The candles. All the candles have been extinguished but a few, and the screen is not a television, just the giant blackened living-room windows. Outside, the blizzard has returned, snowflakes crashing against the glass before sliding down, the hint of howling wind breaking through the double-glazed barrier. Behind the wintry deluge the sky is thick with dark-gray clouds, making it impossible to tell if it's day or night—how long has he been out?

What happened? He casts his mind back to the time before he woke up, before he lost consciousness, only to find a big gaping hole where the memories should be. How much has he lost? He tugs at little bits of threads in his mind. He has a few images, some smells and a few words. He pulls them together to weave into a narrative and stitch over the holes in his memory. A weekend away. They drove down

97

in the car, a girl sleeping in the seat next to him. He kissed her against a tree, the heat of her tongue on his, the freezing cold surrounding them. Was that today? *Ellie*. Her name shoots through his mind like a bullet. His head snaps back. The room feels empty. Where is she? His head, still so heavy, rolls again, then falls like that of a dozing student during a boring lecture, his mind on the edge of consciousness. He keeps falling. Inside a dark well. Inside his own body. In the darkness, he sees her frightened face. Ellie. The idea she needs him, is scared, waking up dazed and confused somewhere alone, is the incentive for him to finally lift his head and keep it up.

His mouth opens, but the words get stuck, insects caught on the flypaper of his tongue. He clears his throat several times until he dislodges the one that he needs.

"Ellie." His voice is barely a whisper. "Ellie?" Her name breaks on his dried lips. He swallows whatever saliva he can salvage and sucks in the air. "Ellie?"

A low rumble, somewhere else in the house. "Ellie, is that you?" Each word burns his throat.

Upstairs. Footsteps, the mumble of voices, maybe? The crackles of the fire pop in his ears, the heat presses against his body, echoes of memories fighting their way through compete with whispered words. So many pieces of information his mind can't process, clashing, pulling him in different directions only to leave him spinning inside his own body with bile rising in his throat.

Ellie. He anchors his mind around her name to stop being swept and pulled under the waves of information swirling around. After a few deep breaths, the onslaught ebbs, and he remembers foreboding words she said to him, words he dismissed. Her voice whispers to him as images flash in his head. The kitchen, surrounded by an opaque darkness, Ellie's silhouette turned toward the silvery tint of the window, what he mistook for childish fear, *I think I saw something outside.* Flash. In the forest, lost in their kiss until the snap of a branch broke their embrace. Flash. Her body flat against his, the dying heat of her mouth on his. The apprehension in her voice as she said, *I feel like someone's watching.* Maybe he should have listened.

Ellie; the lull amid the storm raging around and inside him. He must get to her, ensure she's OK. In his swaying impulse to rescue her, he lurches forward, but his limbs refuse to move no matter how much energy he puts into them. He is fused to his chair. Like his mind, his body is now something else, refusing to respond to his orders. His thrashing and the swaying of his head get to be too much. A musky fear fills the air, pulls the walls forward, bending them to this new reality he's a prisoner of. The distortion is too much, and another violent bout of nausea overpowers him, its sourness stinging the back of his throat. He breathes slowly to keep the sickness at bay.

Commotion. Upstairs, definitely upstairs. Despite his attempt to remain calm, his imagination conjures up dark scenarios where Ellie recoils against the headboard of the master bed, trapped prey as a featureless individual inches toward her. She prays for him to come and rescue her, and he's stuck down here, unable to get to her before she's engulfed by the intruder's shadow. He tries her name, but it dies in his throat before he can open his mouth.

He was wrong to assume they were safe here, alone and shielded from the rest of civilization. Anyone could have broken in, any stranger forced by the storm to look for shelter and finding an opportunity to take more.

Steven concentrates on his breath, lets each inhalation clear the fog, painfully aware that each second he isn't moving is one more second that Ellie needs him. A second closer to the worst happening and him not being there to stop it.

An echo. A familiar sound. His name elongated. A low rumble that morphs into the faraway gallop of feet running down wooden steps. In the silence that follows, the soothing rhythm of breathing fills the room somewhere behind him.

"Steven?"

His mind latches on to her voice to pull itself from the hole in his memory. His lids too heavy to lift, he concentrates on his mouth.

"I'm here."

Ellie's blurry face zooms in and out of focus in front of him. Hair disheveled, the eyes of an animal that wants to flee. He blinks, adjusting his vision until the lines of her face become clear, but something seems off.

"How are you feeling?" Her voice is distorted like in a bad phone connection, her eyes darting all over his face. Their constant motion reawakening the nausea at the back of his throat.

Her hands leave his legs to cradle his face, steady his flopping head. Her blurry smile appears before him, and his heart swells up in rhythm with the stretch of her lips as relief inflates in his chest. She's OK.

"What...what—" A fit of dry coughing interrupts his question.

"Just wait," she says before disappearing. Without her support, his head plunges forward before snapping back into position.

She returns in a flash, and with her the edge of a plastic circle pressed against his lips. The rush of water floods his mouth with a welcome freshness. He gulps it down; rivulets spill on either side of his mouth, water dribbling from his chin, dampening the collar of his shirt. He doesn't care. He downs the entire contents. The sudden rush of hydration improves more than just the dryness of his mouth; his lungs expand fully, tasting the clean air, his vision finally settling into focus. His strength returning, he leans forward to take Ellie in his arms, feel her weight against his chest, making sure for himself that she is indeed OK. Now he can take her by the hand, grab the car keys and escape far away to safety, but his arms still refuse to cooperate.

"What happened?" he asks her, but his question is met by a silence that stretches between them, thick and uncomfortable until it becomes unbearable. While he waits, his mind fills in the blanks with a new terrible scenario, one where his amnesia doesn't result from an intruder attacking them but from the combination of drunkenness and a fall down the stairs which broke his back, leaving him paralyzed from the neck down. The threat of a stranger replaced by a far more terrifying one.

"How bad is it?" This time she answers with a stillness in her eyes and a slight crease of her brow. He sees the pity she has for him. The feeling repulses him. The last thing he has ever wanted is to be pitied. The idea curls his fingers into a ball strangling that pity. His fingers. He can move them; he can't be paralyzed. A delirious relief floods his chest. The self-diagnosis gives him the confidence he needs to finally look down.

Both arms are bound on armrests by several layers of duct tape. He leans forward as far as he can. His legs are bound too, but it's not a chair...He is bound to a wheelchair. He struggles against his restraints, but they won't budge. The intruder theory springs back into his mind.

"Ellie, go grab a knife or something."

"I can't."

Her response and matter-of-fact tone shock him into silence. Maybe whoever tied him down has coerced her, threatened her with unfathomable things if she doesn't comply with their instructions. At least she appears unhurt, but who knows what her clothes might hide.

"Cut me loose before they come back." Her eyes widen as they flicker past him to something, or someone. The instigator standing watch behind him, silently controlling her. If he concentrates, he swears he can hear the soft rhythm of their breathing.

"Ellie, I understand you're scared." Each word that comes out of him requires all the energy he can muster. Her eyes flicker from his face to a spot above his right shoulder. How did they get here? This was supposed to be a romantic weekend, just the two of them getting to know each other better. All the clues he dismissed are crowding his mind once again—the forest, the darkened kitchen. Until they are bleached by a light. Blinding lights in his mind. He concentrates on them until the fuzziness recedes. Headlights, their pale glow reflected in his rearview mirror on that last stretch of road. A shadowy silhouette behind the wheel of the mysterious car, watching his Lexus as it makes the last turn into the private road hemmed by the forest. The same silhouette slipping inside the house while they are out for their afternoon walk, hiding upstairs until their time came. His mind refuses to go further.

"Ellie, I know you're scared but you can do this."

Without another word, she unfurls her body until she towers over him. The curtain of her hair falls across her face. When she pushes it back her expression has changed.

She looks like someone new, someone he doesn't recognize. Leaning in, she brushes away the wisps of hair clinging to his damp forehead, her eyes locked on his.

"Why would I untie you, when I'm the one who tied you up in the first place?"

21. Ellie

His mouth's agape, but he has no words. He stares at me with blown-out pupils full of a mix of shock and disbelief. My lungs shrivel in my chest and anxiety trickles into my veins. I haven't felt this nervous since the first time we met, at the café he likes to go to near his school. When he sat there, perfectly dressed, shining brown hair styled in a quiff, deep-set blue eyes hemmed by a neat but fully straight brow, with me dripping on my chair, tendrils of hair plastered on my cheeks like seaweed on rocks, feeling positively un-attractive. Despite it all, he liked me that day; enough to ask for my number and call later to confirm the details of the bar we should meet at for drinks.

"Ellie, what the hell?" he asks with a voice mixed with anger and confusion. "How did you…"

"I just slipped you a little something." My weight shifts from one leg to the other, nervous energy buzzing down my arms.

"How? When?"

"You're not a woman. You've never been taught to be cau-tious of accepting drinks you didn't see mixed in front of you."

"You drugged me?" His eyes widen, pupils still saucer-sized, a ring of blue clinging to them, like the cat experien-cing the unnerving feeling of being a mouse the first time it meets a dog.

The information slackens his fingers around the chair's armrests. There is nothing more to say right now; I just have to wait. It has to come from him, in his own time. Anxiety creeps back along my spine. The urge to walk it off is strong, but I fight it. Running has been my coping mechanism since my late teenage years. Swallowing miles, music in my ears, until all I can think of is the burn in my thighs and the rhythm of my breath. Grinding my worries under each step pounding the pavement.

Rooted to my spot, I wait for his next words.

"Why, Ellie? Just tell me, why?"

"It's just part of a little game. Something to make the weekend...more interesting. I wanted to do something different. For you." I peer at him from under my lashes. Please, forgive me. I need him to forgive me.

"What the hell, I'm tied up," he says, struggling against his restraints. The whole expression twisting his face demands that he be let out.

"It's part of a game I read about. I wanted to spice things up for our anniversary." He responds with an arched brow. "I thought we could do something special, be more adventurous. I don't want us to become one of those boring couples."

"You didn't need to drug me. If you wanted—"

"I know, it's just I didn't know how to ask you. Do you forgive me?" There is a tinge of remorse in my voice as I chew on my bottom lip. His silence is an invitation for me to continue. "You play, and I promise you'll get lucky. Very lucky. Please? Just indulge me." My lips brush against his as I pronounce the last words.

I kiss him, and he doesn't resist. He parts his lips, his tongue invades my mouth. I can still taste the remains of gin on it. I push back against him, fighting him for control of the exchange until his back is flat against the chair and his head tilts back. I break it off, leaving him panting.

He breaks the silence first. "What's the game?"

I smile. "You're gonna love it, I promise."

I retrieve the stack of papers from the coffee table, where I left them earlier. Perching on the back of the sofa, I savor this moment of anticipation—shuffling pages, reviewing the order—the thrill of being on the edge of the board before diving in. Once I speak, it will all go into motion, the weight of my words tipping the first domino.

"So, professor, I thought we would test your knowledge of literature. Famous texts and their authors."

"All right…" The word tails off with uncertainty.

"Let's start with an easy one: 'To see a World in a Grain of Sand and a Heaven in a Wild Flower, hold Infinity in the palm of your hand, and Eternity in an hour.' Who's that from?"

Pride stretches a smile on his face. "William Blake." Vanity knows no bounds, not even those of duct tape.

"Good, professor." Smiling, I pull my sweater over my head, before tossing it to the side. Standing now in my socks, leggings, and a thermal tank top over my bra. His attention perks up, straightening his spine.

"How about 'I am no bird; and no net ensnares me: I am a free human being with an independent will'?"

"*Jane Eyre.*" This answer rings in the air.

I smile, hooking my thumbs in the waist of my leggings. Anticipation and flames from the remaining candles shine in his eyes. If he were a wolf, he would be licking his lips by now. Instead of carrying on with the expected, I bend and remove my socks.

"Oh, come on."

I smirk at his apparent disappointment. "You know, all good things…"

"I know, I know."

Flicking through the pages I settle for the next quote.

"Now this one. 'We loved each other with a premature love, marked by a fierceness that so often destroys adult lives.' Any guesses?"

Under his silence, his brow furrows. Recognizing the quote but searching, trying to place the sentences on the right page, in the right book. I jump off the back of the sofa, closing the distance that separates us until I settle on his lap. Mouth close to his, I repeat the words, almost brushing my lips against his.

"Can I have a clue?" His lips pucker at the last word, almost turning it into a kiss.

"'She was Lo, plain Lo, in the morning, standing four feet ten in one sock. She was Lola in slacks. She was Dolly at school.'"

"*Lolita.*"

The name comes out as a whisper, carried by his warm breath on my skin still seasoned with a hint of gin. Staying on his lap, I wiggle out of my tank, leaving us with just my bra, leggings, and his hard-on pressing on my buttocks. Even tied to a wheelchair he's enjoying the play, maybe secretly relishing being the subject in my game. Discovering there are pleasures to be had in surrendering, in the anticipation.

"What do I win?" he asks, eyes leering at the hollow point between my breasts, the future reward for his next correct answer that waits under the cotton of my bra. My body the prize he is entitled to if he says the right word. In that moment, I watch the features of his face blur as he becomes an effigy of those who lay their claim on us: the guys who've grabbed my ass at parties or in bars, the older man who followed me for five blocks when I dared to deny him a smile and an answer, the date who placed my hand on his dick as we kissed for the first time.

He is so predictable. How nobody has seen through him

is a mystery. People can develop a selective blindness to what they do not want to see, spinning stories to distract from what's in front of them.

"Last one. 'I can't stop thinking about you.'" He looks at me blankly. True, the words are a cliché, appearing in lots of different novels. I move toward him.

"How about: 'Nobody has ever made me feel that way before'?"

Still no spark of recognition from him. Despite the drugs and restraints, he's still unconcerned, comforted in his belief that he knows me, that I am no threat. I'm Ellie, his shy girlfriend, the girl who blushes whenever he gives her a compliment, the girl who always lets him have it his way, makes it all about him. Safe, predictable Ellie. My actions don't deserve an afterthought. He's so oblivious, so blinded by the shine of his self-assurance he hasn't even wondered where the hell the wheelchair came from.

I wet my lips. "Maybe this will help." Leaning, cheeks almost touching, the next clue a whisper in his ear. "'Thanks for last night, Professor H. J xxx.'"

The last sentence hardens the muscles in his body, digs deep grooves in his smooth forehead in realization at who the author is. His right hand struggles against his restraint.

For the first time, he has no clever answer, no words. I've stolen them all. All his innate confidence melts from his face, and a new kind of excitement tingles in the tips of my fingers. The air is heavy with the shift of power inside the room, for the first time in our relationship. There's so much I want to tell him.

His eyes dart all over me. He is worried. I'm no longer safe and predictable Ellie.

Even worse than that: I know about the texts.

I know about her.

22

February 12

You spotted me today after I hid badly behind a cypress tree on the opposite sidewalk like a third-rate Nancy Drew.

You said, "What are you doing here?"

Grabbing me under the arm, the pressure of your fingers digging into my flesh, you hurried me across the road before ushering me inside your building.

The familiarity of your apartment felt alien to me as I writhed around, unsure where I fitted any more. The air was different somehow, a tangy citrus scent lingering in the room, then it hit me—it smelled of her.

You sat beside me. Your cologne barely concealed the smell underneath, the smell I used to know so well, the smell that used to be on me.

"I love you," I blurted out. I had never said it until now, not because I didn't mean it but because I was terrified of what your reaction might be.

You sighed again, and that little puff of air was more soul-destroying than all the words I had imagined you might have said. I stared at the wall behind you. I pictured an unmade bed, a pillow dented with the imprint of her head. The images liquified in my eyes, and I tried hard not to blink.

You wrapped your hands around my fist as you said, "What do you have in here?"

You peeled my fingers away to reveal a folded piece of

paper in the nest of my palm. You opened the photograph, and all color drained from your face.

"Do you realize how much you could hurt me with this?" Your voice bellowed, twisting me around your disappointment until it wrung me so tight I thought I might shatter. "If it fell into the wrong hands?"

You snatched the picture from my hand and without a second glance tore the paper version of us to pieces. Ripped right through my smile, turning our story into confetti.

23. Steven

The cheap leather flecks under his nails as they scratch grooves into the armrest. How can this be? He's always been careful with J. and he's never given Ellie any reasons to doubt him. The tape tightens against his wrists and ankles, robbing him of the right to subtract himself from her implied accusations by walking away. She's tricked him. He didn't think she was that kind of girl. The kind who likes to play games, especially these kind of games. A silence has settled between them, uncomfortable and heavy with all that's not been said. Steven's sure she has questions; he has too, but in his case asking them would imply there is some truth in what she's found. In the hearth, burning logs crackle and snap loudly like bones being stepped on.

"So?" she asks as she leans against the window, slanted body, her shoulders only pressing against the glass, arms folded under breasts, ankles crossed. Face closed, she looks down at him; he has to twist his neck to the side to look back. Something is different, but he can't quite put his finger on it.

"I'm waiting," she adds.

Her eyes. They have a coldness he has never seen before. She's become a void, as if someone has scooped what makes her Ellie out of her body.

"I have no idea what you're talking about." He shifts in his chair to cross his legs, forgetting for a moment they are still bound to the footrests.

"Cut the crap, Steven. I know. I just want to hear you say it."

There is a harshness in her voice, the control, her general demeanor; he has no idea who the girl in front of him is. As if she has been switched while he was unconscious. This is insane. They should be in Stockton, taking a stroll down the waterfront, ducking in and out of antique stores. She would have threaded her arm inside the crook of his elbow, asking his opinion to help her choose something for her apartment. When she'd found it, he would have insisted on buying it for her, just to see that smile of hers lighting up her face. Purchase made, they would have sat at a local café with bistro tables covered in gingham tablecloths, one of those places where the menu would have claimed that all ingredients were sourced locally and owned by someone who had wanted to escape the stress of living in a big city. Instead, he has wandered into this nightmare. Around them the room pulses with the orange glow coming from the fire, shadows heaving as if the walls were alive.

"It's nothing. One of my students playing around. That's it, I promise—"

"Really. 'Thank you for last night.' That's a prank?"

"I helped her with an essay, that's all."

"Do you think I'm stupid?"

"Why would I cheat on you? It makes no sense."

"You're so much like your father."

The last word whips the air with the sting of an accusation. The unexpected mention of his old man throws him. This is the last place he would have imagined the old bastard's shadow to follow him. If Ellie had met him then she would have had a worthy target for her anger, but she never did. He made sure of that.

"Why are you talking about my father?"

"Because you're just like him, aren't you?"

"How would you even know?"

For her only answer, she drops her gaze toward the window, her face obscured by the curtain of her hair.

He senses there are things she doesn't tell him. Surely, she couldn't be one of them—one of his father's wide-eyed college students. He retraces the steps of her life, searching for the path that would have intersected with Professor Stewart Harding. But in truth, the life she led before they met is mainly a mystery he had no real motivation to solve until now. Is this where the answer lies?

"Just tell me the truth," Ellie asks. "Please."

She is too upset with him for this to be about his father. This is about what he's done or hasn't done, and her feelings for him.

"You haven't answered my question."

"You haven't answered mine," she replies.

"Can we just talk about—"

"We are talking, and I'm asking you to tell me the truth."

Where is the girl who peered at him from under her long bangs? Who always asked for his opinion and listened, hanging on to his every word? He looks at her pinched lips, the angry eyes. It's the same face, but he doesn't see his Ellie, the shy, indecisive girl—the girl who made him wait. Six dates before she agreed. The wait had driven him crazy in this age of instant gratification, but that delayed anticipation had made the reward all the more satisfying.

"I am. I promise—"

"Don't." The word falls like a knife cutting through his lies.

This isn't her. Somehow this isn't her doing. He ransacks his mind for a clue. Someone had to lead her down this path, turn the Ellie he knows into this spiteful girl in front of him.

"You might have taken me for an idiot until now, and I might have allowed it, but it stops now. I know, so there's no point in lying. It's just insulting. I've seen the texts. I know about her."

Her last sentence chills the marrow in his spine, stiffening it. It can't be a coincidence. Word for word what J. said in her last text to him.

He pictures J. and Ellie, perhaps inside the familiar space of Norman's Café—but he doesn't want their presence to spoil his usual haunt, and they wouldn't have wanted the risk of running into him anyway. Instead, he relocates them to one of those trendy places where mismatched living-room furniture makes for hip seating arrangements. He pictures J. slumped on a battered old sofa, while Ellie rests on the edge of a green velvet armchair, wringing her hands, and her eyes shining under a heavy glaze of tears. Trying to reconcile what J. tells her with the certainties she has about what she and Steven have, his commitment to her. Their relationship fracturing under J.'s accusations.

"Sorry. I don't want to hurt you, but I thought you should know."

"It can't be possible. He wouldn't do that to me. To us."

"Look, don't take my word for it. Take his."

J. sliding her phone toward Ellie, maneuvering around their oversized porcelain cups. Ellie with her usual cappuccino, the white froth unspoiled by cocoa dusting. *Coffee and chocolate should never mix,* she told him once with a solemn face. Ellie, staring at his words on J.'s screen.

"Anybody could have sent those."

"Check the number they came from."

Each digit of his cell number a nail in the coffin of Ellie's trust in him. Each blink frees a tear from her lashes.

How could he have been so reckless? He never should have trusted J.

While Ellie waits, he ransacks his brain for the appropriate response, but a persistent pain throbs behind his eyes, making it hard to stay focused. All around him, walls of plaster and glass box him in, the room looming over him. Outside, the wind swirls with such force, crowds the air with so many flakes, that he can't discern anything for certain anymore. If he's right and she's seen J., she knows she has nothing to fear; she eclipses J. in every way possible. After all, she's the reason he put an end to whatever had been going on with J.

"It doesn't mean anything; she doesn't mean anything. You have to believe me."

"Why on earth should I believe you?" All her defenses are up, her arms are tightly crossed, hands on her elbows, her face a mask of hostility. There's no way in.

"She's just a girl, she means nothing to me."

"Nice—so you're just using her."

"No, that's not what I meant. I had a moment of weakness; she threw herself at me."

"Are you saying it's her fault?"

"It's…"

"You could have said no."

"Ellie, please."

"How long has this been going on?"

"Not long. I regretted it as soon as it happened. Is this why you tied me up? There's no need for that. You're safe with me. I would never hurt you."

"You just did."

Silence falls in the room, like the snow settling outside. Shaking her head, Ellie pushes herself off the window and walks over to the fireplace, the outline of her body highlighted by the orange glow from the flames. Her shoulders go slack, and her hands disappear into the thick mass of her hair. Seeing her like this saddens him. He never wanted to hurt her, he never intended for her to find out. It just happened. The way J. had looked at him...he didn't know how to say no. Not to her but the idea of being with her, the excitement of being wanted, desired. She doesn't mean anything; it certainly doesn't mean he cares for Ellie any less.

"How could you?" Her words are barely audible over the sneers of the fire.

"How did you know?"

"Does it matter?"

"I'm so sorry. Can you please untie me?"

"Sorry you did it or sorry you got caught?" Her words are spiked with a contempt he has never witnessed in her before.

"I never meant to hurt you. Ellie, look at me." She ignores his request, staring at the darkness outside, the light from the stars obliterated by the thick cloud cover. "Please look at me."

He needs her to look at him. He can convince her, make her understand, but he needs to make a connection first. Once his eyes hook on hers, he will find a way in, a way to make her see. J. has underestimated the bond he shares with Ellie. She's a good listener, always has been. The day they met at Norman's Café, she was reluctant at first, but he strung the right words along that earned her trust and her phone number. He knows he can gather the words she will respond to, the right combination to express remorse, which will earn her forgiveness, get him out of his restraints and out of this chair. If he can forgive her for the lapse in judgment which led her to drug and restrain him, surely she can forgive his.

"Is she the only one?" The question comes as she's still looking at her own reflection or maybe the forest behind, he can't be sure.

"Ellie..."

Before he can add more, she's in motion, closing the distance between them until she crouches in front of him, her arms a warm weight on his lap.

"Tell me the truth, Steven. We can get through this but only if you tell me the truth."

There's an urgency to her words. Her fingers lace with his as she waits for him to answer, the look on her face asking him to not break her heart further. In the dim light, Ellie's skin glows bone pale, giving her a ghostlike appearance, as if she's not really there anymore. For a moment he regrets that this is not just about some stranger attacking them. At least he would know how to protect them from that kind of assault.

What to tell her? If she only knows about J. then why hurt her further, but if she's aware of everything and she catches him lying...His forefinger scratches the leather covering the armrest. What's the right answer? The right thing to say can be so different from the truth. The rising noise of his nail against the leather grates on him, yet he cannot stop. All the while her eyes are on him, pleading, unwavering.

He has been here before, many years ago. Same eyes, different face. They belonged to his mother. She looked at him with the same distress dripping from her gaze when he was only thirteen. He'd just returned from spending a few days with his old man, who was on his latest book tour. He sat at the kitchen table the morning after he came back—school was starting soon—while his father pushed on west alone with the determination of the early pioneers. His mother piled the questions on as she dropped his favorite French toast onto his plate. He stuffed his mouth with the warm cinnamon dough so his words were sporadic and stodgy.

He stood as soon as he'd swallowed the last piece, the legs of the chair scraping against the floor tiles. Before he could take a step, his mother's hands stopped him, heavy on his shoulders. She fixed him with the same gaze Ellie has on him right now. His mother's question back then not so different from Ellie's; his answer identical.

"No," he replies. "There's no one else."

24

February 25

You apologized with one of your smiles that sends me free-falling inside my own body, telling me you hoped I understood but you would have to miss our private sessions from now on, but you had so much work at the moment. I can't remember what you said next. It's all a blur.

I forced myself to put on what I hoped was a convincing smile. "Of course, I understand. It's fine." It's not fine, it's far from fine. If fine was the sun, I would be the planet the farthest away from it. It's not fine, it's a boulder crushing me, it's my heart ripped into pieces, it's a pain so visceral it drove me out of the room and into the nearest bathroom stall.

I asked you later, "Did I do anything wrong?"

You said, "I don't know what you mean. There's nothing wrong. You read too much into things. I'm just busy."

Sometimes hurt becomes something else. Like how you can collapse a piece of paper into an arrangement of layers to become a crane, a lotus flower, or a butterfly. Sometimes my pain doubles over, collapses into anger, and I think—you cost me my happiness and maybe, just maybe, you should just pay for it.

25. Steven

With a sigh, she stands up, her fingers slipping away from his. The tape around his wrists stopping him from going after her.

"Can you please untie me, so we can talk properly?"

"Why would I untie a liar who clearly has no respect for me?" she replies, the stack of paper she used for her earlier game back in her hands.

"Ellie—"

"No others, you said?"

"Yes, but—"

"Then what do you call this?"

She throws a couple of sheets of paper, which land on his lap. Looking down he feels ice grow down his spine again.

"The elusive J. is a redhead, if I'm correct, isn't she?"

Sweat pools in the hollow of his armpits, soaking the fabric of the shirt beneath his sweater. The grainy pictures are of a girl with long blonde hair, wearing lacy white underwear peppered with tiny embroidered flowers, the digital date and time stamp screaming at him in the bottom right corner. He curses himself for taking the shots, for his moment of weakness. He just wanted to indulge her that day. He should have said no. He doesn't need the photos. He remembers them all.

A. loved posing for him. Despite the low-quality printout, the expression of contentment is clear on her face. The way she always looked after they had sex.

He stopped seeing her not long after he started dating Ellie. He met her at the public library, where she was doing research for a project. She bumped into him as she flew up the grand staircase, knocking his books. Her profuse apologies drew a smile to his face. He loved the way she fingered the pages of her notebook as she listened to him. They agreed to meet up again two days later, when he kissed her for the first time in the astronomy section. She tasted of cherry and pressed her body against his, hard—an offering he couldn't refuse. She opened up to him quickly.

"I grew up in foster care. Mom's a junkie, Dad's a cliché sperm donation who didn't stick around. Nobody's ever cared what I do. Always been my own person."

She met him whenever he texted her, grateful for the attention and the experience of a man, not a boy. She held his hand the first time he took her inside his bedroom, his fingers intertwined with hers the same way Ellie's had a moment ago. The photos had been her idea—they had been sleeping together for a few weeks by then.

On his lap, the pictures come to life. A.'s pale limbs lift off the paper until he sees her sitting on his bed like she had been on that particular day.

"Do you think I'm beautiful?" she had asked him as she hooked her bra.

"Of course you are," he'd replied, kissing her swollen lips. They'd just had sex, and her cheeks were still flushed with the red of orgasm.

"I want to pose for you." She'd reclined on the bed, offering herself. "Would you take my picture? I want to see what I look like after you've come inside me."

He'd been happy to indulge her request, and she'd lain before him exposed, vulnerable, and completely trusting. After a few snaps, he'd tossed his phone aside and engulfed her body with his, only releasing her into the world thirty minutes later. The relationship fizzled out quickly after that.

She had been a bright shooting star whose light distracted him for a moment. He should never have kept the pictures but whenever he looked at them, cursor hovering, ready to drag them over to the trash icon, they reminded him of how he had felt that day, and, his chest inflated, he smiled at the screen and left the files in his computer folder.

His refusal to delete them proves a weakness which angers him. A.'s frozen gaze, which had never been captured on paper before—only lived in pixels on his screen—leads him to question how the grainy photos have landed in Ellie's hands and ultimately on his lap. A storm arises inside his chest, locking his jaw, tensing his arms, muscles straining against the tape as shame curdles into indignation.

"You went into my computer behind my back?"

He would never have thought she was one of those jealous types who riffled through personal possessions, disregarded boundaries because they felt entitled to every single part of the other's one life, leaving them no privacy. How did she even know to look for them in the first place? Nobody knew about them, not even J. *Certainly* not J. The only person who knew... fear doesn't allow him to finish that thought. A. must be involved somehow—it stings of her impulsiveness. That free-spirited nature that had attracted him—how she would pull him deep into dark spaces between towering bookcases, on the edges of getting caught; how she would undress him as soon as he closed the door. Was this the price to pay for ending the brief moment they had shared together—her sabotaging his chance at a happy relationship by telling Ellie?

His mind directs a new scene, A. loitering outside his

apartment building, waiting for him to emerge but instead seeing him with Ellie. Later, she would have approached Ellie, telling her everything, rocking on the heels of her boots like a wrecking ball gathering momentum before smashing through his relationship. Now all that was left was for him to get impaled on the pieces. He's never understood this need to cling to such petty vindictiveness, so often present in women. Why not just move on with dignity?

"You've cheated on me, with not one but two girls, and *I* should be the one ashamed because I went into your computer?" She towers over him, forcing him to tip his head back to look at her. "You're unbelievable."

Leaving him stuck in his seat with her accusations, she crosses over to the loaded cart and pours herself a drink. She downs two fingers of gin before refilling her glass. The metamorphosis continues. The "Ellie" he knows doesn't chug down alcohol like this; she sips it like a child, drinks it slowly, hoping to tame the bitterness with small baby steps. She isn't someone who gulps it down without flinching.

"How could you do this to me? To us?"

He racks his brain for the words to explain this has nothing to do with her, with them, that their relationship is something that exists on a different level than those girls. They satisfy a desire, scratch an itch. They are superficial, insignificant compared to what he experiences with her.

"Can I have some water?"

"What?" His unexpected request narrows those big eyes of hers into slits.

"Water. Could I have some more? My mouth's still very dry, and I'm still feeling nauseous. Please?"

With a sigh, she leaves the room. Like he's become an inconvenience to her. Without her scrutiny and her incessant questions and accusations he can finally think.

The only reason she can hate him this much is because she's hurting. Pain is causing her to lash out, and the extreme reaction means she loves him. His actions wouldn't have hurt her to such an extent if she didn't care. A., J., whichever one told her hasn't managed to snuff all the love Ellie has for him. He knows this brand of hurt, that reeling pain. He has a name for it; one he hasn't thought of in years. Zoey.

When she gets back, he will tell her, show her how much she means to him. He will say anything that will get him out of this chair. If his complete and absolute apology is the price for his freedom, then he will lay the words at her feet.

The air in the room shifts, and the smell of vanilla and jasmine drifts around him. His skin bristles at a light touch like the brush of spider legs against the exposed skin at the back of his neck.

"Is someone else here?" He cranes to see if someone's behind him, but his question is only met by the bloody cackles of the fire.

The perfume lingers, as well as an elusive memory carried by the scent, something familiar he cannot place. The blurred etchings of a face, a smile. Not J. Not A., not C. Definitely not Ellie. Someone else.

Before he can add definition to the features, he is blinded by an explosion of light from the chandelier above as Ellie strides back into the room. He squints, blinking until his eyes adjust to the sharpened environment, and he rehearses in his head the words that will win her over.

26. Ellie

In the kitchen, I don't bother with a glass. Tap gushing, I gulp by the mouthful out of my cupped hands until it hurts. The water leaves me breathless. I splash some on my face, but it doesn't help. This is harder than expected. But I have a reason, one stronger than anything else, stronger than any pity he could conjure out of me. He can only blame his arrogant overconfidence for this situation. He's confused meekness for naivety. He truly believed I didn't see the phone—always turned facedown—on the table at dinner or next to the sofa, the quick flip around and checks at regular intervals, how it was purposely stashed away in the pockets of coats and jackets. I've always wondered if this was a premeditated habit or a subconscious defense mechanism. As I lean against the counter, the heart pendant weighs against my skin.

Recently there have also been increased trips to the public library for research papers as well as the increasing number of plans canceled or changed at the last minute. But I didn't make a scene; didn't demand explanation; didn't stop having sex.

As the empty bottle fills up under the tap, I finger the silver heart. The smile on Steven's face this morning when I opened the box. Him flipping pancakes, the smell of batter sweetening the air in this very room not so long ago. My confidence snags on a splinter of doubt.

The face I need waits behind my closed lids. Memories follow. One rises above all else. Our kiss, that night away from prying eyes at the party, unfolding inside, feelings heightened by the risk of getting caught. The memory washes away any lingering doubts. What Steven's done flashes in my mind, and the prickle of tears stings my eyes. A couple of rogue tears escape, which I mop with the cuff of my sweater.

Nobody but us. The words run over my tongue several times like prayer beads. In the privacy of the kitchen I take my time and stitch myself together again.

"Listen, I have something I want to say to you." Steven's words surprise me as soon as I step back into the glaring light of the living room.

"Don't you want a drink any more?"

"No. Listen, Ellie."

His face has changed as if he's morphed into someone else while I wasn't looking. I wasn't away that long, I think. Gone is the spiteful, defensive Steven; now a more serene version of him sits in the wheelchair, the lines on his face smoothed out, his right hand stretched open, fingers fanned out. I stare confounded at the odd gesture until I slip my hand in his. I brace for a sharp tug, an attempt to break my fingers, instead his thumb strokes my skin.

"I'm sorry."

"You are?" The apology coming from him surprises me even more than his effort at a loving gesture. It strips me of all emotions. He wears a genuine expression of remorse on his face at odds with the Steven I know.

"I've hurt you, when I never wanted to hurt you. I was a fool, a fucking idiot."

The F-bomb, unheard of in his mouth; even when he stubs his toe on the corner of the bed, he won't go as far as a "damn it." Not even on the day I spilled coffee on him by accident.

"Do you really mean it?"

"I was scared to fully commit, and those girls, they were... I messed up, but never again. If you give me another chance, I will never hurt you again the way I did." His promise comes with a squeeze of his hand, which I return, to both our surprise. His fingers are cold, perhaps from the tape slowing his blood circulation. Outside, the storm has dulled into a drift of snow. My gaze flickers toward the kitchen.

"Forgiveness is earned with actions, not words."

"All right. I'll go to therapy, as often and as long as you want me to attend."

"You would seriously do that?" The question catches in my throat. Maybe scaring him was enough. If he had therapy, he couldn't go back to hiding behind his denial, finally admitting what he did.

"I would." He nods.

"But how could I trust you?"

His face lights up at the question. "Go upstairs. Check my bag."

"I don't understand."

"I can prove it. Check my travel bag in the bedroom closet. Small inside pocket, you'll find an envelope. Bring it to me." I felt my brow furrow. "It'll make sense. I promise. Please, Ellie."

With a flick of the switch, warm orange light floods the bedroom. The perspective from the second-floor windows adds drama to the storm outside. The wind whips snowflakes into a frenzy, gusts sending them crashing against the glass. The forest has been erased under the heavy blur of snow. A long howl from the wind draws a shudder out of me.

Steven's bag waits on the closet shelf. It's empty, its contents either hanging here or neatly laid out in the ensuite.

I open the small pocket. The envelope is crafted out of expensive parchment-like paper and weighs heavy in my hand. I could just open it now and be done with it, but I carry it back downstairs.

"Thank you," Steven says when he sees the envelope in my hand. "This isn't how I planned it, but go ahead, open it."

His face narrows with expectation as my finger slips under the unsealed flap. The front of the card reads "for the woman who has everything" in a slanted and looped font set on a background of watercolor flowers. I don't know whether I should be flattered or mildly offended by the statement. I can feel the outline of something hard beneath the paper.

Steven's eyes beckon me to open the card. Inside, instead of the diamond ring I dreaded, a simple key secured by Scotch tape. All of this for a key.

Steven licks his lips. "It's a key to my place. I planned to give it to you later today. I want you to feel you can come and stay at my place any time. And that's not all," he adds when I fail to produce any response to his gift. "You can check my phone or emails anytime you want. No more secrets between us." His lips open in a smile which extends all the way to reach his eyes, one that widens the crack in my demeanor. I shake my head. But there are still secrets. Secrets I know he's still withholding. And secrets he doesn't know I have.

"I don't know…"

"Ellie, look at me." Despite my better judgment, I comply with his request. His eyes shine with a genuine ardor. "I was stupid. You are the only one that's ever mattered to me. I was kidding myself, but not anymore."

The only one. "And the others?"

"All those girls meant nothing to me."

I let go of the key. For a moment, I'd forgotten who the

man sitting in front of me was. Someone who only hours ago pushed my body on to the dining-room table, the solid edge digging into my stomach, the patina of the wood chafing against my cheek, my eyes focused on the tall indoor ficus tree in the corner, counting its leaves in my head, before he stumbled and couldn't go through with it.

"They mean nothing? All of them?"

"Every single one."

27

March 15

I watch the other girls, just like I used to. Sitting in the cafeteria, standing in the hallways. The way their faces become animated as they speak to you. Genuine smiles, wholehearted laughter that reveals the gleam of white teeth or stretches the shine of lip gloss.

I watch them, and I wonder...How many others are there?

28. Steven

The metal seized under him as frustration rumbles deep in his throat. He fights the chair itself as much as what it represents.

How could she do this to him? She threw his apology, and his gift, right in his face, didn't even consider it for five seconds before dismissing his good intentions, rejecting him. He's never given his key to any girl he's dated before. His apartment, his sanctum sanctorum. Doesn't she understand the magnitude of his gesture, of what it says about the depth of his feelings for her? She outstayed all of the others. The brushed steel of the key catches a glimmer from the fire, taunting him from where it fell. She dropped it onto the floor, the gesture of a child disappointed in a new toy.

Anger gathers in the back of his throat, strains against his rib cage. The chair convulses in response. It slants, threatening to topple over. He doesn't care. His entire body feels like a pipe bomb, but before he can explode Ellie strides back into the living room. He swallows his anger, heart pounding against his ribs. Her eyes narrow at him. His body slackens. He shouldn't give her what she wants—to get a rise out of him. Instead, he straightens his spine and props up his shoulders.

She perches herself on the edge of the sofa and smiles at him, while her hands gather her hair before she twists it up into a loose bun, head tilted back, the gesture exposing her throat. Not so long ago he couldn't get enough of kissing those delicate lines; now he thinks of all the things he will do to her once he's free of the sticky tape yanking at the hair on his wrists with each move. The lessons he will teach her. If only he can find a way out.

Hands still high in her hair, the sleeves of her sweater fall back, revealing new tattoos around her slender wrists. He frowns at them until he sees them for what they are—the bruises he gave her when they had sex. Hard to believe that, only a few hours ago, they came together on this very floor. The exact same people they are now. Harder to believe she already despised him that much then. The depth of her deceit leaves him light-headed; he's trapped in a house in the middle of nowhere with the complete stranger she has become.

In the absence of an elastic band, she releases her hair. It falls back, spilling over her shoulders in waves, giving her a wild look, as if she were raised in the woods stretching behind her.

P. used to do that with her hair too: coil it on top of her head, only to let it fall. He never understood the reason she did it. Why take time to do something knowing it has no purpose, that it will fall as soon as you let go.

"I would have never taken you for such a heartless girl. I can comprehend being upset, but it doesn't give you the right to drug me and tie me to a damn chair." Heartless, but not very clever. She will have to release him eventually. And what does she think will happen then? Unless she plans to drug him again so she can leave without him coming after her.

"You're a liar and a cheat, but you're the victim here and not me. Interesting," she replies with an even tone, head cocked to the side. "And it's woman, not girl."

"I still don't deserve this." Anger tightens his lips. The tension she creates in him is new, his shoulders stiff with it.

He rolls his head, until he hears the crack of a vertebra. A small release that will do for now.

"How old are they?" She addresses her toes. He hates that she has the confidence to walk around barefoot.

"What?"

"Those girls. However many there are." She looks up at him, a gaze so cold he would rather she was still checking her feet. "How old are they?"

He sits, the unwilling participant in some TV game show, but the twisted kind where—if he gives the wrong answer—he will lose more than $50,000. The fake leather under his palms is clammy with his sweat.

"You know the answer."

"I do, but I want to hear you say it."

Looking away from her arrogance, his eyes settle on the bar cart. The familiar bitterness of a whiskey or a scotch would be welcome, but he won't ask. He runs his tongue over his teeth, and stays silent.

29. Steven

She towers over him. He's normally the one who towers over her, being a head taller. He loves how he can get her to tilt her head back when they kiss. Not just Ellie. All of them. Their faces always turned up waiting for him to kiss them. Yes, there's always an age gap. So what? There is one between him and Ellie, too. She still waits for an answer that won't come. He won't give her the satisfaction. There are so many questions he wants to ask her, but he's not sure he wants to hear the answers anymore. They each tug at the silence, but she's the one to let go first.

"OK, I'll tell you. Kids. That's what they are—kids. Little girls."

Her last words offend him, passing her judgment as truth. Little girls. Little girls play with dolls and plastic tea sets, they do not wear lace underwear. Little girls draw unicorns and wear ankle socks, they do not wear makeup and do not look at him the way those girls do. Those girls stood on the line marking the beginning of womanhood, they were the ones offering their hands, asking him to take them over to the other side. He would hardly call J. a little girl, not the way she pursued him. Or A., the way she posed for him. He remembers them all, and none of them were little girls. It's common knowledge girls mature quicker than boys. He's sure Ellie herself must have been a precocious teenager in her time. *Kids.* No matter how much she's hurting, he won't allow her to twist the facts to fit whatever narrative she has drummed up in her mind.

"It's not what you think."

"It's exactly what I think. Age of consent is not a fluid concept. Can you imagine what this would do to your reputation if it got out?" she asks, walking over to the bar cart. The question stiffens him.

"Do you want one?" she adds before he can ask what she means.

"I would, but I'm a bit tied up right now," he answers without a second thought. "And still dehydrated."

She snorts at his sarcasm, and for a split second their past relationship resurfaces, that ease of conversation. They could have been having a casual chat and one last drink before heading upstairs to bed, but the rift reopens straightaway, and the reality of his situation swallows him again. She grabs the bottle she filled in the privacy of the kitchen earlier on. He should refuse out of principle, but the lure of fresh water is so great, he almost salivates in anticipation. The bottle rises to his lips.

"I'm all right, actually," he says, twisting his head to the side, the words and his tongue stuck to the roof of his mouth.

"Don't be ridiculous," she replies, angling the bottle at his mouth.

"Damn it, Ellie, I've changed my mind."

She observes him in silence, her gaze dissecting his face, the soft plastic of the bottle crackling under the pressure of her fingers. Her face slackens as she sighs. Bringing the bottle to her mouth, she takes a long gulp and makes a show of swallowing.

He simply nods in response. Once more the bottle comes to him, this time his mouth latches on. He takes a long sip. Water floods his mouth, and he enjoys the slight pain swallowing down big gulps. Once he starts, he cannot stop until the bottle is empty.

"Seriously, Steven. How could you?"

"It just happened. A mutual attraction, a need."

"Mutual? You're kidding, right?"

"I'm not." He frowns. "I assure you it was all consensual. Please don't turn me into one of those guys."

"What guys?"

"Those creeps who pursue women and can't take no for an answer. I've rescued you from enough of them to know. Like that man at the bar last week or the guy from the gallery."

"Unbelievable. You think you're some white knight in all this?"

She stares down, wiggling her nose at him until she rubs it with the back of her hand. His shoulders stiffen. That gesture, both familiar and alien to him at the gallery that night. The familiar face, but not for the reason he initially thought.

He had gone to Ellie's studio with the intent to surprise her with some late-afternoon ice-skating at the Bryant Park rink. He went every year, usually alone, a simple pleasure slicing a path through the ice, hands clasped behind his back while his worries—poorly written essays from students, the rejections that came with every publication, his old man's humble brags—melted away like the shavings of ice beneath his skates. His own little tradition, which he wanted to share with her.

The impulse had carried him downtown to her apartment building in the West Village. With the elevator out of order he climbed the stairs two at a time. He couldn't wait for her to take her first step on the rink, her hand in his as he'd guide her on the ice. He was lost in the idea of the two of them treading the space around others when the crescendo of barrelling footsteps invaded the stairwell before his shoulder connected with another.

"Sorry, man."

The act had been so negligible he didn't even respond. Steven slowed down and turned around in a reflex to catch who had apologized. A shock of auburn hair and a neat beard, the other man had already resumed his trip down the stairs, lost in his own thoughts, and rubbing his nose with the back of his hand. By the time Steven reached Ellie's floor, the stranger had slipped out of his mind; he didn't recognize him a few weeks later when he caught a glimpse of him outside the gallery with Ellie. Her urgency to leave all of a sudden on that night takes on a new dimension, one where he wasn't the only motivation.

With one seemingly irrelevant detail, all the elements line up like the different faces on a Rubik's cube. The stairwell. The gallery. Then a couple of weeks ago, she arranged drinks at the bar where they had had their first date. She cozied up to him the whole night as he drank bourbon and she sipped vodka sweetened with cranberry juice. She wrapped herself around his arm, pressed her hip against his. They kissed in the intimate shadows of their booth, their lips moving fast. She went back to his place, tipsy and eager. Lying in his bed afterward, she told him about her surprise for him—a long weekend away together in Chesapeake Bay. The warmth of her body against his, she waited for his approval. How could he refuse those eyes? They shone bluer than ever that night.

The exchange glimpsed through the window of the gallery has been stained with a new meaning. Not someone bothering her, but someone she knows well enough to mimic their mannerisms; someone conspiring with her. He just needs to figure out what they want.

Ellie stares at him, rubbing the top of her arms. The oversized sleeves slimming her arms more than they already are. Those arms he held above her head as she lay on this very floor under him, those arms that couldn't move under his grasp. Those arms that would never be strong enough to move his dead weight onto the wheelchair after he lost consciousness.

Those arms crossed in front of him are the proof he needed to be sure. They are not alone.

30

March 19

Vee keeps asking me what's wrong every time we speak on the phone. Even on Monday on WhatsApp. I feel so stupid, embarrassed just thinking about what's happened. It will be a million times worse if I have to say it all out loud. I never told her about you because you told me it was our secret. But now you're gone, and I feel like one gigantic fool. I betrayed her, and for what?

Mom keeps asking what's wrong too. All those questions, Mom's looks, the pauses between Vee's words on the phone.

And then your silence. Your silence is the most deafening part.

It all got too much, so I jumped in the pool. Ran in a straight line from my car to the water. Under the surface I waited until my lungs burned. When I couldn't hold my breath any longer, I screamed. I let it all out, billowing upward until I choked on the water.

31. Steven

"It can't be consensual," she says, her voice reaching him before she walks back into the room and his field of vision.

"What?"

The main light in the room vanishes without a warning. Something else to add to the list of what Ellie has robbed him of, obliged to suffer her whims and choices, light on or off included. Thankfully the fire in the hearth is still going strong.

He opens his mouth, but before he can protest, anger curdles in his throat. His attention is fixed on her closed hand, his back flat against the lining of the chair.

Indiscretions are not punishable by death, otherwise his father would have been dead decades ago. His old man has done unspeakable things, crossed lines Steven wouldn't dare even step on.

"What you did to those girls."

He hears the words, but the knife is all that occupies his mind. What he did shouldn't earn him a stab in the gut or a slit throat. Or she might have another revenge in mind. Disfiguring him as a punishment. The sharp steel carving a bloody "C" on his cheek. His nausea is back, bile souring the back of his mouth.

If she wants to punish someone then she should turn her attention to Professor Stewart Harding, a man who has wrecked lives in ways Steven is glad his mother has never learned about. Her denial has shielded her from actions that would destroy her.

There were words whispered at collegial committees, insinuations traded over drinks at university functions, just enough details seeping through to create a clear narrative. There never seems to be a defined instigator to those rumors; they spring out of the ether fully formed, roaming halls and slipping into closed rooms, legends that can never be verified, never gaining any real power that could only be endowed by corroborating evidence and proof.

He had been waiting for Jeffrey at some university function indistinguishable from all others when he caught the tail end of one such legend. Even though no name was explicitly mentioned, Steven recognized the outline of his father in the details. The story of a problem that couldn't be solved with a simple procedure at a discreet clinic. A comfortable sum financed by a book advance, the truth buried by a signature at the bottom of an NDA. All in the girl's best interest: she deserved that bright future promised to her. Everything anonymous, guaranteeing deniability.

In comparison to what his father has done, he's merely made a mistake, one he's genuinely sorry for.

"Steven?" He looks up at her face arranged in a puzzled expression. "Are you listening?" She waves her hand at him, but his eyes go back to the other one holding the knife. "Is this distracting you?" This time, she waves the knife at him.

The precariousness of his situation sends a chill between his shoulder blades. Like a man on a ribbon of ice that rims a shore, he must tread carefully. The wrong word can send him crashing through into deadly waters.

"Ellie, please, darling..."

She rolls her eyes at him. "Do you really think pet names are the way out of this?"

Leaning against the sofa, Ellie slices into an apple, before stabbing a quarter, which disappears into her mouth with a crunch. A foaming spot of juice clings to the corner of her lips. Saliva floods his mouth at the sight and the intoxicating sweet smell of the fruit. She carves another piece from the soft white flesh.

Still chewing, she extends the knife, a wedge of apple jammed at the tip. "Wanna piece?"

"No."

She shrugs. "Your loss."

In the silence that follows she works her way through the fruit, shoving pieces in her mouth, turning the flesh into a pulp she swallows. When finished, she throws the core in the fire. Walking back to him, she wipes her mouth and the blade with the sleeve of her sweater.

"Are you going to admit what you did to those girls?"

"What I did? What is it you think I did?"

"We're not talking two kids fooling around in the back seat of a car. You were . . . you are an adult, and they are just children. You took advantage of them."

The chair quakes under his restrained body. "No, I did not. I never did anything they didn't want to do."

"It doesn't matter. You're the adult. Their fucking teacher," she shouts as the knife plunges into the back cushion of the sofa, her hand strangling the handle. When she releases her grip, it stays stuck in the microfiber filling. "That's called molestation."

The ugliness of her last word punches him in the gut, knocking the breath out of him. He's never molested anyone. He's not the kind of man who lurks in the shadows between buildings waiting to pounce on women; he certainly never drugged anyone to take advantage of them. None of them ever said no, and if they had, he would have stopped. It was all consensual, she can't change that. He never forced himself on anybody. The idea of taking a girl against her will revolts him. What kind of sick, twisted game is she playing? The idea she would fabricate such accusations out of scorn brings a lump to his throat, making it hard to swallow.

"How dare you?" The words struggle to escape against his gritted teeth.

"How dare I? You're the one breaking the law with what you've been doing to those girls."

"And what you're doing here isn't?"

"Never said it was. At least I know exactly what I'm doing and own up to it."

"Which is what? Being mentally unstable, a lunatic? Listen, I'm sorry I've hurt you. Sincerely." She snorts in reply. "But that does not justify your crazy way of handling it."

How could he have misjudged her that much? She somehow managed to fool him. To what end still eludes him. This conversation, if you can call it that, feels like an ouroboros—a never-ending circle, taking them nowhere. Eyes closed, he sweeps his memory for a clue, a sign that would have hinted at her disturbed nature.

All that comes to the surface are lazy days in bed, discussions about Keats or Whitman, brunches in the city. The evening not long ago when they attended a wine-tasting event at some new bar in the Bowery. She confessed she didn't know much about wine. He showed her how to check out the color and opacity, before smelling to identify the different aromas, and finally tasting it on your tongue first before swallowing and noticing how the flavor changed. They sipped Burgundy, Shiraz, Cabernet Sauvignon. Each time, her eyes searched his face for his opinion and guidance. She waited for him to deliver his verdict. Several glasses later, they swayed into a yellow cab, her a lot drunker than he was. In the back seat, she had lunged for him and kissed him with determination. Her newfound confidence tasted of cranberry and a hint of licorice from the Pinot Noir they'd had. He might have glimpsed the real Ellie in that cab, hiding inside the straightforwardness of her kiss.

When his eyes open, she hops off the sofa and comes to lean over him, hands resting on his knees. The silver heart dangles in front of his face, mocking him—the symbol of his foolishness, of how she owns him. Has she slept with the man from the gallery, the man who must be here somewhere, or helping her somehow? He tries to imagine her with that stranger moving on top of her but he can only see himself. Behind her, the flames animate her hair with an orange glow. He sees Medusa.

"How can I make you understand how much of a pervert you are?" Her unwavering eyes are ready to turn him into stone.

The word unleashes a wave of savage energy that sweeps over him. Reaching out, his hands snatch fistfuls of the hair dangling in front of him. The strands twist around his fingers, roping her in and yanking her head down. She cries in pain. He doesn't want to hurt her. He respects women, but she's forcing him to be that man.

"Enough. Untie me. Now." Another rotation of his wrists, showing her his resolve, and she whimpers. That close, he can smell the alcohol and the apple on her breath mingled with the scent of her fear.

"Let go of me."

In response, he tugs harder and she hisses in pain. His pull drives her down, a knee almost to the ground. He has her where he wants. He feels the weight of her hand shift off his legs. He sighs in relief, waiting for the sound of tape being peeled off his wrist. Instead, an electric pain shoots from the heel of her hand crushing his balls. His fingers spasm in the knots of her hair, twisting her face, but she doesn't yield; instead her claw digs deeper into his flesh. The pain blurs his vision and folds his body, his head jerking into her face before he surrenders. She staggers back, falling against the sofa, leaving tendrils of herself still dangling between his fingers.

He straightens himself. Despite the pain burning in his groin and the other throbbing behind his forehead, he looks at her in the eyes, jaw clenched, waiting for her revenge. He's never hurt a woman before. He abhors violence, the blunt instrument of the weak-minded. But she has forced him to stoop to that level; she can only blame herself for having driven him to such an extreme. She drugged him, strapped him to this chair, she refused to listen. What does she expect? Every man has a breaking point.

Glaring at him, she runs her tongue over the new ridge splitting her lower lip, smearing the blood on her teeth.

"Time to teach you a lesson, professor."

32

April 4

I can't talk to anyone. It's all my fault anyway. I only have myself to blame. I got into your car. I called you. I asked to stay the night. I wanted it to happen. I said yes, every time you asked. Yes. Yes. YES. You never forced me. I remember it all.

The world had gone home, and we were the only ones left. Pushing the heavy double doors, we stopped at the top of the stairs, admiring the downpour. Sheets of rain falling so hard and tight it blurred the cars in the parking lot. My crappy driving skills versus the deluge. I didn't like the odds. You wouldn't let me drive anyway. My knight in shining armor. My Mister Rochester.

We were off, your long legs giving you the advantage. Backpack over my head I sprinted behind you, reaching the passenger side as you pushed the door open from the inside. I dropped, a drenched bundle, onto the upholstery. Despite our race we were both soaked to the bones. We stared at each other—two drowned rats—and burst out laughing.

The rain had drummed on the roof of the car, pelted the windows, steamed up the inside. The noise around us deafening, imprisoning us in this glass and metal capsule, the world outside grayed out of existence. The air thick with the earlier warmth of the day.

You leaned across to open the glove compartment. The blood pounding in my ears. The proximity of our bodies.

Your breath cold on my wet cheek. Eyes screwed shut, my lips crashed on yours so hard I felt the outline of your teeth under the flesh. Up close you smelled of damp and cologne. You didn't pull away. Not immediately. But you didn't linger much.

You said, "You can't do that."

I wanted to run away, for the storm to swallow me. Yet, I stayed in my seat, staring at my hands limp on my lap.

"It's OK," you said. "It's just a mistake. I won't say anything. Let's just forget about it. It'll be our secret."

33. Steven

Eye-watering pain radiates from his groin. His body wants to double over, but it can't fully because of her, because she has strapped him to this chair. He takes shallow breaths through gritted teeth. The living room swims under the tears building in his eyes. Head tilted far back, he waits for it to pass. That's all her duct tape will allow him to do, and he'll be damned if she sees him tearful. When the pain finally dulls to a manageable ache, the first thing he sees is the blade protruding from the soft furnishing—a totem to her madness.

Merely escaping is not enough anymore. He needs to get out of here, but first he needs to find out how she knows and, more importantly, what she's planning to do with this knowledge. The hair bristling on the back of his neck tells him this little *huis clos* she has been orchestrating is not simply the lashing out of a scorned girlfriend.

His mind conjures up the guy from the gallery again, the messy mop of auburn hair, the scene glimpsed through the bay windows—and his presence earlier in Ellie's stairwell. Strapped in this chair, he can no longer afford to believe in coincidence. There must be something he's missing.

He shifts, the tape biting into his wrist. He hates feeling this helpless and confused. His ability to think has been pilfered by the drugs she polluted his body with. He craves the comfort of certainty and misses stretching his legs, stretching his arms above his head. Snatching back his freedom dominates his immediate future. Further on lies how he will deal with Ellie.

Oblivious to his pain, she perches on the sofa. Her hair is now swept up and secured with an elastic band. Hair up and face scrubbed of makeup, she looks so young. Her arms are crossed against her chest, holding her copy of Dostoevsky's *The Devils*.

Not that thing again. The book has been living in her bag for the last month. He was first introduced to it when she met him for dinner at Gramercy Tavern. By the time she had arrived, he had started working on his second bourbon.

"So sorry I'm late," she said, sliding into her seat.

"One more bourbon, and I would have thought you'd stood me up."

A flush of shame darkened her cheeks a lovely shade of crimson at his simulated scowl.

"Sorry. I got held up at the library trying to get a book I need for my next assignment."

She'd dropped the hefty paperback on the table. Leaning across, he slid the book toward him, cocking his head to check the title. The cover depicted a bearded man in a white shirt and black waistcoat reclining on a stripy pillow. The white letters cutting against the black background read "Fyodor Dostoevsky—*The Devils*."

"I could have lent you my copy."

"I needed the special edition with the missing chapter. Of course, it took the guy on duty ages to find it for me."

More likely, the assistant took his time to spend as much time as possible with her and might have even flirted a little, hoping he could score a number or a coffee date. It was irritating that it had delayed her, but he didn't blame the guy and he wasn't threatened by him. Ellie was his, and the way she looked at him that night, there was no space behind her eyes for anybody but him. In the end, he would have been happy to buy this guy a drink for making her late. She was eager to earn his forgiveness well into the night.

The book had scarcely left her side since then. Soon, he resented its presence, as if she had taken a Russian lover. They were never truly alone anymore, a corner of the book jacket peering from under a sweater tossed on her desk, or the bearded man peering from under the flap of her bag, spying on them kissing or having sex. A silent observer to their relationship, judging him with his stern, elusive look.

And it's here now, tucked inside her embrace like an accomplice. Related somehow to the lesson—she says—she has to teach him.

"What are you planning to do with this?"

"I thought some of the themes in that book could be relevant to our conversation."

"Let's make this clear: this is not a conversation."

"I thought we could have a look at the missing chapter which was later added back to the published version." She opens the book and flicks its pages until she finds the right section.

"You must be joking."

"*I kissed her hand again and took her on my knee. Then she suddenly pulled herself away and smiled as if ashamed, with a wry smile. All her face flushed with shame. I was whispering to her all the time, as though drunk. At last, all of a sudden, such a strange thing happened, which I shall never forget, and which bewildered me: the little girl flung her arms around my neck and suddenly began to kiss me passionately. Her face expressed a perfect ecstasy.*"

With steady eyes following the lines of letters, she reads effortlessly as if she has read this passage so many times the inked words are no longer necessary for her to know what she should say next.

Behind her shoulder, the relentless battering of snow has dulled to a light drift, and only darkness persists. He wonders what time it is. Late afternoon, he guesses. Not that he will ask her.

"Do you do that too?" she asks, looking up from the pages.

He buries himself in his silence. He could discuss Dostoevsky's style and argue the validity of the translation when the missing chapter was finally found, but that's not what she wants to hear. When he talks, she doesn't listen; he won't indulge her anymore. His backside hurts from the prolonged sitting. He shifts his weight about, but all it does is rearrange the pain. She has taken all options away from him, even his ability to cross his legs.

He looks past her to the monochrome canvas of the forest, the undisturbed blanket of snow reminding him of how utterly alone they are. Nobody to hear him scream, no concerned neighbors to check up on them, or borrow a clichéd cup of sugar. He has to give it to her, she—or they—chose this place well.

He sits there, a literature teacher devoid of words. Whatever he says will be twisted until it fits the shape of her narrative, so he gives her nothing. Every girl he has ever been with has been attracted to him. He never encouraged them or took them on his knees. He never asked J. to stay behind and talk to him, to stand so close he could smell the mint from her gum on her breath. He never demanded that A. pose for him. How could he be responsible for their choices?

The fleeting scent of vanilla and jasmine catches in the air, a breath next to his ear. He squirms around, to catch a glimpse of the void behind and the source of the perfume, but there is only so far his spine will twist. The scent dies, and its origin still remains a mystery.

"When all was over, she was confused. I did not try to reassure her and no longer fondled her. She looked at me, smiling timidly. Her face appeared to me stupid." She doesn't look at the pages this time, her eyes never straying from his face, appraising his reaction to Stavrogin's confession.

"Is it like that for you as well?" He detects a flicker in her voice, a rustle of sadness, but before she says more, she clears her throat, and the weakness is gone. Maybe he just imagined it.

"What do you want me to say?" The question sighs out of him.

She sits on the edge of the sofa, the book a rampart between them, her body shielded behind it like a fortress. He remembers their walk in the forest, her head tilted up, her mind lost in the twist of branches ahead. *There are things she doesn't tell him.*

"I loved them for as long as I was with them," he adds, legs struggling against the duct tape, forgetting he cannot cross them, the way she does right now.

"Love?" The word has her jump off the roost the sofa has become to her.

"You know, you'll have to let me out some time." He ignores her question, pins and needles in his backbone. "You can't keep me in this chair forever."

She paces in front of him like a dangerous bird of paradise, thin black legs disappearing under an oversized sweater, a motley down in blues, reds, and yellows. Even her head is shaped like a delicate bird's, with those high cheekbones and huge eyes. He has spent hours staring at those eyes in bed or over tables at restaurants or bars, trying to decide if they are blue or green. They remind him of those mood rings girls used to wear when he was a kid. After all these months he still hasn't made up his mind. But never did he see in them

161

a hint of the ruthlessness he has experienced in the last few hours.

"Please, for an academic you can't be that stupid. You didn't love them, you loved how they make you feel." Right now, her eyes shine a cold jade. In the background, a log collapses in the fireplace and sends flames leaping as if conspiring with Ellie in a show of indignation.

"Are you pretending to be a shrink now?"

"Spare me the sarcasm. It's a fact, you loved the way they looked up to you, put you on that pedestal you crave so much. With them for a moment, their uncontested attention, pulling you out from under Daddy Harding's shadow."

"Fuck you."

"The saddest thing is you don't even realize that you want what you hate most."

"What do you mean?"

"Come on, admit it. It's the truth, classic psych 101."

She's wrong. None of them have anything to do with his father. Why won't she stop bringing him up? She is just making up assumptions to fit her wild theories and justify her deranged behavior. She offers him an alluring smile, a hybrid between a smirk and a pout. The same one she had given him yesterday, listening to Chris Isaak. A lifetime ago. How she resisted him, how he enjoyed the thrill of taking her, how she allowed him to push against the soft limit of what was permissible, how his desire soared when he claimed what she was withholding. But he never forced himself on her, if she had asked him to stop, he would have. He's not that guy. Not with her or any of them.

He's the kind of man who always opens doors and gives up his seat on the subway for women, who always sends them flowers, lavishes them with expensive gifts. He got her that dress she wore last night because he knew she would look great in it. He always knows what looks good on her. Every time they go out, he always pays for drinks or dinner. Always happy to help her out and give her advice. It drove him crazy when she made him wait, but he respected her choice.

How can she imply that he forced himself on any of those girls when he's the kind of man who's always been there to rescue her every time men have been bothering her? When everything about his actions shows that he's one of the good guys?

34

April 6

Sometimes in the dead of night, it comes back to me. The clamminess of Tom's fingers, the fizziness of the beer in my mouth, the fermented taste of his tongue.

The cold touch of his fingers under the layers of my skirt brought me back. They traveled up like ants, getting close, too close. His hand crept up my leg. His fingers were not yours. I pushed them back. Too fast. I was so stupid. Fingers clawing at the line of the bustier. Fingertips cold from the chilled beer cans.

I asked him to stop. I'm sure I did. My shouts filled the small space of the car as I pummeled his shoulders until I pushed him away from me. The harshness in his eyes sent my body against the door.

He said, "You're such a fucking tease."

Was I a tease? I got into his car. I pressed my body against his. The hard-on pressing against the black fabric of his trousers accused me.

I stumbled out of his car. His insults chased me down the street. He called me a slut, said what did I expect, and I was asking for it. And when I still wouldn't let him, he called me a stupid dyke. I kept running long after the words faded away.

Because of him, I had no way of getting home.

Because of him, I called you. You said I could call you any time, if ever I was in trouble, so I did. Your voice was heavy with concern. Concern for me.

Because of him, I learned that you cared. You just said, "I'm coming to get you."

Is it crazy that I'm still grateful to you for that? Even knowing how it ends, I would do it all over again.

April 7

On the evening news they showed a house near Orlando, Florida, being swallowed by a sinkhole. It unfolded on screen as it collapsed into the darkness, there one second, then gone from the world.

I burned Jane. I used the barbecue in the backyard, dropped her on the grill before dousing her in lighter fluid. I watched her being engulfed in flames, all four hundred and forty-eight pages of her story, of her deceit. I watched as the flames curled the paper, blackened the words, turned her into ashes.

One ember landed on the back of my hand, branded the skin with a tiny red triangle. I rubbed it during class while I fantasized about telling you what I did. Would you be mad? Could I drive you to touch me? Slap me, knot your fingers in my hair?

I wish I had someone to talk to. I wish I'd told Vee about you back when it all started. It's too far gone to explain it all now.

35. Steven

She stands in front of him, eyes shining with defiance, more blue than green. He studies her face, teeth clenched, holding it all in. The low light has sharpened her cheekbones and the narrow bridge of her nose, erasing all softness from her face.

"What about you?" he asks.

"What about me?"

"You're not one of these girls, so if that's all I'm after, why am I with you?"

She shrugs at him in response. The answer of someone who doesn't have a valid argument. He's seen it before. That rise and fall of shoulders which populates the classrooms at Richmond Prep whenever he squeezes students a little harder, pushes against the scaffolding of their argumentation and sees it all fall apart. Only last week, Hunter Markham surrendered with the same hollow response Ellie just has. His mouth cracks into a thin smile, but it doesn't live long.

The little victory tastes like ashes. In a short few hours she has ruined everything. His hands retreat into fists, fingers curling on to themselves. Fingers which stroked her cheeks, fingertips she kissed before they roamed the expanse of her body, now they crave to close around her throat and stop the lies and hatred that spill out of her. He stares at her, and amid the rage there's a kernel of grief for the girl he used to know, the girl he loves. Ellie's gone. The girl he's left with now wields the power to ruin everything.

He runs his tongue over his teeth, but it doesn't ease the dryness.

"Actually, any chance of another drink? I could do with one right now."

"Sure. Do you want a bourbon?"

"I thought we were out."

"I lied."

The clink of ice cubes hitting the bottom of the glass has never sounded so good to him, loosening the knots in his shoulders. She presents him with the two fingers of amber liquor, and he should say no. His mind needs to stay clear if he wants to outwit her and get out of whatever she and whoever else might have planned for him.

Under Ellie's guidance, he takes a short swig, and the acrid taste of malt hijacks his mouth. His eyes close as he opens himself to the soothing burn of the alcohol trailing down his throat before hitting his bloodstream. He pushes back against the glass to indicate that he's finished.

As she lowers the glass, a drop sits heavy at the corner of his mouth. Just as it slides down, she wipes it with the pad of her thumb. A familiar gesture. He remembers them all.

Back during his time as substitute teacher, his relationships had a natural expiration date. Once his placement was over, he would be gone. They always knew that. His single status meant he could easily be sent from one state to the next. Sometimes they made it harder. N. cried on his sofa for an hour when he called an end to their time together.

"What will I do without you?" The words hiccupped between sobs.

His instinct urged him to wipe the tears away with the pad of his thumb. He did nothing. Any gesture toward her at this stage would be seen by her as an encouragement, a signal, things might not be completely over, that there was still a chance. Even an inconspicuous hand on her knee could be the butterfly to bring a hurricane down on his life. He couldn't let that happen, so he folded his hands on his lap. In the end, she understood and left his apartment with red-rimmed eyes but resigned.

T. hadn't been that easy to persuade; she had deluded herself she could keep him interested by being more daring. Honestly, he did enjoy some of her entrapment—that time in his car after she called him, crying late at night to pick her up. She pretended she was stranded at the mall after a late-night film. He shouldn't have, it had been such a reckless endangerment of his career, but it was a risk worth taking, one away from witnesses and his work. But when she kissed him in his classroom where anybody could have walked in, he ended up having a quiet chat with the school principal.

"I'm worried she's developing some unhealthy crush on me, and to be honest with you it's making me uncomfortable. I think there are some problems at home which might add to the whole situation."

"Teenage girls," Forsyth—that was his name—had said, patting Steven's back. "Don't worry, I'm glad you came to me with this."

Yes, he remembered them all. But they weren't able to hold his attention for long. Until Ellie—the girl who stayed.

Ellie's eyes on him now are a lily pond of blue speckled with green. In the hollow of the moment, the last several hours don't exist, and he is back flipping pancakes for her as she moves around the kitchen, searching for mugs.

"Ellie..."

Her name in his voice acts as the wrong trigger; her face closes, and the light that has flickered seconds ago dies along with his hope to reconnect. He watches her retreat inside herself like a body that sinks deeper under dark water until it completely disappears from view and all that is left is a smooth, impenetrable surface. He shifts around in his seat as much as he is allowed by his restraints. Despite the move, the fabric of his shirt still sticks to his back.

Light from the dying fire recedes, allowing shadows to grow tall and mingle to slowly form a veil of darkness in the living room.

Before he can say anything that could put her on a path to resurrect the Ellie he knows, she starts reading again.

"I walked up and down and then sat down on the sofa. I remember everything up to the last moment. It decidedly gave me pleasure not to speak to Matryoshka, but to keep her in suspense; I don't know why. Did you play games with all those girls you seduced?"

"No! Do you think we are in some kind of nineteenth-century novel? Seriously, listen to yourself, Ellie."

"Are you sure?" The slight twitch in her tone and her slow delivery unnerve him, as if she is privy to some information that eludes him.

He won't let her play mind games on him, not any more than she already has. He is a respected college professor, a reputable author, and who is she? Nothing more than a little girl upset that she isn't the center of attention.

She flicks the pages again until she finds a new passage, with such dexterity he wonders if she had it all marked in preparation for tonight.

"About eleven o'clock the doorkeeper's little daughter came from the landlady at Gorokhovaya Street, with the message to me that Matryoshka had hanged herself."

As she reads, or rather recites, the face which has escaped him reappears in his mind on a wave of jasmine and vanilla. Each of the words Ellie speaks adds clarity to the features, color lines, eyes, lips—a porcelain doll coming to life. He remembers now.

She'd been with him when he skirted around the edge of consciousness after Ellie drugged him. The echoes of a familiar voice calling his name. She stood on a cliff overlooking the ocean, wind whipping curly strands of hair across her face. Trapped in an old memory he had forgotten, grasping at edges that crumbled under his touch as he fought to wake up. Just the outline of a ghost who kept whispering his name. But she was too long ago, almost a decade, and on the other side of the country. She couldn't possibly be with them tonight.

He searches the lines of Ellie's face, the tension in her brow, for a clue. She gives him nothing.

36. Steven

She snaps the book shut with such a force, it jolts him in his chair. "She killed herself. Used, discarded, and ignored. All she had left was to jump." The words tremble on her breath as she quickly turns away from him. She could be crying, but he can't be sure, until she wipes her face with the back of her hands.

"Are you all right?"

"Yes, I'm fine," she replies, a tremor still in her voice.

When she faces him again, moisture clings to her lower lashes. Even though his feet are plagued with pins and needles, his ass has gone numb, his back is stiff and drenched in sweat, all because of her, he feels a strange pity toward her. Her mask of confidence is wearing thin. She doesn't know it yet, but soon he'll ask her to untie him, and she will. She hugs the book tight against her heaving chest as if it could somehow comfort her.

"Do you need a drink?"

She just nods and doesn't bother with a glass; instead she takes a swig straight from the bottle. She doesn't return it to the cart. Her hand strangles the glass neck as she walks to the fireplace. She douses the dying embers with a generous splash of bourbon, which sends the renewed fire into a frenzy, flames shooting up, licking the back stone. She throws another log in as an offering to the fire, feeding its fierce appetite. She lowers her hand toward the flames, straddling the line between discomfort and pain until she retracts it, shaking off the feeling. The fire should be the least of her worries right now. Despite the heat, Steven sees her shiver.

After she frees him, he'll tie her up and lock her inside one of the spare rooms for a few hours while he has a well-deserved sleep in the master bedroom. Once he's rested, he might be inclined to hear her plead her case to be driven back to the city instead of being left stranded here. He was wrong. Whoever that guy was at the gallery and in her apartment block, she looks too vulnerable to have someone in the house helping her.

"Do you think he should be forgiven?" Her voice is barely audible over the sharp snaps of the burning wood.

"What?"

"Stavrogin. That's the whole point of his confession to Tikhon: look for absolution. Should he be absolved just because he confesses?"

Despite his unwillingness to engage in her twisted game, her question awakens the academic inside. His mind wanders back to their conversations on his sofa, discussing which Brontë sister was the most influential—Charlotte for him, Emily for her—or the validity of Anaïs Nin's *In Favor of the Sensitive Man*, and every time the fervor with which she defended her positions. Their debates animated her: she would lean forward, gesticulate, fired up by the argument, until she fell back into her seat either triumphant or frustrated, if he got the better of her. Their literary jousting always ended in laughter, or one of them trying to derail the exchange with devious tactics: mouth, tongue and the more than occasional stripping of clothes. She advanced to where he sat on the couch like a great feline. He watched her, elbow on the armrest, head resting on his knuckles. She popped the buttons of his shirt as she enumerated the reasons why "The Raven" was one of the best Gothic works ever written.

The memories linger at the back of his mind, heavy with nostalgia.

If a Russian outcast can be forgiven, surely there is a case for her to forgive him. She remains silent, and her eyes stay on his face as if appraising him and the validity of his argument. They seem more green than blue now that she sits in shadows. Propped against the back of the sofa, she looks up at him. He's tempted to use that reprieve to pile on the words and the arguments until she caves under their weight. But that won't work with her anymore. A word from him now is more likely to trigger her than to be of service to him. It's her move. Opening her mouth, she brings the bottle to her lips but thinks better of it.

"Are you sorry for what you did?"

"I am." The words leap out of him. "Of course I am. I never intended to hurt you."

"What about them? Are you sorry for what you did to those girls?" Her eyes shine on him like scissors that could slice through his restraints. She needs to hear the words, so he gives them to her.

"Of course, if any of them felt hurt by what I did, I'm sorry for that too."

The glimmer in her eyes dies and with it the idea he might be freed soon slips further away from his grasp.

Getting up from the ground, she moves away from him and faces the window. On the other side, the cloud cover is tinted with a purple shade. He can't remember the last time he saw the sky or even the sun. Other things that don't exist here, like civilization or the passing of time. He has no idea what time it is. He could have been stuck on this chair for minutes or hours.

"How sorry are you?"

He opens his mouth but finds it empty of words. Silence

grows between them, palpable and noxious like thick weeds or a fungus. He can almost taste it, furry on his tongue. Beads of sweat run down his spine while he ransacks his mind not just for the right words but the right combination: like for one of those digit-locks, if he could only find the right sequence.

"What do you mean?"

"How far are you willing to go to show remorse?" she says, addressing her reflection in the window.

Turning and rubbing at the little crust of dried blood at the center of her lip, she moves toward him. He never meant to hit her, she must know that. He's not that kind of man. Only hours ago on the mezzanine he rescued her from going over the banister. That reflex sums up who he really is. The chair she's pinned him to has brought out the worst in him—not even the worst, someone entirely different, as if he had suffered some kind of mutation. Her hand cups his cheek, her skin a warm familiarity he leans into, hoping to reconnect, to remind her of the man on the mezzanine, the man she kissed in the woods and made pancakes with. Anything to get out and away.

"You let me out of this chair, and I promise you, I will show you every day how sorry I am for what happened."

"I have something in mind..."

"Anything for you," he says before twisting his face to kiss her palm still on him. It tastes of salt.

She leans forward, and a metallic click echoes while she unlocks the chair's brakes. Released from his static position, she flips him around, and the world of the house behind him exists again. He feels like he's been reacquainted with an old friend. Everything is as it should be. No tall man with a mop of auburn hair, not a sound from upstairs. Just the dining table and beyond it a sliver of the checkered floor of the entrance through the open door. The sight relaxes the muscles in his hand—he hasn't realized how cramped his fingers have been until now. But his new position is only temporary. She grunts behind him while she steers the chair around the dining table. Slowly, she wheels him across the threshold and into the lobby.

The light in the lobby shines like the sun. The intense brightness blinds him, and he blinks several times until the familiar shapes of the lobby emerge from the whiteness.

"Blood running cold" is a melodramatic expression he has often underlined twice in red in students' essays. But as the lobby comes into focus, a chill spreads under his skin.

Secured to the first-floor banister, coiled tight around the dark mahogany, a rope dangles, white and thick. One a climber would use as part of their gear to scale a perilous mountain side.

One that ends in a noose.

37

April 20

I stood in the bathroom earlier. Hurting. My body vibrating from pain. I've been hurting since I left your apartment. I haven't been able to breathe since leaving you. A critical piece of me is still trapped in your place. Holding the scissors with a trembling hand, I slipped and stabbed the skin. The shot of pain overshadowed everything else better than the icy shower had, and the pandemonium in my mind quietened for a moment.

I sat on the toilet. The side of the bathrobe parted and revealed the white skin and the blueish veins like underground rivers. Scissors wide open, the sharp tip pressed against my skin until it dimpled the flesh. I dragged it in a loop on my inner thigh until an infinity symbol pulsed red and hot. I opened myself to the pain. It overtook me. Nothing else existed anymore other than the burn of the red line.

38. Ellie

Fear breaks the perfect lines of his face and rearranges them in an expression I have never seen on him before. Something visceral has taken hold, unrefined. Even before any explanation, he has taken the rope and its meaning seriously. Whatever vague ideas he has in mind, they are far from the truth. Despite the fear, his arrogance remains; he still believes he knows what this is all about. He doesn't. Despite all the hints he refuses to understand.

"What the hell is this?"

"Your chance at redemption." I position myself between the chair and the noose, but his eyes are still fixated on the rope in the background.

After the dimness of the living room his eyes haven't adjusted yet to the brightness of the entrance, and he blinks at me with squinty eyes, disoriented. A few minutes ago, he looked like a man convinced he had worn me down and was about to be liberated, but as usual his smugness and over-confidence have led him astray.

"My what?"

"Redemption," I repeat with a smile and greater enunciation.

His mouth twitches as if chewing on words he doesn't want to say, truths he doesn't want me to know.

My hand dives under the hem of my sweater and fishes out the packet of cigarettes stuck in the waistband of my leggings. I slide one between my lips and light it with the flame in my cupped hand. A long drag, and smoke fills my mouth until I swallow it down. It slithers down my throat, slows down my heartbeat, mellows the stiffness in my neck. Head tilted back, I exhale that first drag and I can tolerate him a little better.

"Since when do you smoke?" he asks, his face screwed in disgust.

In lieu of an answer I walk to the kitchen and grab a mug. As I fill it, the hiss of water reaches the foyer, and Steven's disembodied voice reaches me.

"Could I have some water too?"

No "please": another layer of his manufactured civility gone. Cigarette wedged at the corner of my mouth, I pick up an extra mug. Denying a thirsty man water accomplishes nothing. We still have a long way to go. Back in the grand entrance, his lips part for the porcelain rim of the cup I hold for him. The gurgles he makes resonate in the spacious environment of the foyer, which is the size of a small New York studio. Everything in this house has been super-sized, including the staircase with its glass, wood and reinforced-steel fixtures. Taking a long drag, which hollows my cheeks, smoke fills my lungs, and I savor the thrill of withholding information—a tantalizing foreplay only heightened by his barely concealed frustration. His eyes stare at the loose wrist and my hand holding the cigarette.

"Which one do you hate most, the cigarette or the tattoo? Or are they both equally filthy habits in that skewed moral compass of yours?"

"I can't comprehend that need to degrade your body like that." He shrugs.

"Frowns at someone inking their own body but has no issue abusing that of a teenage girl—that's some serious ethical relativism there, professor."

His only answer comes in the form of the scratch of his finger against the fake leather of the armrest. Is he aware of what he's doing? The chair rattles with the frustration of a caged animal, and an exhilarating fear shimmers down my back. If he gets out.

One wrong move and I could get hurt. Badly.

Abuse. Even if I know what he's done I still find it hard to say the word. He's the perpetrator, I'm the accuser, and still the word that makes me and others uncomfortable, catches in the back of our throats, so we hide it inside more bearable approximations—molesting, sexual assault—but he needs to hear it, face what he's done without lessening his act with easier words.

"How much is your sham of a life worth to you? For your systematic statutory rape of students to stay a secret?"

"What are you saying?"

"I have pictures, names, dates, all your little secrets, ghosts of relationships present and past. How much are you prepared to give for your reputation to stay as pure as that snow outside?"

He scowls in response, the disdain on his face unmistakable. "So this is what it's all about—money?"

So pitiful. Why do these men always assume everything has to do with sex or money? But I'm curious to see where this will lead.

"What do you mean?"

"This is why you and your boyfriend orchestrated this entire thing. Tricking me into coming here so you can scare me into paying you for your silence."

"My boyfriend?" The accusation is unexpected. Taking another long drag, I scan my memory for a moment or situation that could have implied I have a boyfriend.

"Tell me, did you set up this whole thing from the start? Or did the two of you come up with it after we started dating?"

"You've lost me here. What boyfriend?"

"Are you one of those con couples they show on *America's Most Wanted* or something far seedier? You can drop the charade." His voice rises as he twists his head around. He waits in silence for someone to step out of the shadows, to make their grand entrance and prove his shrewdness. The dramatic moment he's engineered climaxes, then shrivels into an awkward silence.

"Or maybe he's waiting nearby to pick you up once this is over?"

"Where did you get the idea that we're not alone?"

"Come on, I'm not stupid. There's no way you could have got me into this wheelchair all by yourself."

The look of smugness which takes over his face would be infuriating if he wasn't so wrong. Instead, it curls the corners of my mouth.

"Sorry to disappoint you, but that was just me. The pack-strap carry method. You should look it up. So much knowledge out there, only an online search engine away."

"Even if your boyfriend's not—"

"What makes you think I have a boyfriend?"

"You can drop the pretense. I've worked it all out. I saw you together."

"When?"

"Sasha's gallery opening. I saw the two of you talking outside. Saw him coming out of your building once. You tried to usher him away outside the gallery, but I still caught you. You two seemed very cozy."

My laughter explodes in the lobby, reverberating from the high ceiling and bouncing off the tiled floor. Once it has taken hold of me, I cannot stop. It overtakes my whole body, rocking it until my sides hurt, and tears dampen my cheeks. In the middle of the checkered floor, Steven is sulking in his chair, glaring at me. His face is almost enough to send an aftershock of laughter through my body.

"Connor's not my boyfriend, he's my cousin," I say, the last tremor of laughter shaking my voice. "And for the record he would be more interested in getting into your pants than mine."

Connor. Sweet wouldn't-hurt-a-fly Connor. Connor, who would cradle spiders, taking them outside when I wanted to stomp on them. Connor, whose answer to every problem is shakes and fries. It's true: in some way he was there at the moment of inception, the time when the first decision was made. But this is nobody else's battle.

"Doesn't mean anything. He could have put you up to it."

"I'm a big girl, Steven. I don't need some guy pulling the strings."

Dropping the cigarette stub into the mug, I fish another one out of the pack and light up. The nicotine and tar feel less toxic than my proximity to him right now. So typical of him to think a man has to be behind all this, that I couldn't carry this out on my own. Our entire relationship has been saturated with the advice he dishes out—which I've never asked for—based on the deluded idea that he knows best.

Time to crush that belief.

"It's very simple. I am giving you a choice. I can tell the Board of Education about your systematic statutory rape of students and underage girls, provide them with names, dates, pictures. I will destroy your career, and even more: I will destroy your precious reputation."

Stepping forward, I lay my hands over his, and the scratching stops. As my body fills the space in front of him, he has no other possibility than to look right at me and the determination which imbues every fiber of my being.

"You will never be able to teach, or prey on, a young girl

ever again. You will be known as the disgraced son of Professor Stewart Harding." Words are a weapon, and the last sentence stabs him in the gut as his eyes bulge heavy with terror at the mere prospect of a permanent fall from grace. "Or…"

I walk away to drop the tower of ash at the end of my cigarette into the mug, where it fizzes when it hits the water. The unfinished bargain builds inside him, and the sound of rattling metal fills the air. The rattling of the wheelchair under his body has become a Morse code of his feelings and frustrations, one I'm still learning to decipher.

"Or what?" He stares at me with an unblinking gaze which I withstand with one of my own. No more submissive Ellie, looking down or peering at him from under her lashes. Every moment I am stepping out and away from her, expelling her like a ghost I have allowed to possess me for a while, until she has served her purpose.

"Or you can take the honorable way out. Commit suicide by hanging yourself, and I promise you I won't say anything. You'll die with a pristine reputation. Who knows, your premature death could elevate you to heights you could never have reached alive."

My cigarette butt hits the bottom of my cup with a hiss.

It took us a while to get here, more than the three and a half hours' driving time. The weeks corralling the evidence— the excuses which tasted bitter, the kisses which smelled like someone else, the pictures which looked like children's faces, the text messages, their secrets stitched with xxx. The hours scrolling through listings, looking for the right stage, the right kind of forlorn getaway, somewhere it could be nobody but us—and the ghosts of all the others. Houses skidded past in a blur. But, as they say, when you see it you just know. The tall windows, the jagged lines tucked between

186

the ocean and the woods. One look on Google Maps and a few clicks to zoom out showing only green for miles to confirm how perfect it was. And it hasn't disappointed so far. So much has already happened. But we're still not there yet.

A mumble from his mouth slithers through my thoughts. "Sorry, what?"

"I said: come on, this isn't funny anymore. It serves no purpose." A pause. "Plus, I really need the bathroom," he says, with a smug smile on his face.

39. Steven

His smile vanishes with Ellie as she walks out of the room without a word, leaving him alone with a full bladder. She has abandoned him here, when everything he knows about her tells him she should have sympathized and released him from this damn chair. If the theatrics of the rope and the noose aren't the desperate antics of a scorned little girl or the scare tactics of a blackmailer, what is she after? The more he knows, the less everything makes sense. The less *she* makes sense.

He is beginning to doubt how much he ever truly knew about her. Apart from a predisposition to listen to him and her love and study of literature, she's a mystery he has enjoyed until now. The fact she didn't try to get him to meet her friends or, worse, her family has always been a benefit. He went to her studio apartment a handful of times but he never paid much attention to any photographs that may have littered the place, happy for them to spend most of their time at his place—far more spacious.

His blood slows down with a chill at the horror that, in fact, there were no photographs in her apartment. Who has no personal mementos on display? Even he has a scatter of photos: his graduation, his gown-clad tall frame sandwiched between his parents; being the best man at Jeffrey's wedding; receiving the Samuel Sewall's Essay Prize. He scans his memory of her place and he can't picture a single keepsake from her past, no family or friends staring at him from behind cool glass, no proof of a life before she met him. Same with all their conversations: no real stories from her childhood, teenage years, nothing more than a passing anecdote here and there. *She* would curl up on his sofa, chin resting in her hand, listening to *his* stories.

Each recollection unpicks a stitch in their relationship until the whole thing completely unravels. Every assumption and decision he's made so far has been based on his knowledge of her. But he has absolutely no idea who the woman he's trapped with is. She appeared to him fully formed and drenched on the tiles of Norman's Café, but he has never cared to find out where she came from, who she was before he met her. For all he knows she could have walked out of some psychiatry facility and right into his life.

And still, despite everything she's put him through so far, the humiliation, the spiteful remarks, he still can't reconcile this cruel and conniving Ellie standing in front of him—the girl plotting his downfall—with the Ellie from their relationship. He hates the part of him which still clings to her. The girl who surprised him at work only a month ago. The pale winter sun sunk below the mountain range of skyscrapers which dwarfed the high-rises and brownstones in the foreground. He had just stepped through the double doors of Richmond Prep and into the crisp wintry afternoon after everyone else, delayed by a call from his father.

The call might have ended, but his old man's voice stayed with him like an earworm burrowing deep into his patience, eating at it. The sly digs disguised as humorous or innocuous comments about his job—"Read your essay in the *North England Review*. Nicely done, my boy, one day you'll get to have a book of yours published like your old man." *My boy,* Steven's jaw hardened at the colloquialism the old bastard deliberately adopted whenever he referred to him, forever freezing Steven at an infantile stage.

Standing at the top of the steps, he had been debating swapping his afternoon coffee for a couple of bourbons when he spotted her—unmissable in her oversized coat, a bright red island amid a sea of navy uniforms. She looked up at him. From a distance, the glaze of tears shone in her eyes before she quickly turned away. He discarded the dreadful phone conversation on the porch as he flew down the steps and parted the sea of students to get to her.

He reached her just in time for his thumb to crush the tear which had spilled onto her cheek.

"Is everything OK?"

"It's nothing," she sniffed.

"Tell me."

"It's silly, really."

He lifted her chin so she could see his determination. "Tell. Me."

It surprised him how much he genuinely wanted to know.

She looked at him for a long time before she answered, "Just a stupid misunderstanding with a friend."

She punctuated her statement with a heavy sigh which urged him to pull her close until the weight of her head pressed against his chest, forgetting for a moment his aversion to public displays of affection, especially in front of his students and colleagues. Her body, hardened by the wintry wind swirling around, rested heavy in his embrace.

"What's that?" He nodded toward the small cardboard box in a pretty pastel green which she held onto by its strings, knocking against his leg.

"You told me the other day that you'd never tasted Magnolia Bakery's banana pudding."

"You remembered that?"

She nodded. "I only had one class today so I thought I'd bring you some. You really need to try it." Her words were light, but her tone was still laden with whatever sadness lingered inside. She transferred the weight of the package to him. The strings had left red lines on the inside of her fingers. "Anyway, you must be busy. I'll leave you to it."

She'd already stepped away from him, ready to be swallowed by the tide of students heading home, when his free hand caught hers.

"Hold on." Bourbon and commiseration could wait.

"I don't think it's a good idea right now."

"What do you mean?"

"I really should go." Her words were at odds with the look in her eyes.

"You don't expect me to eat all of this by myself, do you?" The question didn't require an answer; he knew how to make her feel better. "Come on, let's go."

She followed him home but had somehow disappeared somewhere inside her own head, and they walked in silence. He didn't want to pry, though he couldn't help wondering what exactly had happened. But all of that changed once they reached his apartment. Whatever worries they both had were shed and left pooling on the floor next to their clothes.

She kept her eyes tightly shut as he ate banana pudding off the shallow dip of her stomach, licked the cream off her skin, leaving behind the shiny stamp of his saliva. Hungry, he moved up to find her lips, and his body collapsed onto hers, dessert squashed between their stomachs, spreading on their skin. Before he could kiss her mouth, she flipped around, staining his expensive Egyptian cotton sheets. He didn't care. Head buried in his pillow, she offered herself to him.

Later, he lay on his back, one arm tucked under his head, the other wrapped around a naked Ellie, their bodies and the bed sticky with the remnants of pudding, a heavy waft of banana and sugar hijacking the air in the bedroom. He felt the flutter of her damp eyelashes, her breath falling on his chest. After a minute, she slipped out of his embrace and headed toward the bathroom. Propped on an elbow, he watched the listless roll of her hips as she crossed the room. She reminded him of a fawn testing its legs for the first time.

"I'm going to get a drink. Do you want something?" he asked.

Without turning back, she shook her head. "No, thank you." Her voice slightly shaky from what they had just done.

A couple of hours with her and he had forgotten all about his father. She had painted over the resentment that had been bubbling under the surface before he'd seen her waiting for him, washed away the sourness that a conversation with his father always left in his mouth.

"No, thank *you*," he breathed, as the hiss of water slithered its way into the bedroom.

But in truth: he doesn't know what she does or who she sees when she's not with him or at NYU. He never asked who that friend who upset her was, and it has never been a worry for him, until now. Now she is acting like those unhinged women in films, TV series or in the cheap newspapers they sell at supermarket check-outs, ruining a man's life out of some misplaced entitlement or because of some sort of perceived wrongdoings.

He sits alone, surrounded by the pungency of her cigarettes, which mingles with the sourness of his own sweat. He aches to escape, stand outside just to fill his lungs with crisp, clean air. How did he get here? And still another scent rises, carrying a memory which tugs at him, fraught with a strong chemical scent.

40. Steven

M. was sixteen, and he was a twenty-five-year-old substitute teacher who had just started his second teaching assignment. After his PhD, he had had the urge to flee college academic circles where his father's shadow roamed.

She sat in the third row of his English class. She tossed her long black hair around and chewed the end of pencils with a mouth wet with pink gloss. On warm days, she would twist that hair before stabbing the loose bun into place with one of those gnawed pens. She was a magnetic pole, always drawing his gaze back to her between two and three on Thursday afternoons.

Before work, he had taken to going swimming every other morning right at opening time, the local pool ideally located between his overpriced studio and the school. The early hour meant he had the place all to himself except for a lone lifeguard slumped over in his high chair, arms crossed and head falling on his chest. For forty-five minutes, Steven sliced the water back and forth until his arms ached, refining the muscles, burning whatever fat would dare cling to him. Body immersed, his mind latched on to his father, strolling around Coopers Beach the previous summer, while every acquaintance commented how perfect a body he had for a fifty-four-year-old—his old man's physique a better subject to marvel at than Steven's excellent academic achievements.

She had appeared one morning—roughly a month after he started attending—clad in a red athletic swimsuit. She slipped into the lane the farthest away from him, swimming a nonchalant breaststroke, chin tilted up, or staring at ceiling tiles while doing the backstroke. Her aloofness intrigued him. His rhythm slowed down as he paused in between laps to observe her.

Every time she would come in shortly after him and slither into the water, never saying a word or even acknowledging his presence, always leaving before he finished. His head would break the surface, and she would be pulling herself up the ladder—dripping—or already walking away, the red waterlogged spandex alive with the roll of her hips. The smack of her bare feet bounced off every tiled surface, announcing her departure.

It had been an unremarkable morning, nothing to differentiate it from all the others that had preceded it. Towel in hand, he rubbed his hair and face dry in the privacy of his cubicle when a knock at the door interrupted him. Had he forgotten his goggles by the side of the pool? As soon as the lock clicked open, she slid in. There was barely enough space for both their bodies; certainly, no space for explanations or questions, it was in silence she pulled down his Speedos before going down on him. He staggered back against the wall from the boldness of her act and the warmth of her mouth.

When he dared look down, the right shoulder strap of her swimsuit had twisted around itself. She must have sensed his gaze because she stared at him from under her lashes. Kneeling in front of him, exposed, offering herself to him, gray eyes asking for approval, a show of his enjoyment. Her gaze didn't leave his face, as she continued, taking him deeper. There was something incredibly erotic in her gaze, the lock of hair plastered on her cheek. That look of submission overwhelmed him, spasmed deep inside, until he couldn't keep it in anymore.

Her boldness contrasted with a shyness nestled in her silence. It wasn't just sex, it was a connection; he instinctively knew she wanted to be seen, acknowledged. They never exchanged a word. It was a mutual agreement they never made but was somehow implied. He would leave the door unlocked and she would slither in, always in the same red swimsuit. Two bodies wedged in the confined space surrounded by the smell of chlorine. Since then, he can't go to a pool without the flitting memory of M. crossing his mind in some kind of Pavlovian response.

Their affair ended the same way it began—without a word, the day he stopped going to the pool when his assignment ended.

He saw the same look again at St. John's Catholic school in Boston. He was complimenting one of his students about her essay on *Jane Eyre* and her precocious comments. She too wanted him to see her. H. A beauty spot lived under her left eye, so black it looked drawn on. Cupping her cheek, he used to stroke that tiny mole with the pad of his thumb. She had eyes as green as the turf at Fenway Park. He didn't really follow baseball, but when in Boston...

He remembers them all. Each a unique experience, a story that belongs to him. He gave them the validation they craved. He saw them, told them they were beautiful, that they mattered. They listened to what he had to say, sought his advice. He showed them how much pleasure there is to be had, the right spot to kiss and touch.

One of them stands out from the group. The face that solidified amid Ellie's recitation of *The Devils*, the one she couldn't possibly know about. In his mind she stands on a cliff, wind whipping her hair.

W. With each passing moment, everything makes less and

less sense. Vanilla and Jasmine. Strange, the details that stay with you.

"Do you still need the bathroom?"

"Yes, desperately." Ellie is back, and he waits for her to use the knife or the pair of scissors she has fetched, but instead she smiles at him, an empty water bottle in her hand. His stomach tightens with disbelief at the sight.

"Are you kidding me?"

"Nope."

"Untie me now," he spits at her, the edges of duct tape biting into his skin.

"No."

"Fucking untie me now," he shouts as the chair rattles hard under his rage. She responds with a stony silence that fuels his frustration, the wheels from the chair lifting dangerously from the floor. Once he has burned through his anger, the chair stops moving.

"Finished?"

He won't dignify her with an answer.

"I'm not untying you, so you have two options: either you use this bottle, or you piss yourself. What's it gonna be?"

The cruelty of her words and steadiness of her tone tell him the Ellie he knows is gone. He is now trapped in the middle of nowhere with a stranger and he has no idea what she's capable of. But the horrifying consequences of this will have to wait. For now, the humiliation of pissing himself is too shameful for him to bear.

"The bottle," Steven says, the words barely escaping through his gritted teeth. He will never forgive her for this. He has never been treated with such disrespect. How can she do it to him?

His zipper goes down, and as he closes his eyes his mind

detaches himself from the situation. She takes him into her hand, and for the first time he doesn't grow hard at her touch. He lets go of his pride irrevocably as the warm stream of urine hits the bottle. How did he get here? He has never sunk so low in his life. Whenever he gets free, he will make her pay for this. She can't keep him tied up forever. Humiliation reaches absolute rock bottom when she shakes the last drops out of him, before zipping him up.

She leaves him alone with the acrid smell of urine to dispose of the bottle and its contents. And he unleashes his rage.

41

April 23

Every day at school, I have to see you. I have to sit in a freaking classroom, trapped for an excruciating hour with you. I get to watch you ignore me, smile to the other girls in class, chat with Ms. Winters in the hallway. Yesterday, I stood by your desk at the end of class, bristling, waiting for you to look up and see me, but your eyes stayed firmly on some paper on your desk.

"Could I talk to you about my assignment?" I said, the words trembling on my lips.

You didn't say anything, you just sighed, as if the will to live was slipping out of you. It rocked through me and sent me running. I ducked into the nearest girls' bathroom. In the privacy of a locked stall, I found a spot of skin, and then found a release.

School assembly afterward about the dangers of the Internet. Apparently a girl over at Jefferson High had chatted with this teenage boy online who turned out to be a forty-year-old creep.

You sat on the podium with the other teachers, shaking your head like the rest of them at the tragic situation. Never looked once in my direction. Principal Harvey urged us in her usual whiny voice, "If any of you has experienced anything like this or if you are concerned about a friend or someone you know, you can speak in all confidence to Mr. Gibson, or one of your teachers. We are here for you."

Here for me. The fifteen-year-old. Who knew what she was getting into. Sitting at the top of the bleachers, I looked down at the podium.

How can I tell any of them, when they're all on your side?

42. Ellie

The light comes in too bright, for a moment turning my eyes into slits. It shines white around the bathroom mirror, bleaching my features. I look pale, gaunt; I still don't recognize myself.

I've been Ellie for so long—days which have stacked up into weeks, into months. The warm bottle trembles in my hand. I set it down before clutching the edge of the sink, searching for myself behind the mask in the mirror. It's like finding my way in the dark, feeling around until I stumble upon something familiar. I ease back into my old self; shrug off the coyness I've been wearing for him. Shed it like an invisible snake's skin discarded on the bathroom floor.

I pull out the picture. Just looking at it reminds me of who I truly am. But recognition drags along with it the pain which has been locked deep inside. It surges like a wave carrying my heart into my throat, drowning my lungs. It softens my legs and drives me to the floor.

Z...Y...X...W...

Lost in backward recitation, the pain—starved of attention—dwindles to something manageable, a dull pinch in my chest. If Dad was still around and knew I was still getting those panic attacks, he would come himself and drag me back home. *This wasn't the deal, Bug,* he would say in that gravelly voice which scared everyone, except me. I miss him so much. He knew how much what happened had messed me up, he literally had a front seat that day, and still he trusted me to deal with it—up to a point.

After it happened, I wanted to get back to the real world. Dad's reluctance at letting me move on my own to the other side of the country proved to be the main obstacle, but I had Doctor S. on my side.

"Do you think she's ready?" he asked as I hovered by the window of his home office, the air on the terrace heavy with the smell of burned meat from one of the neighbors having a barbecue. I imagined Berkeley, how I would fit in there, saw myself in the quad, with friends around me, even though they still all had the same face.

"I think she has made tremendous progress, and it's the next step for her," Doctor S. replied. Thanks for Dad and his habit of using speaker phone for most of his conversations.

"But does she still have…" My throat tightened at the sound of my father's faltering voice. The urge to run in and throw my arm around him overwhelmed me, but I remained still and hidden.

"I cannot discuss my sessions with your daughter and what we talk about, but I'm confident that she's ready for this next step in her life."

Dad replied with silence. I could visualize him on the other side of the glass, reclining in his swivel chair, the back straining under his weight, fingering the stack of papers on his desk or maybe fiddling with a pen as he processed the information. No matter where we lived, his office always remained a constant in all the houses we called home.

"Are there any precautions we should take?"

"I've already recommended to her one of my colleagues who can see her in Oakland, and of course I'm available should she feel the need to speak to me."

There was a lump in my throat at her words. There was still a part of me that feared being away from her. She knew the words to make me taller, the words to make me believe I would be OK, the words that made the pain bearable.

"Thank you for this."

"She told me that you have a house in the area."

"Yes, in Monterey. I'm planning to reopen it so that we can move back there."

"So she will have a backup system at her disposition, should she need it."

"Thank you, doctor. I'll let you know if I have any additional questions."

In the silence that followed the click chiming the end of the call, I waited for a throat clearing or a shuffling of paper, anything I could interpret as a clue.

"You can come out, Bug."

I smiled at the thrill of my trespass being discovered. "Aren't I too old for that nickname?" I said as I walked through the open window.

"Never gonna happen, sorry." He paused. "Berkeley, then." The fake stern expression on his face didn't fool me. As much as he knew I was hiding, I always knew when his mind was made up and which way it leaned.

"Thanks, Dad," I said, finally able to throw my arms around him.

"Now scoot," he said. "I have a call with the state attorney."

The bottle tips over the toilet; Steven's piss hits the water with a hiss, the stringent smell—overpowering that close—rising from the bowl. I smile at his humiliation as I flush it down. He's always been so self-assured, but I have made a chip in the veneer, a crack I can slither into and do some damage. Maybe I could carve him and see what he is really made of inside. Would his anatomy reveal how compromised he is? Would his organs show specks of mold, the progression of darkness, or has the rot completely overtaken him down to his marrow?

My mind skirts around what Steven would do to me if he got loose, what those fingers which scratched the leather of the armrests would do if they roamed over my skin, wrapped around my bones. All in a place where nobody would hear me scream. But it's not about me. That's what he still doesn't realize.

Steven breathes downstairs. I'm not ready to be reunited with his contempt and anger, the false indignation which oozes out of him. Sitting on the rim of the tub, I light a cigarette. Above the bath, the window slices the wall, filled with a direct view of the ocean. The storm has relented, unable to sustain the energy it needs to fling waves against the shore. All that energy, and nothing has changed: the house is still standing, the forest hasn't yielded either.

Another drag settles in my lungs, the smoke swirling inside me. On the other side of the glass, the ocean slithers like black oil, lulling my heartbeat. It almost looks inviting, but under its sedated appearance the water is freezing and the undertow strong enough to sweep you under and out. Sitting on the edge of the tub, I feel like a survivor on a raft, hoping to make it to shore by morning. The filter burns my lips, jolting me back to attention.

Even though it hasn't appeared all day, the sun has now vanished, the clouds blackened by night's arrival. The cigarette stub hisses under the stream of water from the tap before I drop it in the wastebasket. Instead of leaving, I light up again, staying with my memories of Dad a little longer.

Dad. He would die barely a year after that call to Doctor S. One more death for me to survive. His strong heart worn out from worrying so much about me. As I lean against the wall, my face is bathed in tears. Tears for his absence, and because a good man like him is dead while a man like Steven still has a pulse. Because, without Steven, Dad would still be around. But then—if Dad hadn't died, I would never have learned the truth.

43. Ellie

The light in his eyes has shifted, the glare now coming from a burning hatred rather than an intense fear or contempt. The cool demeanor of Professor Steven Harding has melted and left his body, diluted in his urine, to reveal the raw man underneath.

"I will never forgive you for this."

"Peeing in a bottle should be the least of your worries right now."

"You're crazy. Delusional. How many times do I have to say it? I did not take advantage of anyone. They never said no."

His tirade makes me drop to the floor, where I sit cross-legged. The dominance of his ego is exhausting. A giant monolith he has erected to himself which blocks his perspective and bounces everything back to him. It really needs to be crushed into a fine sand, exposing him as the fraud he is, leaving him with nowhere to hide.

My restraints have robbed him of more than just his freedom, they have also snatched away parts of his confidence. There was a piece in the *Washington Square News* recently about Dr. Albert Mehrabian and his book *Silent Messages*. The article explained that he found that only seven percent of any message is conveyed through words, thirty-eight percent through certain vocal elements, and fifty-five percent through non-verbal elements—facial expressions, gestures, posture, etc. . . . Looking at Steven stuck in his chair right now I wonder how much of that fifty-five percent has been impaired.

"Only because you groomed them."

His genuine or more likely fabricated lack of awareness brings me to my feet, working through my frustration by pacing the checkered floor. The queen can always move in any direction, but in this game the king is stuck in a perpetual state of check, learning that he's not omnipotent.

Catching a gleam from the flames, the signet ring on his little finger winks at me.

"You are so much like your father." I nod toward the ring. "Even received his seal of approval."

"This isn't a seal," he replies, wiggling his little finger. "It was a gift for receiving my PhD."

"Or a gift for the apple not fallen far from the patriarchal tree? Sorry, I know you detest clichés. But remember, I've done my research like any good student. I know all about Daddy Harding and his philandering ways. Quite sure a few of them were below the age of legal consent. Both of you saw us as a means to an end. Stroke your egos and dicks in the process."

"Seriously, Ellie?"

"Picking the lonely ones, making them feel special, giving them just the right amount of attention to make them think they have a chance, so they'll be the one who throws themselves at you, and you can delude yourself that you've done nothing wrong. Making them believe they are Jane Eyre and you're their Mr. Rochester."

I search his face for a reaction. He really is the most skilled of predators, one who ensnares with compliments, taking an interest to seduce his prey into lying down in front of him, willingly offering herself. So cunning that I almost fell for it on our first date. A few drinks lowered my guard, as the world slurred around us. I got caught on the hook of his smile. He chose his environment well, the miasma of voices and the live band conducive to a manufactured intimacy—his warm breath on my neck, the pressure of fingers or a hand on an arm each time we had to lean into each other to continue our conversation. I lost myself within his charms, falling fast for the persona he has refined over so many years. In the end, I had to apologize and sit on a toilet in the bathroom for a few minutes to gather myself, tame the rhythm of my heart.

The abundance of details about his technique has kick-started a little vein pulsating under the delicate skin below his left eye. If this were a poker game, I would have just found his tell.

"Where did you get such stupid ideas?"

"I have my sources." The little twitch flutters faster under his eye, and I enjoy the physical distress my words are creating. "I'm surprised you never slipped up and called me my darling Jane by mistake."

That's when I see it, what I've been waiting to see in his eyes since I've strapped him to the wheelchair—a flash of genuine fear.

44. Ellie

I stand, he sits, and the silence between us flows, a river dividing us. Around us, darkness gathers; it is barely late afternoon, and we have already lost the light, not that there has been much of it today. To think there are places on earth when nights swallow days and stretch for months of darkness, where the closest to sunlight is a smudge of light on the horizon. It's only been a day, and the lack of sunshine is setting me on edge.

Losing the light has deepened the shadows and nudges last night's fears. Abandoning Steven, my attention drifts upward. I scan the second-floor landing, expecting to catch the silhouette of a ghost, a memory or an intruder, standing in a corner or by the railing, looking down and judging us. For a split second fear runs an icicle finger down my back. My eyes keep searching the darkness until Steven clears his throat.

"Stop acting like some kind of victim, Ellie. Nothing I've done gives you the right to do this."

His persistence in making this all about me and my inability to deal with what he believes to be a minor betrayal is infuriating, yet so typical. It crawls under my skin, pricks of electricity stinging across my shoulder blades and the backs of my arms. Unable to look at him and all his delusions any longer, I storm out of the foyer and into the living room. Walking by the ficus tree, I snap one of the leaves which I roll between my fingers. How can he still think this is only the volatile retaliation of a scorned woman? The sight of the rope and the noose has failed to scare him into an admission of guilt. I scan the room for something I can use as a threat, jolt him out of his state of disdain. The brass of the fireplace tool set catches my eye, until the obvious stares at me from the back of the sofa.

When I go back to him, the sight of the knife in my hand stops his jerky movement. He tenses his fingers around the armrests and pushes his body into the back of the chair. Even his fear is predictable. The closer I get, the straighter his spine becomes, stretched to a point where his vertebrae might disconnect from each other. No matter how much he tries, he has nowhere to go. The edge of the blade dimples the skin below his cheekbone and severs his breath for a moment as he turns his face away.

"Don't move," I order him. "You wouldn't want me to cut you by accident."

He complies without any resistance, without saying a word. Under my guidance, the knife runs down the length of his face until it meets the corner of his mouth, tracing an imaginary line, the same path I used to trace with my finger when I pretended to want to take things further in bed. The exhilaration from the act is overwhelming, unlocking impulses I didn't suspect existed. Anger recedes, my chest tight with the thrill of what I could be capable of, the satisfaction and pleasure which would be derived from hurting him, to be the architect of his pain. I wonder how much pressure I would need to apply to break the skin, draw blood to the surface?

"What do you think would be a fitting punishment? Maybe a big great gash on your cheek would be appropriate. No more dashing good looks to appeal to young impressionable girls. But then..." With a slight added pressure, the knife edge strains a little deeper still without breaking the skin. In his strained throat his Adam's apple bobs like a puck on a High Striker, measuring the force of his terror. "…the scar could get you their sympathy."

With a smile, I navigate the narrow bridge of his neck with the knife, before continuing down the plain of his chest. His panicked look ping-pongs from my face to the knife, desperate to keep an eye on my resolve, as well as track the knife and its intended destination. Halfway through, the edge of the tip nicks the stitches of his sweater, tearing a small hole.

"Sorry."

I smile again. Under the blade, his chest frets with shallow breathing. A rank smell permeates from damp patches under his armpits, where the wool is a darker shade of navy.

When the knife reaches the hard line of his jeans, I linger, running the blade alongside the denim border that stretches just below his navel. Below his clothes lies skin covered with a soft down I have kissed many times. I could slice the layers of wool, cotton, skin and finally the wall of taut muscles from behind which feet of tightly packed intestines would spill out onto his lap. Among it, would some of his secrets slip out too, coated with warm blood? The idea is enticing but not part of the plan. That would be too easy, and he doesn't deserve an easy outcome. During the entire time, my eyes never leave his face; I wonder if he can read what I'm thinking.

I resume my travel down his body. When the knife reaches his groin, the rest of his body hardens under the fear. I maneuver the blade in a circle, dragging it slowly under his ball sack.

"Or I could just cut off your balls, make sure you can't hurt any of them ever again. Would you prefer that to being outed as a sex offender? Would this be a fitter punishment, professor? Losing your balls instead of your career?"

"You're crazy."

The blade does another lap around his groin, the sharpened steel grating against the denim.

"You think you're such a great guy, don't you? A man who treats women well because he pays for everything and—what?—gives up your seat for them on the subway? Dinners, expensive gifts and common decency don't make you special or entitle you to do whatever you like. Women are not playthings, Steven. You can't just buy us and then dress us up like some kind of doll. The fact you listened to those girls and were nice to them when everybody else ignored them doesn't mean they owe you. You can't wreck their lives and then act as if it's all their fault, say they asked for it."

"I haven't harmed anyone. They can tell you." He licks his lips before he continues. "And if I hurt their feelings, then I'm truly sorry." Head bowed, I look at the knife, my knuckles white from strangling the handle. "Stop acting as if I killed someone."

I unfurl, knees stiff from the crouching. I need to get that knife away from him. From me. The idea of slashing his throat to cut off the lies coming out of him is too much of a temptation right now. Back in the living room, I leave the knife on the sofa.

In the foyer, shadows have stretched now to such lengths that they touch and congeal into a uniform darkness. With a click, the white glow of the chandelier floods the room. It hasn't struck me until now that the long stems of glass descending from the ceiling give the appearance of a gathering of icicles looming over us. Even though night has been banished from the room, the light casts an artificial coldness which draws a shiver out of me.

The delusion that he can't be held responsible is so embedded in him—a weed that has a strong hold, its roots tangled so deep into his mind. It will require longer than I estimated to get past it, yank it out to reveal the truth suffocating beneath. But I won't stop until I do.

45. Steven

As soon as Ellie has been swallowed again by the darkness of the kitchen, Steven struggles with the chair. But, in the midst of another fit against his restraints, he freezes.

On the left, the tape has slackened around his wrist. If he twisted his hand enough, he could slide it out. He works on it with short tugs. He rocks his left hand, eyes fixed on the knife resting on the back cushion glimpsed through the open door. The blade protruding motivates him. Escape is not just an abstract anymore. It's within his grasp. He can do it. Just break what seems unachievable into manageable goals: first get out of the chair, then grab the knife, then get out of here.

She's lost it, but whatever that was with the knife is the least of his worries right now. Those three words she said earlier keep churning over in his mind—*my darling Jane.*

She didn't say that she never met J. or A., but neither of them have knowledge beyond their own relationship with him. So how does Ellie seem to know so much? The tape chafes his skin, but he doesn't stop. He has to second-guess every moment of their relationship, especially the moments when he wasn't there. They've never bothered him until now. What did she do when he jumped in the shower without her? The morning after they slept together for the time, he had found her perusing the living room, but he might have unknowingly caught her snooping. He had woken up with only the warmth where her body had been in his bed, so he went looking for her, found her in his living room wearing

219

his shirt, fingers running along the spines of magazines and reviews neatly lined up on a shelf. He leaned against the door frame, taking in the sight of her moving inside his space and his clothes.

"What are those?" Turning around, she offered a smile perfectly framed by her tousled hair. A flawless blend of innocence and sexuality that tightened his stomach.

"Reviews and journals I've been published in."

"Published...Like what?"

"Mainly essays, articles, some reviews."

This would normally be the time when he would offer to pay for a taxi fare after promises to call and make plans for later, but he caught himself enjoying her lingering.

"Would you read some to me?"

"I don't want to bore you."

"I'm sure you can make it interesting."

She turned back toward the row of magazines. He didn't let her leave until Sunday morning. Ellie—the girl who stayed, but had it been really his choice?

Under this new, unforgiving light his earlier grand gesture of giving her a key to his place has withered into a foolish act. Humiliation swells in his chest so hard, he might just choke on it. Most likely she's just helped herself and already has one. In his mind, she breaks into his apartment while he's at work, pulls out drawers, leafs through his papers. He let her in, and she's abused his trust in the worst way possible. He promised he would never let them in.

Zoey. The name rises to the surface of his mind along with the sour taste of betrayal. He hasn't thought of her in years, not allowing himself to revisit this part of his life, although he's lying. Sometimes late at night on the rare occasion he cannot sleep he wonders what could have been if things had been different between them: if he would be standing here a different man. If he would be here at all.

She was getting lost trying to get to her Social Justice course when he walked into her.

"Social Justice is overrated," he told her. "Come and have coffee with me. Cappuccino? Latte? Mocha? Please say something before I get to macchiato. I'm not sure I can handle a macchiato girl."

"What's so terrible about macchiato?" she laughed.

"Come with me, and I'll let you know. It'll be far more riveting than your lecture, I promise."

She was so unlike him, an oddity he had fallen for. College was for experimentation, and Zoey was the perfect subject. She enjoyed marches and protests, refused to eat anything that once had a face and wore too much kohl around her eyes. Being with Zoey was like chasing a kite dancing in gale-force wind, something exhilarating that always left him out of breath.

"Come with me to the Hamptons for Labor Day weekend," he said as she lay on his bed, her naked body sheltered inside his Princeton sweatshirt. She had become a permanent fixture of his dorm room, one he was ready to introduce to his home environment and his parents.

"You sure? I think I would stick out like a socialist sore thumb out there."

"That's the whole idea, you can ruffle some old Republican feathers, make things interesting."

It didn't take long for him to convince her to come, but it took longer for her to convince him to take a bus instead of the train or hitch a ride with one of the other students heading that way. The experience left him feeling unclean in so many ways. Three hours in an oblong tin can on wheels with a busted air-conditioner, every seat occupied by a body ripe from the heat. Everyone glistening with perspiration under the blistering sun hitting panes of glass, all surrounded by stale air flavored with the bitter scent of humans trapped in a heatwave.

When they stumbled out of the bus, they decided to forego the house, instead dipping in the waves of the Atlantic Ocean to cool off. By the time they made it to his parents' home, their skin was tight from the salt and the baking sun.

"Hello?" He sent the word out, a search party looking for signs of life.

"Steven." His mother appeared shortly after her welcome reached his ears. Joy shone in her eyes. She advanced on him, arms outstretched into a forlorn invitation to a hug. She smothered him while he bided his time, wondering what Zoey would think of the scene. After an uncomfortable amount of time, her arms released him.

"Hey, now, Mr. Harding," Zoey said, a huge grin on her freckled face as she shook his father's hand with an enthusiasm that punched through the heaviness and dispelled the awkwardness of the previous moment. His father's lips stretched into a thin smile as Steven imagined his old man swallowing the corrective "It's Professor Harding, actually" jammed in his throat.

Oblivious, Zoey moved to his mother, leaving behind her usual trail of patchouli before she hugged her under his father's skeptical gaze and an arched eyebrow. Zoey lacked a crucial component to earn his father's approval: respectability. He could already picture his old man, referring to her over lunch back in the city as his son's rebellious phase.

"Fuck me, your father's an asshole," Zoey said as they got undressed that first night for bed. The hours of darkness hadn't dampened the heat outside. On the contrary, the night had pushed it down, and they slept naked under the thin cotton sheet. He had watched her at dinner arguing with his father about state welfare and immigration policy—the hardened Republican and the idealistic Democrat jousting over two bottles of Merlot.

"I'd love to," he joked as his mouth trailed down her torso to the cup of her left hip, which housed her tiny bird's footprints tattoo—a homage to her favorite song—close to where her golden hair curled, although those had been waxed off a few days ago.

Round two took place on the patio the following day over a lunch his mother had organized. Tired of the arguments and counter-arguments, Steven had scooped Zoey from the bench before leaping into the pool feet first with all of her cradled in his arms. He loved how she made herself as small as possible, nesting against his chest as she braced for the impact with the water. As their mingled cannonball broke the surface, she shrieked. The shock of the cold water hardened her nipples as they emerged, her soaked t-shirt clinging to her skin. Wiping the water off his face, he caught the heels of his father's loafers walking through the patio doors. At the table amid leftover food and glasses stained with the dregs of red wine, head down, his mother folded and smoothed her napkin.

The following day was the main event: the Hardings' annual Labor Day party. Friends and family gathered in small groups on the terrace or under oversized umbrellas to hide from the relentless sun. The temperature had crept up again overnight; it was now officially a heat wave. Tucked under the shade, Steven got cornered into a conversation with their elderly neighbor—Edna something—who insisted on knowing every minute detail of his life at Princeton.

She smelled like a thrift store, a mix of mothball and slight mildew. Somehow this shriveling old woman smelled like Zoey's clothes.

"Your father must be so proud," she said, resting on his arm her desiccated hand covered in a papery skin and liver spots barely hiding bulging blue veins.

"Sure is," he lied. The only person his father had ever been proud of was himself, and certainly not about Steven going to Princeton when his old man had been a Yale alumnus.

As the old bore went on about her time at some godforsaken college, he scanned the scattered groups, searching for Zoey's blonde mane and her slightly reddened shoulders under the brown tan.

"Would you excuse me?" He left without waiting for a response.

He hopped from one group to the other, but Zoey was nowhere to be found. Abandoning the furnace of the outside, he slipped through the open French windows in the hope the innards of the house would hold some answers as to her whereabouts.

She stood in the kitchen, half her body leaning inside the giant fridge.

"What are you doing?"

"I came in to get something and can't for the life of me remember what it is. I've been enjoying the welcome cold from the fridge and running a massive electricity bill for your parents," she laughed, closing the door. Despite the cold, her cheeks seemed still flushed with heat. "Let's go for a swim," she said, her fingers finding their way through the slits between his.

"Have you seen your father?" his mother asked as they exited the house.

"I think he went to the bathroom," Zoey replied, squeezing his fingers.

After the sun sank behind the houses hemming the coast, the party—like many others—moved on to the beach, everybody awaiting the annual firework display. Once again, Zoey had gone missing in the crowd. The first explosion of fiery green and pink ignited the night, and she wasn't there to share the moment with him. With every eye fixed on the sky, he backtracked toward the line of houses.

He found her by the Meyers' house, her body sandwiched between an old palisade and a silhouette not unlike his own. The next denotation of vivid gold in the sky illuminated Zoey's face, her tongue deep inside his father's mouth.

The blow of seeing his old man and girlfriend together left him feeling slightly concussed. Steven froze, his eyes following his father's arm down until it disappeared inside the V of Zoey's opened denim shorts, his fingers inside her as his wrist rubbed against the bird feet inked on her skin. He still couldn't look away when she broke off their kiss, throwing her head back in abandonment, offering his father an expression of pure pleasure that had been his alone until now.

The fizz of the next swarm of pyrotechnics being launched severed the connection, and Steven ran away. As he trudged across the beach, sand filled his boating shoes. He removed them before launching them at the ocean. He returned when Zoey and the whole house were fast asleep. The following morning, at breakfast, he remained silent. His father reached for the jug of fresh orange juice the maid had prepared because his father didn't like the one from the supermarket. In doing so he exposed his wrist and the patch of skin that had rubbed the night before against Zoey's tattoo.

He never confronted his father about it. He never told Zoey either. They slept together a few times in the following weeks after they got back, but every time her tattoo was exposed, images of her with his father detonated in his mind like flash grenades. He stopped calling her and avoided her around campus, which wasn't that hard, as they both had circles of friends that didn't really intersect.

He never brought a girl home after that. He never let a single one of them in. He never fell so hard again. Until Ellie.

46. Ellie

The kitchen is sunk in a darkness lit only by the light spilling from the foyer. After an evening cooking dinner in here, I'm attuned enough to the layout of the room to find my way to the other side without stubbing a toe or banging a hip on a corner. I had to escape the silent storm in the other room, even just for a moment.

Even though I know what I want, I linger in the shadows, elbows resting on the bruise-colored granite worktop. Despite all my motivations, this is turning out a lot more difficult than expected. I feel drained, as if Steven's disregard and resistance have been feeding off my energy, sucking the very marrow from my bones. Slowly I inflate my lungs, allowing them to strain against their bony cage.

The skin from grapes—spilling over from the fruit bowl—feels smooth under my fingers. I pluck one before popping it in my mouth. It rolls around on my tongue before I trap it between my teeth. Testing the integrity of its skin, the pressure of my molars pushes the flesh against its thin membrane. When I'm ready, I squash it, pulp oozing out from its casing and the juice flooding my mouth.

Under the rush of sugar, I pop another one in. Their taste always takes me back to that summer, a salad bowl full of grapes standing between us. She peeled their skin with her teeth, the thrill coming from the patience required. Her wanting to know if she had what it took. We sat in her garden, blades of grass tickling our bare legs. The sun baked our shoulders, hers lightly reddened and littered with a constellation of freckles, whole galaxies of them that had bloomed under the heat. Grape trapped between her fingers, her teeth worked on the skin. In an unadulterated joy at her success, her mouth stretched into a smile. She was different from me in that way, and yet similar in so many others.

In the privacy of the kitchen, I use the break to get reacquainted with myself. I unfurl fully, stretching my arms, my spine, my body. Being alive is so much more than merely a heartbeat in your chest or a breath in your lungs. I become my own again, not someone fashioned to an image that would entice him, would keep him interested and tethered to me until I could lead him here, unsuspecting.

My true personality has been hibernating at the back of my mind for months now, remaining silent every time he expected me to stroke his ego, not saying no when I wasn't in the mood for it, not gagging or biting when I first took him in my mouth, but screaming in my own head every time he spoke to a teenage girl. I disguised myself behind smiles, a demure demeanor, looked at him through the distorted length of adoration. I lived through the scary moments when I forgot who I really was, lost in the intensity of a kiss, the tenderness of a gesture, when not only did I buy my own lies, but his as well—the pretense of the caring man. But as the air climbs into my lungs, the corners of the picture tucked inside my bra prick my skin, welcoming me back from a relationship which has tested the edges and limits of my sanity.

The fridge is humming behind me, a low buzz that drowns everything else out until it's all I can hear. Just that noise. Like whirring flies over a rotten fruit or a spill of blood. My nails press against the hard worktop, their tips at breaking point. I'm swept by a sudden urge to smash the damn thing until the noise is dead, but I shouldn't waste my energy. The rage I nurture belongs to someone else. My hand closes into a fist as I hold on to it, an emotion so often denied to us, being told that anger is unbecoming, unladylike. Whatever happened to us we should bear it with a fucking smile or dignity. Men like Steven shaking their heads, their disappointment wrapped inside heavy sighs as they call us emotional or hysterical. Finally, I am owning my anger—I have every right to it—harnessing its power for my self-determination.

The air fizzes behind me. For a second, I expect the empty space to be filled with the presence of death incarnate, tight fiery curls catching a sliver of light. I imagine sallow skin, milky eyes looking through me, blue lips smiling.

I turn around, and the room is empty. I don't know whether to be relieved or disappointed, but I know what needs to be done next.

47. Ellie

In the foyer, I feel the hatred rolling off Steven.

"You will end up behind bars for this," he barks, little bubbles of saliva foaming at the corner of his mouth.

He interprets my silence as an invitation to continue. "I might have been inclined to be lenient before, but that's over. As soon as I'm out of this chair and this damn house I'll be pressing charges."

Wrapping my hands around the chair handles, I struggle to wheel him out of the foyer and back into the main room, as if he has gained weight in the last few hours, anger turning into lead in his body.

"Do you hear me? I'll sue as well. I'll sue you, Ellie. You'll end up on a psych ward. You'll never recover from this."

He twists his head from side to side to get a glimpse of me, draw my attention, but I remain silent. When he realizes he won't get a rise or an answer out of me, he stops. I'm not Ellie anymore. He's not used to women who don't comply with his will. Come to think of it, he isn't used to women full stop, preferring the malleable minds of young girls.

The chill I felt earlier still hasn't left; it has spread icy roots like frozen veins under the skin of my arms; rubbing them achieves nothing. I throw a couple of logs onto the ashes. Poker in hand I stab the dying embers in the hearth until they glow back to life.

"You'll need to add some paper if you want it to catch," Steven says, offering an opinion I didn't ask for.

The newspaper pages crumple into tight balls under my

fingers before they land in the fireplace. Even though he's a literature teacher, I'm sure he would rather *The Devils* was used to resurrect the flames, but the book is here to fuel a different kind of fire. After a bit of poking around, a flare licks the logs, leaving black tongues on the soft inside of the wood. Heat corrupts its white flesh; once it has a taste it will continue working into a frenzy until it has consumed it all.

On the wide screen of the windows, a scene—dulled by the double glazing—unfolds, one where an unforgiving wind batters the dark silhouette of pine trees and lifts the dusty layer of snow off the ground, tossing it around. The storm has regained its strength. On the ocean side, silent waves crash on the sand, adding to the drama of unhinged nature without a voice and the ocean throwing itself against the earth, pummeling at it like an angry fist against a chest. The only soundtrack to the mayhem outside dulled to wheezing, and the mild thumping that penetrates through the double glazing.

"Have you heard about the Law of Unintended Consequences?" I ask, my eyes still fixed on the defiant landscape manhandled by weather.

"What?" His voice sounds distracted. I turn to him for his full attention. His squirming stops.

"The Law of Unintended Consequences. Have you heard of it?"

"Seriously, you want to discuss sociology now?"

I shrug in response.

Confusion spreads across his face, lining his forehead. The tumult of emotions which has settled on there at one stage or another since he regained consciousness offers such a contrast to the control and self-assurance which are usually a permanent fixture of his personality. But this new battery of emotions—fear, confusion, and guilt—are only skimming the surface. Deep down, he's still the same man.

The only other time I've witnessed such distress in him was not long after we started dating. We agreed to meet at Norman's Café after my last class of the day. He had arrived first and was waiting for me, my usual cappuccino already on the table. I smiled, pretending to see thoughtfulness instead of control in the gesture. As I sat, he pulled me in for a kiss, a hand resting on the back of my neck. Eyes closed, I imagined any other lips on me to stop me stiffening under his touch.

"Good day?"

"OK," I answered as I rummaged in my bag. "These were in the main hall." I smoothed a creased leaflet before sliding it across the table.

The confident façade crumbled under the heavy frown of his brow, as his eyes follow the line of words centered and bolded at the top in an Arial 16 font.

I recited the title I had already memorized. "*An evening with Professor Stewart Harding. Monday, October 24.* That's your father, isn't it?"

My question was met by a stony silence heavy with the smell of caffeine. Of course, I acted as if I hadn't noticed how unnerved he was.

"Should we go?" When he didn't respond again, my hand rested on his. The unexpected contact of skin drew his eyes away from the badly photocopied face of his father until they found mine.

His fingers gripped the leaflet edge, his clear discomfort almost tearing the paper. "You know that nonfiction piece I mentioned the other day? It might get published in the *New*

Yorker." He pushed the leaflet back toward me. I guessed he expected it would be recycled like most paper which found its way into my hands, hoping to watch me fold up his father's name until it disappeared under a new shape.

"Steven, that's amazing. Did they say when?"

"Nothing's confirmed yet. Do you want a muffin?"

"Sure."

Twisting in his seat, he motioned to the waitress.

"So?"

"So what?"

"Your father's thing. Do you want to go together? Time for me to meet the old man?" I joked.

"No." The word rushed out of his mouth. Taking a long breath, he composed himself, pinning back his default charming smile on his face. "No, it'll be boring. There's a new play on Broadway, let's go to that instead."

"Are you sure? I mean it's your dad. Don't you want to support him?"

He snorted at my assumption. "He doesn't need my support. Come on, my treat." But his smile—still stretched tight—never reached his eyes.

Steven is hidden under a thick glaze, a shiny reflection distracting from what lies beneath. I still need to dig deeper, excavate it all, and leave him a hollow shell which I can then fill with terror and shame, crushing his spirit until there is only one means of escape.

"The belief was popularized by Robert K. Merton," I continue. "According to him, unintended consequences can be broken into three categories"—I count them down on my fingers—"unexpected benefits, unexpected drawbacks, and perverse results."

"You're seriously doing this."

"Us being here is not an unexpected benefit of your actions."

Gaze cast down, his eyes refuse to meet mine. I pause, the silence a ghost hand lifting his chin before he speaks. "Which one of my actions do you think is responsible for this?"

"I thought *The Devils* would have provided you with the clue."

"Again with that old argument. You're not like those girls, so if that's all I'm after, why am I with you?"

"Because I give you exactly what you crave and what you normally get from those girls. Someone vulnerable, who looks up to you, strokes that damn ego of yours. I just have to use a pinch more sexuality than those girls to keep you reeled in. Don't you ever wonder why I lasted so long? Because I'm the girl who always says yes."

The chair hums with his anger. I can see that, finally, it's dawned on him that he was cheated into a relationship, cheated into granting me access to his feelings. That in this relationship, he has been the clueless one from the start. It stretches my mouth into a smile.

Everything I've done has been to lead me to this moment. My life for the last three years consisting of tirelessly speculating, gathering, planning each move in my head and in notebooks I later burned, watching flames licking the paper until the ideas on them turned to ashes. I nurtured scattered puzzle pieces until I could fit them together into a workable plan. Now that the time is finally here, apprehension mixed with excitement tingles in the tips of my fingers. My tongue sticks to the roof of my mouth, but I resist the lure of the bottles on the cart. Instead, I wedge a cigarette at the corner of my mouth. The trembling flame in my hand makes it hard to light it. After a long drag, a plume of smoke escapes from my mouth, along with the nervous energy which has been buzzing inside me.

"I'm tired of your games." He doesn't even try to hide the exasperation in his voice. For him, this is still just child's play—the tantrum of a spiteful little girl.

"So am I. So am I."

My bag sits on the sofa, where it has been waiting until now to come into play. The large notebook which has been with me for so many years catches on the side of the bag's zipper—a final witness ready to testify. With great care, I free its corner from the metal teeth. My fingers run along the faded stickers: the peace sign, the Nirvana smiley, the Peter Pan and Wendy, the last one a gift I bought for her at the mall the day we went to see *(500) Days of Summer. Oh my god, I love it, it's perfect*, she had said with the biggest smile, smothering me in a hug, my face deep under the canopy of her fiery curls.

But it's not time yet for the part the book has to play in all this. Instead, I take a few sheets of loose paper which have lived folded against the shelter of the hard cover. The pages shake in my hands. They are merely a prop for comfort; their words are etched on the vault of my skull from countless readings. As always, seeing her handwriting fills me with a sadness mixed with the joy of our memories and time together. I could and still can read her moods in the letters, her impatience in the sharp angles and straight lines of capitals, grooves of frustration she dug into the paper with her ballpoint, sloppy cursives of boredom.

At the corner of my eye, Steven waits. Sweat stipples his forehead. I track a bead as it slides down his temple all the way to his neck, where it disappears under the collar of his shirt.

Maybe he does remember.

48

May 9

Dear Vee,

*This wouldn't have happened if you were here. I don't blame you;
I blame myself. I wish I had your strength; I wish I had told you
sooner. I wish I had told you the truth. I tried once but I chickened
out. I didn't want to disappoint you.*

*He is older, much older than what I'd let on. He's not a senior at
a nearby high school or even college. He teaches literature at school.
Our school. He replaced Mr. Marsham while he was on long-term
disability. I thought he liked me. He did like me, but I did something
wrong, messed up, and he stopped liking me. No more afternoons in
his bed, his smell now gone from my skin. I inhale a bit deeper when
I pass him in the hallways or on the way to my desk. Capture for a
moment the scent of memories that bring tears to my eyes. Yes, you
can say it, I'm fucking pathetic. I just can't help it.*

*He acts like I'm just another student, as if the last few months
only ever existed inside my head. Sometimes, I wonder whether I
hallucinated our whole relationship. Maybe I was the mad wife in the
attic all along, and not his darling Jane, as he liked to call me. But I
didn't. It was all real. No fantasy can hurt this much.*

*I obsess, looking for what I've done wrong, what led to him leaving
me. It keeps me awake at night. Lying down, I look for answers on
the white expanse of my bedroom ceiling, but there are only shadows
up there. I play and replay it all in my head, every conversation, every
gesture, but the mistake I made is still hiding, driving me crazy.*

In the privacy of my head or my bedroom, I review everything. I unspool all those conversations I've had with him, dissect them, strip the flesh from words, all the way to the bones, peeling the skin off every gesture I've made, hoping to find a cancerous cell, the one that infected my relationship with him and led him to carve me out of his life. I can't think about anything else. I can't sleep. It keeps me up at night, distracts me in the car, torments me when I watch TV, has caused my grades to crash. Your steadiness is an ocean away; without it I just falter. No one to tell me to stop or show me how. Mom kind of knows something's up, but I can't tell her, she would never understand, and I'm scared how she would react. She would just take the whole situation to an all new level of worse.

I went to his apartment yesterday, slipped a letter under his door. The mailbox was too impersonal. He was out, but I still pressed my ear to the wood, listened to the silence on the other side, remembering my time at his place, the slight ruggedness of the carpet under my bare feet, my words and moans sliding along beams of light filtering through the blinds. Leaning against the door, the memories rose in my throat: so many they jammed and starved me of air. I escaped down the stairs too fast, stumbling over the last few steps before my body crashed against the tiled floor of the lobby. Pathetic. I've been pressing on the fresh bruises on my skin to remind myself I'm not really a ghost.

In my letter, I've asked him to meet me at Cypress Point. If he comes it'll mean he still cares about me, at least a little bit. I told him if he doesn't, I might do something stupid. The last time I saw him, he was so mad, so angry at me. That can't be our last exchange; it can't end like this. He has to come. I reminded him of the assembly, Principal Harvey's advice to talk.

I needed to tell you; I suppose this letter is kind of my confession. I want you to understand. So I'm sending it all to you, so you can read it—sorry it's all torn up—and so, hopefully, you can forgive me.

I think about that night, you know. I'm sure you'll guess which one. I was too stupid to realize it back then, and then I was worried I got it wrong, so I didn't say anything, but after all that has happened here, I wish I had done something, said something to let you know. I'm sorry I never found the courage until you were on the other side of the world. I just mess up everything. Even us.

You won't get this for a while. Who freaking knows how long snail mail takes in this age of instant messages and replies? Chances are, you'll get it all after I meet him. Although, he might not come, and if he shows up, I have no idea what he might say or what he might do. You should have seen him when he found the picture. He was so mad. The way he tore it apart.

If he doesn't come. I don't know. I don't know anything anymore. Sometimes I want it all to stop, his words and my thoughts crowding my mind, the way he looks at me now—a break, just to melt into the ground, cease to exist for a little while. But then, I hear your voice whisper in my head, my one and only true friend, my best friend. No, you're even more than that. You're the one person who has and will always love me. Maybe I can hang on just long enough for you to come back.

Nobody but us.
Wendy

49. Ellie

"You're her friend. The one who went to Europe." It isn't a question. A flicker of recognition twitches on his face. The truth has opened his eyes wide—seeing me for the first time. The real me, without Ellie standing in the way. The only person who knows that his pathological need for validation has a body count.

Wendy. Despite all the years that have passed between then and now, the pain hasn't ebbed. It lives under my skin, waking up at the slightest prick. Memories of her constrict my throat, and it hurts to swallow. Tears are swelling at the verges of my lids, and I feel my lashes bow under their heaviness. The drops will fall with the next blink. I swipe them quickly with the back of my hand, as my throat keeps burning. The edge of another panic attack tingles at my fingertips. Now is not the time for this.

"You're Wendy's best friend." It stumbles out of him as if he hasn't meant to speak out loud.

My jaw tenses; her name in his mouth grates on me, the way it comes out like breath, as if she's a part of him. I want to carve her out, split him open and extract her from his core, but she needs to stay with him a while longer. He needs to confront the reality of the situation and finally take responsibility for what he's done.

"All this time…"

"All this time. Ellie's just my middle name. First name's Verity, but you knew me—"

"Vee."

My name smashes through the veneer. Vee—I hold the truth to all of his lies, my name is the thief that has broken into his attic, and he now stares at me like Dorian Gray confronted with his wretched portrait. My name leaves him with nowhere to hide. He can't imagine how many times I've wanted to tell him, blurt it out in the middle of sex, sneak the truth right into his ear or in the middle of one of our one-way conversations, where my only contribution was finding new ways to say "yes."

Verity. Each letter a step to lead him to the rope waiting for his neck. Because I know what happened, I know all of what he did to Wendy. I watch the power my name has, how it changes the lines on his face. I can even smell it on him.

"Ta-da," I say flatly. "We finally meet. Just eight years late. I came back to Monterey long after you'd left. You wouldn't have noticed me back then anyway." He frowns at the suggestion. "I was the right kind of damaged in the wrong kind of package."

"Listen. I remember Wendy. She was a nice kid, but..." He doesn't finish his sentence, instead he lets the unsaid fester between us, hardening into a scab until I have to pick at it.

"But what?"

"But nothing happened. I mean, she had a crush on me. I knew that. I was flattered, yes, but it was getting out of control, that's why I put an end to our private tutoring sessions."

Taking my silence as an invitation he continues.

"Whatever she told you, or wrote to you, those are just the fantasies of a young, impressionable girl with a vivid imagination. She got caught up in *Jane Eyre* and invented some sort of fantasy where I was Mr. Rochester and she, Jane. I think she struggled with some bullying going on at school too. I should have said something, but she begged me not to."

" 'Nothing happened'..." I mutter as my nails carve half-moons into my palms.

"If that's the reason you're doing this, there's no need. I don't...I don't deny what happened with the others, J. and...Jamie and Ashley...and I'm sorry about those girls. Wendy, she was sweet, talked about you a lot, but no. She kissed me once, I told her it wasn't right. That's all, I promise she made it all up. It wasn't her fault but—"

"Enough!"

The explosion of shattering glass which accompanies my shout surprises us both. I don't remember grabbing the tumbler or throwing it into the fireplace. I was expecting everything from him but nothing as low as gaslighting the dead—setting her memory alight and burning what's left of her.

"How can you lie like this?" I spit the question in his face. "I knew her better than I know anybody. She was naive, she was good, and she was not some kind of mythomaniac." He opens his mouth but thinks better of it. "Or is that your defense strategy if you're ever confronted, 'nothing happened,' and any accusations are just the fantasies of some unreliable girl?"

"She was sweet and lonely, very lonely and, as I've said, I suspect bullied, but think about it: why would I lie to you about her? I've got no reason to. I don't deny the others—Jamie, Ashley. It makes no sense for me to lie about just one—" My laughter cuts through the flow of lies spewing from his mouth.

"Jamie and Ashley. You think I believe they're the only others? When are you going to stop taking me for an idiot? They're just the tip of the iceberg. How many years have you been a teacher for?"

The number tenses his jaws, and he keeps the answer to himself.

"If you choose for me to alert the media, I'm sure a lot more will come forward to tell their stories."

His lack of shame disgusts me. Retreating behind my memories, my fingers stroke the old leather cover of her diary. She is always everywhere but most of all, she's trapped within the pages of this notebook. I'm in there too, a version of me exists inside, one I had to shed in order to create Ellie.

Before he met me, I starved myself into the teenage body which appeals to him—small and unthreatening. Months to learn to peer from my lashes, be the girl who always listens, nods dutifully when he talks about his essays, his publications, and all his other achievements, never forgetting to congratulate him, never talking about herself unless he asks, not to bore him with the details of her life. The girl who always validates his choice of restaurants, plays, or exhibitions, who learns to make suggestions in such a way he can appropriate them as his ideas when he accepts them, being adventurous sexually without dominating, a girl who never suggests but always agrees, who sometimes feigns doubt so he can have the enjoyment of convincing her, fakes orgasms when necessary, who learns what he likes in bed—which positions, how much moaning stimulates his ego, who looks at him intently when he thrusts inside, who displays her pleasure to feed his pride. What's important is not that she's enjoying it but that her pleasure derives from him and the power he gets from it. The game is rudimentary enough to make cheating—using it to my advantage—easy, although he doesn't know how fucking exhausting being his girlfriend is.

But all of this doesn't compare to the sacrifices which came that night. That date, the fine line of being drunk enough to go through with it but not so much I would let something slip. The first time I had sex with him, the feeling of his fingers crawling on my skin, how I climbed into a little box inside my own head and shut an imaginary door, leaving the place vacant and willing for him. Holding myself together long enough to get home, walk inside the shower and become undone under the stream, dissolving into a puddle on the mosaic floor, sobs lost among the water. But something even worse was to come, more shattering than a breakdown—the intolerable betrayal of my own body, whenever I came under the rhythm of his body, from his fingers or his tongue, how I despised myself in those moments. I doubt I will ever feel whole again. No matter how much I have damaged myself, it was for her. It will all be worth it.

"Why all this?"

"Sorry, what?" I ask, my attention still focused on what I had to give up.

"Why the sham of a relationship? If you thought I did something wrong, why not just go to the authorities?" His last sentence narrows my eyes into slits. Even now he still can't admit it. As a literature professor, he knows the importance of words and what they convey... *If you thought I did something wrong*—placing the onus on me, my assumptions.

"Because I wanted you to experience the betrayal. The person the closest to you turning on you. Know the hurt you have inflicted. You took my best friend away. You ripped her out of my life and used her for your own gratification before breaking her into a million pieces."

My legs ache, but I stay standing. I open the diary at a random place, and the memory I read pulls my lips into a faint smile.

"Not just my best friend. You took away the first person I loved."

"But I've told you already nothing happened with Wendy. How many times do I have to say it?" His voice is even, as if the smooth tone would hide the inflammatory nature of his comment, not stir the beast inside me.

"I don't believe you. I believe her."

50. Ellie

No matter where I am, my memories always take me first to the same place—her mother's notorious annual charity benefit. By the time I arrived, Wendy languished next to her parents, an eyeroll away from terminal boredom. The baby-blue dress she wore reminded me of those long ballerina tutus, the rustling skirt a soundtrack to accompany her every move. She should be twirling inside a music box to an audience of rings and tangled necklaces. Fiddling on her spot, she kept plucking at her top, earning disapproving glances from her mother. The constellation of freckles on her cheeks lifted when she saw me. She promptly abandoned her mom and dad to come and greet me with a hug as her parents kept talking to some old couple.

"Thank God you're here," she said as I enjoyed the warmth of her bare arms on my shoulders and the tickle of her hair on my cheek.

"God had nothing to do with it, unless she controls the traffic-light timing down Fremont Boulevard."

"At least this year this whole thing won't completely blow. Seriously, it's so boring."

"Who are your parents talking to?"

"The Michaelsons. He works with my dad."

"If they have as much money in their pockets as wrinkles on their faces, your mom's charity is in for a big check."

The audible snort erupting out of Wendy flattened her mother's lips into a thin red line.

"Come on," she said, pulling me along. "Let's get the formalities out of the way."

Wendy's mom had rearranged her lips into a wide smile by the time we reached her. "Good evening, Verity."

"Hello, Mrs. Katz, great party."

"Thank you."

"And thanks for inviting me."

"It's nice for Wendy to have someone her own age here." She rested her hand on Wendy's shoulder.

"I'll make sure she has a good time." My promise erased any traces of the smile on Mrs. Katz's face.

"Regina?" The lure of a new donor provided enough of a distraction for us to make a clean getaway and disappear inside the crowd.

"Now what?" Wendy asked once we reached the other end of the ballroom.

A quick look around revealed we were surrounded by a forest of elegant gowns, dinner jackets, and stern looks; the women looked like colorful Christmas trees dripping with sparkling ornaments and garlands of several carats. On the entire length of the room, a row of French windows opened onto the patio and beyond that the hotel's garden.

"Wait for me outside," I instructed her.

She headed for the terrace as I weaved through the mass of people in the opposite direction. A few minutes later I followed in Wendy's footsteps and headed outside. Despite the time of year, the night air was still heavy with the warmth the sun had left behind. Along the darkened path, the murmurs of the ocean mingled with the muffled conversations from rich people pretending to have a good time. Both followed a similar rhythm, but the rise and fall of voices coming from the ballroom lacked the conviction of the ocean. Dad loved telling me that the first time I witnessed the sun setting behind the ocean when I was four, I cried for hours, convinced the sun had fallen and melted into the water. Wendy laughed so hard the first time she heard the story.

I found her waiting for me on a bench, her pale skin radiant under the sulfur glow of the garden lights. I shook off the prickling in my back and swallowed hard. "Let's get our party started."

"How did you get those?"

I dropped the tray of amuse-bouches and a bottle of champagne next to her. "A magician never reveals her tricks." She pouted in response, and something tightened inside me. "OK, I bribed a waiter fifty bucks."

Half a bottle later, we had demolished the neat rows of miniature food, and our cheeks were flushed from mouthfuls of fizzy bubbles.

"You are such a bad influence," she hiccupped. "Please never change."

I smiled. "Nobody but us."

"Nobody but us."

She raised the bottle and took another swig of it. As she swallowed, her face scrunched, smashing together her constellation of freckles.

"My mom is gonna kill me when she finds out."

"Stop hogging the bottle." I snatched it before she had finished. Foam dribbled from her chin, and we both laughed until our jaws ached.

I swallowed a gulp of bubbles, my lips cupped around the bottle's neck in the same place hers had been. The crunch of shoes on gravel interrupted our little party when one of the waiters walked over to us, a cigarette wedged in the corner of his mouth and a crooked bow tie around his neck.

"Do you girls have a light by any chance?"

"Sure," Wendy answered, tossing the lighter she retrieved from her bag.

"Since when do you—" I whispered, but she just shushed me in response.

"Thanks."

Taking a few steps forward, he handed the lighter back to her after taking a long drag which turned the tobacco into a bright orange cinder. Standing closer to the light, I could see the line of pimples dotted along his hairline. He couldn't be more than eighteen, nineteen.

"You've got yourselves quite a little party going on here," he said, smiling at me.

"We sure have."

Now if he could just leave us alone, but he stayed rooted in his spot, busy working on his cigarette. Silence and the smell of nicotine crept into the space between us. Maybe the awkwardness might drive him away.

"Me and my friends get off in a couple of hours if you want to hang out."

Or maybe not.

Wendy's hand covered mine as it lay on the bench and squeezed it, silently communicating her agreement with me.

"Thanks, we're good here."

"You sure? We've got beer and grass." He threw his stub on the ground and crushed it with the tip of his shoe. It left a black smudge on the light cement path. Back on the bench Wendy's hand still covered mine, the heat of her palm making my skin clammy.

"We're sure."

"If you change your mind, just look out for the bonfire on the beach."

We watched him walk away until all that was left of him was the crunch of gravel under his shoes.

"I think he likes you," she said, elbowing me.

"Yeah, right. Also, since when do you have a lighter?"

"You guys can hook up on the beach later."

"You can go and hook up with him yourself."

"No, thanks."

"Why not?"

"Because." Her eyes pleaded with me.

"Because what?"

"I don't want some meaningless waiter to be my first kiss."

"You're such a hopeless romantic."

The champagne had unbridled the words so fast they sneaked up on me. I regretted them as soon as they left my mouth. They dragged her eyes to ground, where she scuffed the tip of her shoes against the cement.

"Sorry."

The fizz tasted bitter at the back of my throat. We sat side by side, arms rubbing, surrounded by the sweet scent of honeysuckle thickening the air, echoes from a string quartet streaming through the open French windows, and the peal of glasses and distant laughter.

"Maybe you could be my first."

"What?"

"Kiss. You could be my first kiss."

"You mean in a *Cruel Intentions* kind of way?"

"Yeah, but without the psycho bitch persona."

I laughed, but it sounded off.

"Seriously," she said. "You're my best friend. Kind of makes sense, really. To have my first kiss with someone who really likes me."

She handed me the bottle. My heart was in my throat. I wanted nothing more than for my lips to meet hers, taste the champagne on her breath, but fear had sealed my mouth shut. The seconds before I answered were the longest of my entire life. Each one of them an invitation for Wendy to utter the dreaded words "Forget about it. It's a stupid idea."

"OK."

By now, my heart was pounding so hard I was sure she could hear it. A breath caught in my throat when she twisted to face me. She took a swig and handed me the bottle. I drank too, but the alcohol didn't soothe the tangled ball of nerves in my chest. The glass clinked as the bottle found the ground. Her eyes screwed shut and apprehension crunched her nose and rearranged the scatters of freckles on her cheeks. She was as nervous as I was.

"Wendy Moira Angela Darling, relax."

Her face slackened, caught between a smile and a hiccup. I glimpsed the beauty of the perfect moment and brought our mouths together. *Nobody but us.* Her lips were soft and they parted in a breath. My hand clutched the edge of the bench. I moved slowly, etching the memory in my mind down to the smallest details. I tasted her tongue, tasted the alcohol the fizzy bubbles had left on it. A bolt of electricity jolted through my spine. The vanilla and jasmine of her perfume thickened the air around us. The artificial light from the lamppost shone through my closed eyelids and turned the darkness pink. It would forever be the color of our first kiss.

Those memories are all I have left.

51

May 10

Does it hurt to die? I wonder if you have time to feel the pain or if it's too quick.

Like blowing on a dandelion.

52. Ellie

Tears stream down my cheeks again, pool in the corners of my curled lips. She could always conjure a world of emotions in me, but her letter, the memory of that night at the benefit, her last diary entry, it's all too much. I mop up the tears with my sleeves before a light rustle reminds me I'm not alone in the room.

"Are you OK?" His question is soft, as if he isn't strapped to a chair, as if I didn't put him there, as if we're only reminiscing about our pasts after discovering we have an acquaintance in common.

"Did you see her?" I ask. "The day she died?"

He shakes his head.

Outside, the snow drifts again, flakes as big as feathers but not as heavy as before, as if the weather is growing tired too. They twirl like the down that burst from our pillows during my first sleepover at her house. The fight and destruction drove her mother to label me a bad influence.

Trapped in a house with the gates of my memories now wide open, images and moments of our lives flooding me, I'm faced with the man responsible for taking it all away, the reason why there never was and never will be any new memories. He ripped her out of my life and then without even knowing me he broke me into a million pieces, shattered me in such a way that the pieces could never fit back together in the same way. I hate that he has memories of her I will never possess or that, because of him, she will never have the chance to make new memories—he robbed her of her chance to have choices, make wrong decisions, find herself, change her mind, become someone different, go to Berkeley with me, rebel, dye her hair pink, become a vegetarian, cry on my shoulder the night she has a drunken Big Mac, not because she slipped but because she loved it. He has killed her in a million ways.

The knife balancing on the back of the sofa cushion calls to me. I stand next to it, considering the idea, running a finger along the blade. It would be so simple—my fingers curl around the handle—just a few well-placed stabs or a red line across his throat somewhere south of his Adam's apple. The end. But the reflection in the window is not mine, it's hers. Her eyes remind me that he doesn't deserve simple and easy. I owe that to her. He needs to be broken until he makes the decision himself to finish it or suffer the consequences for the rest of his life. In my mind, his limp body dangles off the rope.

The Internet and books have provided me with all the necessary information on the mechanics and physics of a hanging. I have gathered useful knowledge along with the useless trivia. The drop from jumping from the second-floor mezzanine with the noose around his neck coupled with the momentum of his body weight will snap his neck, and death will be instantaneous. No chance of suffering, but no chance of being rescued.

On the other hand, kicking a chair he was standing on would result in a small drop. His neck would stay intact, but he would be put in the throes of brain ischemia: a blockage of all veins and arteries that carry blood and oxygen to his brain. With nowhere to go, the blood pressure in the veins of his head would mount until the capillaries in his face and eyes burst. By then his brain would be slowly dying, and I hope Wendy's face would be the last image in his mind as it was engulfed in cold darkness, her becoming his angel of death. Finally, the swell of his brain due to the lack of oxygen would trigger the vagal reflex, causing his heart rate and blood pressure to plummet, and the crush to his trachea would add to the slow asphyxiation. Death would become a bet of what would give out first: heart, brain, or lungs, eeny, meenie, miny, mo...Death would be slow, around ten minutes—an enticing idea, but the chance of rescue or escape would increase too.

"Ellie? Verity?" My first name has an alien ring to it in his voice. "Vee?"

In response, my hand crashes on his cheek, leaving a red outline. The pain of the slap radiates in my palm, until I shake it off.

"Never use that name. Ever."

His eyes harden, and his jaw tenses, but he is taped to a wheelchair, and a look of indignation at being slapped by a woman fifteen years his junior is as far as he can go.

"Striking a restrained man. Does that make you feel powerful?"

"You really don't get it, do you?"

"Then explain it to me." His words roll out like thunder, his anger taking all the space in the room.

Staring at the dying fire in the hearth, I bounce the idea back and forth in my head like the steel sphere of a pinball machine. I didn't plan to share this part of my past. But I'm prepared to do anything to take him one step closer to that noose around his neck.

53. Ellie

London's dampness seeped through my bones. I pulled the zipper of my coat all the way to the top, sealing myself away from the city and its weather. Still the damp cold found its way under the layers of clothing, filtering through my skin, my flesh, until it reached my bones. Even though it had only been a few months, the North Cal sun had faded into a distant memory, one of many things which belonged to another lifetime.

I buried my face inside the coils of my scarf. Everything was smaller here—the streets, the houses, the personalities—and grayer too, especially the sky. Sometimes, looking up, I couldn't tell if I was looking at clouds or the actual sky beyond. The dullness accentuated by Wendy's absence, London a constant reminder that she was an ocean away from me.

On the gray sidewalk, two girls about my age walked in front of me. They leaned as they spoke to each other, the way shared intimacy pulls bodies together, shoulders rubbing, and the puffs of their breath mingling clouds loaded with the secrets they shared. Seeing the shape of their bodies lengthened my strides. I would get home and write a long email to Wendy and organize a proper catch-up on WhatsApp for this weekend—maybe we could watch the same film, each of us on our side of the ocean, and comment on it via chat. Maybe I could even get her to tell me more about whatever she's been hiding from me. I knew there was something she was withholding, and part of me was hurt, but the bigger part of me sensed she was unhappy and was desperate for help.

Slamming the front door, I climbed the stairs two at a time, eager to make a start on my plan of action. Now I understood all those women in Jane Austen's novels, desperately sitting through the agonizing wait for a letter bringing news from a loved one or a dear friend.

"Verity?" I barely had the chance to reach the second-floor landing when Kate's voice chased after me. Even after so long, I could never call her Mom.

"Going to my room."

"Can you come down here for a second?"

My shoulders dropped at her request. "Can it wait?"

"Please, Verity." The flatness of the tone left no doubt this wasn't a question but a request for compliance.

Abandoning my backpack at the top of the stairs, I back-tracked to the kitchen, where Kate sat at the table, a steaming mug in front of her. She had taken quickly to the local custom of drinking tea. Lost inside an oversized cardigan, she looked tiny against the vast expanse of Victorian tiles of the kitchen. The sight sent a chill down my spine. She looked up at me with eyes rimmed by pink lids as she grabbed one of the many crumpled tissues strewn on the table. It wouldn't have surprised me if she had caught another cold with all that damp weather, but a twitch at the corner of her mouth told me this wasn't it.

"Kate?" My voice, barely higher than a murmur, didn't sound like my own.

"Something happened back home."

Silence built between us, a threshold between that moment and the rest of my life. I didn't want to ask, and she didn't want to say. I wished I could have stayed in that moment forever, suspended in the seconds before she shattered my defenses with two words.

"It's Wendy…"

Her name hit me in the chest, before finding its way inside the soft opening between my ribs, burning through the flesh. It wasn't just Wendy's name but how she said it, the syllables fractured by the tremor in her voice. The searing pain pushed me into one of the empty chairs. The name was now in my head on a loop, over and over, faster and faster, speeding up my heartbeat. All so easy: only five letters and I unraveled, not wanting to hear or even imagine the end of Kate's sentence.

"Sweetheart…"

"No." I repeated the word, over and over again, as if laying bricks to build a wall, protecting me from the truth, but still her words found their way between the gaps.

"There's been an accident,"—I continued my litany of nos—"Wendy's dead, sweetheart."

Dead. The word fell heavily, knocked me out of my chair and sent me running to my room. Kate sent words of sympathy after me, but they barely registered. In my room, my body slowly shed the numbness, exposing something raw underneath. Face buried in my pillow, I screamed, screamed until my throat burned, until my saliva stained the fabric, until I smothered all the anger and the hurt in the synthetic filling. She couldn't be dead; she was my age. A parade of memories rose from the depths and streamed through my head, and at the end of each one the truth was waiting to hit me again, bruising my heart. Outside, a bland sky stretched over a jagged line of slated roofs and thin chimneys. None of it made sense, I couldn't imagine a world without her in it.

When I stopped crying, the gray of the sky had been replaced by a pitch black, my bedroom and the inside of my head shrouded in the same darkness. Strands of hair stuck to my damp cheeks. Coming out of my stupor, I vaguely remembered Kate knocking on the door about dinner and then leaving me alone when she received no answer. I sat, looking at the shadows which populated my bedroom, wondering if that was what a place without the girl I loved looked like. Through the window, a thin comma of moon hung high, the dim pinpricks of stars peering from between a few wayward clouds. *Second star to the right, and straight on till morning.* Maybe I didn't have to live in a place where Wendy no longer existed. Maybe I could be her Peter Pan, and we would never have to grow old.

The spill of cold air bit my damp face. One leg over the window threshold, then the other one, bringing me closer to Wendy. Sat on the ledge, eyes closed, I inhaled one last time before flying off to Neverland, but a sharp tug sent me flying backward and inside my bedroom.

"Are you crazy?" The question came wrapped inside Dad's voice. His arms closed around me. They pinned mine against my chest as he dragged me away from the window.

"I have to go. Let me go," I screamed.

"Calm down."

My back struggling against his chest, I kicked and wriggled, but his grip was too strong.

"I have to go. I can't…I can't…"

"It's OK, Bug. It's OK."

In the end, it was Dad's unwavering patience which brought me down. Not my blows, my words or my anger. He just waited until tears spilled down my face again, until my anger cracked inside my chest in a multitude of heaves and sobs, until it stifled my words and they died in my throat. Finally, my legs buckled. Whatever was left of me shattered on impact.

Still, he didn't leave me, his body following me down too. As pain and so much more poured out from all the cracks, the prison of my father's arms became a refuge.

After my stunt, Dad nailed the sash shut to be on the safe side. I was surprised he and Kate didn't confiscate all of my belts and mirrors too. They didn't need to worry; after the meltdown I had in my father's arms I woke up exhausted the following day, and the feeling hasn't left me since, replacing the marrow in my bones with lead. When they informed me there was no way I could make it home to attend the funeral they expected another outburst, but I just dragged my body back upstairs without a word, the blanket trailing behind me.

Dad's assignment got extended, so we stayed in the UK. When we stepped through the glass doors of arrivals in San Francisco airport three years later, for a moment I expected her to be waiting for me, clutching a stupid sign and wearing a face-splitting grin. The moment skittered away, and the harsh reality spread through me like a sickness, leaving me kneeling on an airport bathroom floor, heaving above a toilet bowl. Later that day, I visited her, shielding the puffiness of grief behind sunglasses. Even after three years, the pain was still raw, living just under the surface, ready to awaken at the slightest prick.

She waited for me under a cedar tree. All the preparation Doctor S. had done with me dissolved when I saw those two dates separated by a dash; her whole life summed up in that little line. I hated it. She was so much more than that. I read her name carved in gilded letters, and a faint smile bloomed on my lips. She was not a gilded kind of person; she would have rolled her eyes at that. An origami lotus flower trembled in my hand until it rested at the foot of the stone. My effort, a crude attempt full of hesitant edges compared to her expertise. This was all wrong. There shouldn't be a headstone, or an epitaph calling her "Our beloved Daughter."

During a sleepover at mine, while we watched *A Walk to Remember*, drunk on spiked lemonade, she had initiated a "what should happen when I die" conversation. When death seemed so impossible, you could talk about it with the detachment of youth. She wanted to be cremated, she said, her ashes scattered from a cliff. She wanted to dance over the ocean and ride the wind, she added. The idea had terrified me—not her death, but a world without her in it. I had swallowed a big gulp of spiked lemonade and replied with a nonchalant "Yeah, me too."

She never had the chance to tell her parents. She would never have the chance to tell them anything anymore, do anything anymore.

"How could you leave me like this?" The words tumbled out even before I could realize what I'd said, what I had been holding in, couldn't confess even to Doctor S. or Dad—she didn't just die, she left me.

Grief kicked me to my knees. "You left. You left me. Me." Sobbing hiccups broke my sentences. "Without saying anything, without even a fucking goodbye. I could have helped…I miss you so much. It hurts. It fucking hurts. All the time."

Face and hands pressing hard against the grass, I embraced the ground, desperately seeking a hug from my best friend six feet below.

"Come back, please come back. I miss you so much, I need you so, so much. It's unbearable here without you. It hurts. Please, I need you. Please come back. Please…I'm sorry, I'm so sorry. I wasn't there," I whispered to her, my mouth brushing the earth.

So many feelings dropped onto the grass lumped inside heavy tears. I imagined them seeping down to her. All the pieces of me, scattered over her grave as I lay here. And the feeling of abandonment ran cold in my veins, until I was alone all over again.

54. Ellie

The memories have scared my breath away. The grief swelling in my chest compresses my lungs, rendering them useless. I breathe furiously but take in no air while my heart throws itself against my ribs.

V...U, T...

I lean over the back of the sofa, my fingers grip the cushions, my legs falter. I grip the top tighter, concentrate on the letters.

S, R...Q...

I hang on to Doctor S.'s instructions: *If you feel an attack coming on, recite the alphabet backward.* Slowly, distant echoes and distorted words filter through. I latch on to them until they make sense. They coax me. My face is slick with tears I didn't know I had been crying. Since Wendy's death, I've been feeling like I have swallowed a great big snake. It has lived in my chest, coiled around my organs. At first it was there all the time, then with Doctor S.'s guidance it untangled itself to sleep in the pit of my stomach, stirring only when the emotions get too strong.

"Ellie? Talk to me. Ellie, are you all right?"

Unable to talk, I simply nod before stalking off to the kitchen to fetch a glass of water, which I gulp down, the water squeezing past the tightness in my throat. When I come back, Steven is silent, somewhat smaller in his chair, looking at me with eyes that hold something which could be mistaken for pity.

"I'm sorry you had to go through this." I open my mouth

to reply, but he's not done yet. "And I am sorry about Wendy. What happened to her was a tragedy but nothing—"

"Did she make you mad?" The urge to know the truth sends me to kneel in front of him. "Maybe it was just an accident. Maybe you didn't mean to push her."

I have no idea what he might say or what he might do. Those were her words, the ones that have been keeping me up at night for years, feeding my suspicions. His behavior tonight has proved that he has the potential to harm. So many times he has looked at me as though I am something breakable. If he ever manages to get out of this chair, I can speculate as to what he might do.

"You won't believe me whatever I say," he says when I least expect it. His words might not even be for me. "Actually, can I get a drink?"

I watch him, unsure if I should give in. Like every other relationship, this one is based on a delicate power play.

"Please?"

I'm too tired for mind games, so I get him some water. He looks tired, the thin skin under his eyes puffy and slightly darker. Behind him it's hard to distinguish the silhouettes of the trees from the blackness of the night. In the dark, everything has merged so you cannot tell where one thing ends and another begins. It must be later than I think, but hard to say without my phone to check.

Leaving the bottle on the cart, I turn away from Steven. Eyes closed, I find her behind my lids. I am greeted by her freckled face, her mouth chewing on one of her curls like she always did. Like any girl with curls she was desperate to have straight hair, but I was glad she didn't. Behind the closed door of our bedrooms we shared secrets, and more kisses, disguising them as practice, invented futures where we were still best friends in twenty years' time—or, as I hoped, more—never finding the courage to tell her everything. To love in secret felt safer than the gamble of honesty. If she didn't feel the same, I feared the awkwardness would fester between us until it broke our bond. As long as we had a tomorrow we could always become more. But our imagined futures never happened because of the man strapped in the chair in front of me; because of his needs for adoration, for validation—he robbed me of my tomorrow.

Jasmine and vanilla.

Do I keep on imagining the smell, or did I really bring her ghost with me?

"You think this will help you. That revenge will bring you closure, but it won't. Killing me is not the answer."

I supress a scoff at his Psych 101 rhetoric. Is he still stuck in that deluded stage where he believes he can talk me off the ledge?

"If you don't take the deal then you'll end up on the sex offenders list. You'll be a disgrace in those academic circles whose opinions you cherish so much. When I'm finished with you, you won't even be able to get a job at an inner-city night school. You will never work in education again. I wouldn't be surprised if Daddy Harding disowned you."

The last line hits him in the soft lining of his pride, and he squirms. I imagine the words burrowing deep inside him, climbing the ladder of his rib cage until they reach his throat, where he will choke on their implication, leaving a taste of ashes at the back of his mouth.

"You hate me that much." The end of his sentence doesn't curve into a question. "So, all that time we were together…"

"It was all to get me to this night, to this place, offering you this deal. The chance for you to choose your punishment. I knew I had to get close to you."

"What if I had said no to this weekend?"

"I had a couple of deserted warehouses scouted on the docks by the East River. Quiet but obviously a lot less isolated."

"You've thought about this a lot."

"I've been planning this since I was twenty. I had years to perfect my plan. So don't think there is a scenario that I haven't played out in my head."

"Twenty?"

Twenty—three years of preparing, plotting. Discovering someone has hated him for that amount of time and even worse, someone who has shared his bed, who has smiled at him every time he's said her name, who has parted her lips for him every time he's kissed her, someone who has pinched the soft flesh between her thumb and forefinger every time her hatred has threatened to overwhelm her and spill out between them.

"Since I first saw you, but I wouldn't expect you to remember me. I didn't have the kind of body which would have caught your eye back then," I say as he opens his mouth to protest, but I continue. "No need to pretend. We both know the kind of female form you prefer." He scowls at my statement. "Please, I spent hours at Norman's Café, trying to grab your attention without being obvious. You didn't notice me until the day I walked in soaked, with a see-through dress clinging to my body and a rescue-me expression on my face."

Avenging Wendy had been the fire which burned the body fat and shaped my body into the image I knew would appeal to him, the narrow hips and small breasts, the blur between woman and child. The exterior transformation somehow easier than the interior one, adopting a meek persona, developing the need for his approval, learning to be confident while not burdening him with my issues, unless of course I asked for his help so he could play the rescuer. Whenever I faltered, her ghost appeared in my head to remind me— *nobody but us.*

"How did you find out?" Steven asks. "About me?"

55. Ellie

Dad's office was bathed in silence and the ghost of his presence. I had to escape the throng of people cluttering up our living room to pay their respects. Kate could look after them. I sat in his old leather chair, the one constant, always following him wherever we relocated. He could bear parting with a desk but not his chair. I laid my cheek against the headrest, the familiar smell of tobacco and orange flowers wrapped around me. As I ran my hand along the desk, memories fluttered to the surface—sitting on his lap, pretending to close business deals, punching endless numbers on his calculator. Every drawer I opened held a memory, an image of Dad. The last one was full of junk and, at the bottom, a box labeled "London."

I lifted the lid on that little corner of our lives, rummaging around until my attention snagged on the corner of a craft envelope cluttered with U.S. stamps. I recognized the slanted block lettering even upside down. Once extracted from its hiding place, the package weighed heavy in my trembling hands. Dad hid this from me? The faded postmark told me that Wendy had sent it the day before she died. How could he? But then, with my stunt the night I learned of her death, how could he not?

Alone with the envelope, I tore the flap with trembling fingers. Inside, her journal, torn pages spilling out from between the hardcover held together with an elastic band, and a separate, neatly folded piece of paper that fell on my lap. Taking a deep breath, I opened the sheet.

Dear Vee,

This wouldn't have happened if you were here. I don't blame you; I blame myself. I wish I had your strength; I wish I had told you sooner. I wish I had told you the truth.

By the end of the letter grief had curdled into anger as I thought of the man she had loved, the man who drove her off a cliff and six feet below the ground. Long after the house fell silent after the last guest left, I sat on the floor of Dad's office, the puzzle of Wendy's life without me scattered around. I shifted pieces about, looking for seams that fitted together, making sentences out of confetti. Her death no longer a mystery which ate at me from the inside. In each rip of paper she told me what he did to her, how he tore her apart like the pages of her diary. There I was, putting her back together with Scotch tape. If this was the only way I could have her back, I would take it.

Doctor S.—the therapist Dad and Kate insisted I saw after my extreme reaction to Wendy's death and through the depression that ensued—told me that the anti-depressants I was prescribed only got rid of the symptoms; recovery came with knowing what made you sick. I liked Doctor S., with her pixie cut and oversized red-rimmed glasses. I didn't think I would have been able to talk to a man about the confusing thoughts bumping underneath my skull. I used to sit on her beige sofa once a week, cradling a pillow against my chest, picking imaginary lint from it, until one day I forgot the pillow. I followed her gaze to the other end of the sofa where it rested, and she told me, "You're gonna be fine, Verity."

That man was what had made me sick, or more precisely the idea that he lived a full life, guilt- and consequence-free, when my best and only friend decayed in the ground because of his reckless indifference.

The Internet provided digital signposts, crumbs of information to follow. I studied his picture on the website of the Manhattan prep school he was teaching at, confronting the origin of the sickness. I had to see him, fill out the outline of his body, see it in motion, listen to the tone of his voice. Fate lent me a hand by sending him to New York. Convincing Kate I needed a change of scenery wasn't hard, and I suggested visiting cousin Janet and her son, Connor, in NYC.

Armed with a MetroCard and an address for Richmond Prep, I set out to find him. I had no idea what I would do, what I would say; I didn't even know if I wanted to speak to him. I was just compelled to see him in the flesh.

The school lived under the long shadows of a row of trees lining the street. I chose a spot on the opposite sidewalk and waited. It wasn't long before the double doors flew open, and students spilled out onto the steps, all wearing the same navy uniform. Despite the illusion of conformity, I could pick out who belonged to what group: the popular ones with their nonchalant attitude, that slight cock of the hip; the nerds or shy people, who held their books close to their chest as a shield, or gripped the straps of their backpack, knuckles bleached with apprehension. It was all there on display, the confident smiles pinned on bubblegum-colored lips, the steadfast hands raking through hair, the carefree laughter, the manufactured laughter, too short like a manic hiccup, nervous eyes looking for a friend, a lifeline before being noticed by the wrong people.

Amid this sea of teenagers, he appeared. The man I had studied so many times, suddenly in three dimensions, let loose onto the world. He stood tall, talking, waving, smiling—as alive as she was dead. Anger spread through me, calcifying the ridge of my spine, unfurling into roots which welded me to my spot on the sidewalk. For a few seconds, he looked right at me and frowned. An irrational fear I had been recognized swept through me. Sweat pooled under my breasts, dampened my bra. But he didn't know me, and his gaze went straight through me.

His eyes abandoned me as he checked his phone, sauntering down the stairs before long strides took him down the street. When he turned the corner, his disappearance jolted me into chasing after him. A glimpse hadn't sated me; I needed more. He remained an outline, a shape without substance. I stalked him through the web of the Upper East Side's streets until I almost lost him when he hurried down into the 68th Street station. Electricity prickled my skin, then I caught the quiff of dark hair passing through the turnstile before he disappeared inside the herd of commuters. Panicked, I scanned the crowd until I spotted him, heading for the nearest platform. I rushed after him. He stepped into a car as I was running down the stairs. The shrill signal of the closing door scared me into leaping over the last four steps before launching my body through the nearest set of doors. As the train juddered to a start, I collapsed into the nearest seat, heart thrashing against its cage. When I dared to take a peek, he had remained impervious to my presence and my heroic boarding.

We got off at Grand Central—42nd Street, where I almost lost him again while battling the upcoming stream of people. Finally, I caught up with him as he climbed the stairs of the Grand Central Library. I trailed him until he entered the Economics and Sociology section. A shadow hiding behind a wall of paper, I loitered in the row next to his, running a finger along spines, unspooling titles in my pretend search for a certain publication. In the gap between the books and shelves, I spied him checking his watch and twisting the signet ring on his little finger. A little voice in my head whispered to approach and talk to him. I froze when I realized the voice was Wendy's.

My mouth opened, but before my lips could shape words to catch his attention, a smile bloomed which illuminated his whole face. In the cradle of that moment, I witnessed it—the spark that had drawn Wendy to him, the prickling under the skin.

She looked young, no older than sixteen, dressed in the same uniform as the other kids from Richmond Prep. The expression she wore on her face scared me, a look of complete adoration as if the world started and ended with him. Like the children in that old tale who followed the hypnotizing tune of the Pied Piper, she was bewitched, ready to follow him into bed, off a cliff, or in this case to a shadowy recess at the very back of a row of dusty books.

A silent observer trespassing on their intimacy, I watched the movement of their bodies through the gaps in the shelves. How she pressed herself against him. Their mouths fought each other, trading whispered moans for a gasp of air. On my side of the bookcase, my throat tightened as I leaned closer, nose against the bound covers smelling of old leather. The magical tune of their encounter seeped into me, attracted to the illicit exchange, a willing conspirator unable to look away until his hand vanished under the pleats of her skirt and her face twisted in response. Instead of their tangled bodies, it was the photograph in my pocket that sprang to life behind my eyes, his and Wendy's naked bodies moving under a thin sheet, her head tilting back the same way this girl's had. I saw a white tombstone, two dates separated by a dash.

Out on the entrance steps, I panted, hands resting on my knees, desperately fighting to reclaim the regular rhythm of my breath, the crowd swirling around just a blur of colors through the curtain of my tears.

Grief, frustration, and nausea ebbed under a new flow of emotions, and the undeniable conviction he would not stop. How long before the next girl threw herself off a cliff or under the wheels of a train, another victim falling prey to the selfish solipsism of Steven Harding?

"Hey cuz, you all right?"

The unexpected question straightened me. "Connor? What are you doing here?"

"Dropping off some books. You look really pale." The concern creasing his forehead. Kate had definitely filled Janet in about my fragile mental health, and she—in turn—had briefed Connor. Look out for the fragile, unstable girl—the girl on the edge.

I pasted what I hoped passed for a convincing smile on my face. "Low blood sugar. I skipped lunch."

"Let's get milkshake and fries, then. My treat." Draping his arm around my shoulders, he ushered me away from the library and its dark secret.

Despite Connor's best intentions, I couldn't shake off Steven. He had to be stopped. And I had to stop him. I couldn't go to the cops. It was a he said/she said situation in a society where the words of a twenty-year-old wouldn't amount to much. If I didn't stop him, how long before another girl ended up like Wendy? As I was the sole witness, it was my responsibility. It wasn't just about avenging Wendy anymore. It was about stopping another death. Four months later, I applied for the graduate program at NYU.

56. Ellie

My origin story has robbed Steven of his wit. He stares at the undeniable truth, the creator in front of his creature—for, like Dr. Frankenstein, he made me. A raw humanity trapped in a cage of flesh and bones driven to hatred and retribution. His act of genesis was an unintended one, but like the monster, I did not ask to be born into this. But who is the truest monstrosity: the creature or the creator?

"All of this for something that never happened."

I scowl at him.

"Whatever I say, you won't believe me. Ask yourself, what proof do you have apart from the rambling of a teenage girl?"

Tiredness washes over me. Steven's lies, or denial, or both, gnaw at my resolve, and all that's holding me together is the threads of my friendship with Wendy. Someone needs to stand up for her. I won't let her down like he did, and all the other adults at the time who missed or ignored the signs.

"That time in New York, that was years ago. Why *now*?"

"Do you remember the time I waited for you outside Richmond Prep with banana pudding?"

So many emotions flit across his face that it's hard to know what he really thinks. His silence and clenched fists tell me he needs to hear more.

"I told you I had a fight with a friend, but in truth while I waited for you I overheard a conversation which reminded me why I needed to do this."

The double doors of Richmond Prep burst open, unable

to contain the spill of students and voices that the last bell of the day had unleashed. Groups crowded the sidewalk, friends lingering about, not quite ready to say goodbye to each other, finishing conversations before heading home.

All around me, a tumult of voices, laughter, excitement, the background noises of my teenage years; slowly the surrounding chaos rearranged itself until the tail of a sentence behind me caught my attention.

"…he's way older."

"Wow, I can't believe it. You've got a man. A real man. None of those stupid boys like Justin McGuire and his friends."

"It's so different with a man," the mystery girl added, emboldened by her friend's enthusiasm. "It's so intense. Sometimes, it feels like one of those crazy roller coasters at Coney Island. You know, like the one that drops you from the top."

My fingers tightened, strangling the strings of the package in my hand, the latest prop in my pretend-relationship.

"I'm so jealous. Why can't you tell me who it is?"

"It's—you know—complicated…So you can't say anything. It's a secret."

The last sentence chilled me more than the wintry wind swirling around. In my mind, Wendy fell off that cliff all over again, but she wasn't alone. They were all falling. Lost because no one was there to catch them, because he isolated them. Wendy reached out all those years ago on WhatsApp, but I didn't catch her then either. I was too stupid to understand what she was asking; worse, I didn't listen, because I was hurt and jealous. Whoever had been talking behind me, I would catch her.

I look at Steven in his wheelchair. "What I heard broke me all over again, but would you let me go home? Of course not, what Professor Steven Harding wants, Professor Steven Harding gets without concerning himself with other people's feelings. You dragged me to your place." He opens his mouth, but the time for his excuses is over. "I had to bury my face in your pillow to smooth my screams as you broke me over and over while having sex with me because that's what *you* wanted and deluded yourself that surely I wanted it too. I was barely holding it together when I escaped to your bathroom, but of course you couldn't leave me alone for five fucking minutes."

He stares at the fire, limp hands held at the wrists by duct tape. I don't tell him that by the time I got home that day numbness had worked its way inside every cell in my body, that I survived by spending the night on the floor of my bathroom, swigging from a bottle of vodka until the alcohol had destroyed every memory he had infected with his words, his actions, his presence in my life. I emerged the following morning with a monster headache, an empty bottle and a clear conviction.

"You think you're some clichéd knight in shining armor ready to protect the fair maiden from the monsters when really you're the fucking dragon."

Silence falls in the living room, heavy and cold like the snow outside. Although the threat within the room is much more dangerous than the hostile weather. Playtime is over.

"So, what do you choose?" I ask, shattering the sheet of ice the silence has turned into.

"You're delusional. I told you nothing happened with Wendy. Nothing you said will change that fact. Which language do I have to say this in for it to get through to you? Anyway, do you really believe you can drive me to kill myself?" The words carry an edge of condescension. Even bound to a fucking wheelchair, the man still thinks himself superior.

I linger at the edge of his question, allowing the absence

of an answer to work its way through his thick skull, a niggling worm burrowing deep into his brain, a parasite driving him crazy until it tenses the muscles in his neck.

"I will leave you here. Take the car and drive to the nearest town." The words fall from my lips slowly, so he can weigh the heavy determination loaded in each one of them. "First, I will go to the local police station and tell them how you lured me here on the pretense of a romantic weekend when all along you wanted me alone because I had discovered what you were up to."

"They'll never believe you."

"Is that so?"

"Have you forgotten? You're the one who booked this place. People will know you orchestrated this." His lips stretch, but the smugness doesn't live for very long. The expression of shock he's expecting on my face doesn't come. Instead, I offer him a smile of my own, one that doesn't die. My silence grinds him, eroding the monolith that is Steven Harding's overconfidence into a fine sand I will scatter away until nothing remains.

"You know what the problem is nowadays? People have so many credit cards that they have difficulty keeping track of them. For example, when was the last time you checked the charges on your MasterCard?"

He responds by withholding the answer, like a child. But I can see it's there, behind the barrage of his clenched teeth, the seal of his pinched lips, the words jammed in his throat, burning his cheeks.

"A MasterCard, an online booking form and an email address were all that was required for *you* to book this place. By the way, Mrs. Winslow thought it was so romantic—how you asked for the main phone to be removed so we wouldn't be disturbed."

His silence persists and hardens, sealing him in. He knows I'm right. He knows he's lost. His eyes shine with a new hatred for me. His intentions are displayed in the harsh lines of his face—he wants to hurt me. Badly. Good, I'm no longer a little girl playing a game she isn't familiar with. He's taking me seriously now. I am Frankenstein, and he is my monster.

"Then," I resume, "I will give them a statement, a narrative, and evidence: emails, photos, a diary, a pattern of behavior. They will photograph the bruises on my wrists and my thighs you gave me yesterday afternoon, my split lip. After that, I will head back to the city. I'll speak to the dean of Barnard College, Richmond Prep's principal, the Board of Education, and I'll call the administration at Columbia University."

The Ivy League name veils his eyes with a new darkness and he flexes his jaw so hard his teeth might shatter—something deep inside him has awakened, an upheaval rising with each pumping of his chest.

"I will tell them everything I told the police. Finally, I'll contact the press to tell them my story, or rather your story. I'll tell them about Wendy, show them her letter, which says how she feared what you might do to her. I won't shut up until they reopen the investigation into her death."

"As you say, it's a story. Your word against mine. All you have is a few texts and a couple of grainy pictures. Nothing incriminating," Steven growls at me, the mask of civility finally sliding.

He watches with contempt as my hand pulls something out from inside my bag before holding it in front of his face. His eyes widen under the heavy implications of the scene etched on photographic paper which I guess he didn't know existed—the smiling face of a teenage girl, cheeks still flushed with the lingering warmth of orgasm, the tight red curls tousled from rolling in bed, and behind her, Steven's listless body sprawled out, the sheet barely concealing his nakedness, the features of his face unmistakable despite the angle and amateur framing.

I fold the picture and tuck it inside the cup of my bra alongside the other. Anger whistles through his nose as he forces heavy breath into his lungs while he acknowledges the existence of the proof of his crime and with it assesses the level of devastation it will inflict on his life and future, the raging fire which will destroy everything in its path.

"Did you think she gave you the only copy? Oh, you did," I scoff.

Before continuing, I move close until my lips almost brush against his ear. The next part, a slowly uttered promise that is intended to burrow deep under his skull until it's all he can think about.

"You've got no idea of the connections my father had in the media and the Justice Department. By the time the authorities and I are finished with you, your reputation will have been napalmed, reduced to smoldering cinders. Your future confined to a line on the Sex Offenders Register after you get out of jail for statutory rape, second-degree rape, manslaughter and false imprisonment."

The entire time, Steven keeps his gaze straight ahead, eyes unblinking at some imaginary point, but the strained tendons in his neck and his wrist pushing against the tape betray the impact my words are having on him.

"But you still have a choice. You can stop all of this from happening. A way to keep your precious reputation. To be remembered as an outstanding teacher, an honest man. Better to do it now than a year down the line in prison. What do you say, professor?"

The fire crackles in the background, the protest of the dying wood weakened by relentless flames. Eyes lost on the darkness on the other side of the glass, a silent Steven decides on the length and the shape of his future.

I resume my place on the edge of the sofa, my hands tucked under me to give the illusion of control, body leaning forward, ready to receive his answer. When he's ready, his eyes hook on mine and don't let go. Fire breaks the log in the hearth.

"I need to take another piss," he says with an even tone.

57. Steven

Ellie sighs loudly as she slides off the edge of that bloody sofa where she likes perching herself.

"You're just delaying the inevitable."

"Suit yourself, but it's about to reek of urine in here. It's not like I can just pop to the bathroom." The words roll off his tongue dripping with an aggressiveness he's no longer bothering to hide.

"Fine." She leaves the room to fetch the bottle she has left in the upstairs bathroom.

She knows. Worse, she has evidence. That damn picture, its every detail burning in his mind. It's now or never. He forcefully wiggles his right hand, working its way under the strips of duct tape. He tucks his thumb under his palm as far as he can because the expression "as if his life depended on it" is not an overblown turn of phrase but a cold reality. His skin in constant contact with the armrest has made the fake leather slick with sweat—his fear and instinct for survival lubricating his escape. Thoughts of the things he will do to Ellie once he's free fuel his motivation. Teach her a lesson or two, write them in shades of purple and red on her skin. He'll get that picture back from her, the emails, the diary and all the rest of it. Burn it all in the fireplace. Destroy all her precious proof. Progress has been slow, the edge of the tape biting into his skin, he pulls through the pain, the burn of the polyethylene and mesh dragging. Then, all at once his hand is free. He rotates his arm, clavicle rolling around in its socket, easing the stiffness built up from hours of forced immobility.

A muffled noise draws his attention to the ceiling and the fact he has no time to waste. Twisting on either side, he flicks the brakes off. Pushing the wheel with one hand, he edges toward the sofa and the knife resting on the back cushion, but the uneven motion leaves the chair askew and the knife slightly out of range. Leaning forward, his fingers graze the smooth steel of the blade. He grunts, his shoulder now sore from strained ligaments barely holding him together. She could be back any second. He almost has it but in his eagerness, he taps too hard; the knife swings in the opposite direction, and his hope freefalls down into the pit of his stomach. *Come on, Steven, you can do this.* Holding his breath, he extends himself as far as he can. The raw edge of the tape around his other wrist eats into his flesh; he harnesses the pain that escapes in grunts through gritted teeth. Finally, his fingertips slide across the handle still warm from Ellie's grip.

The knife is in his hand.

Without a pause, he slices through the layers of tape still restraining him. Conscious that the window of time is narrowing with every passing second, he springs up to his feet, but the room violently sways under him. Hands on the back of the sofa to steady himself, he waits for the earth to stop moving. Get a move on, he tells himself. Now.

Fighting against a strong tide of nausea rising up inside him, he staggers across the lobby into the kitchen, careful not to look to his left toward the banister, where the noose is hanging. He flicks the switch, and the hook where the key should hang shines empty. He puts down the knife. Opens drawers. Rifles through their contents. Cutlery and useless junk that rattles under his growing frustration. The clatter bounces off the kitchen's wall, making him flinch. Damn it, he needs to be careful. All she's put him through is making him sloppy. A deep breath helps him steady himself. When he resumes his search, he moves items quietly. Pride dictates that he should stay, wait for Ellie and teach her a lesson. A part that's not really him wants to. But he's not that kind of man, he doesn't hit women. Fear has rearranged his priorities, retribution can wait until he's back in the city. He needs to get as far away as possible, put this place and her bizarre charade in the rearview mirror of his Lexus. He needs to locate those damn car keys.

There's no way out otherwise—without them, he's trapped in a house with a harpy who wants him dead. Even if he grabbed his coat and left right now, how far could he make it in this weather? How far away is the main road and from there, the main town? When he drove down, he barely saw any cars and can't remember seeing any lights from houses. Their earlier walk didn't reveal any hints of neighboring properties. On the other side of the window, the world is a blur of black and white until a mass of copper curls that couldn't be here moves in the glass's reflection. Spinning around, he faces a very real Ellie standing in the doorway. Her eyes flash to the knife that lies on the island between them.

With it, he could force her to tell him where the keys are. They stand, bodies tensed, waiting to see who will make the first move. The knife is closer to him. She can't reach it before he does. The twitch of her hip triggers him into action. He leaps forward. His hand slams on the knife as darkness swallows the room when Ellie hits the light switch.

His sight quickly adjusts as black shapes detach from the shadows. Hatred mixed with adrenaline shoots down his spine, kicking his body into motion. He chases after her, avoiding cupboard edges and door frames before catching up to her on the stairs. Lunging, his hand closes around the bones of her ankle, robbing her of her balance. The noise of her head hitting a step spreads a warmth throughout his chest. As he pulls her down by the leg, the hardwood smacks her back and limbs while he hauls himself up until her body disappears under his.

"Get off me." She struggles, a flurry of uncontrolled swats of her hands, one of them knocking the knife from his hand. Her fear reeks sweet and tangy in the small of her neck. He feels the slender bones of her forearms against his chest, the jut of her hips, the fragile crescents of her ribs—an offering of bones all utterly breakable. In the semi-darkness, he catches the silver glint of the heart pendant. Twisting his fingers around the chain, he rips it from her neck and throws it away. She clenches her teeth but doesn't yield. He doesn't just want to hurt her, he wants to punish her. He wraps his fingers around strands of her hair. Pulls at them hard, until he gets a satisfying scream out of her.

"Where are the car keys?" His words sound more like the low growl of an animal than a man.

"Fuck you." She spits the insult in his face, which offends a primal part of him he has never connected with until today. He needs to break her. Before her hissing has finished, he knots his fingers into her hair and drives her head into the step.

"The keys, Ellie."

"No way." Still defiant, her breath is too warm on his face and spiced with bourbon. Before he knows what's driving him, he's kissing her hard, ramming his mouth into hers. Grinding against her, he squeezes her breast until his fingers find the nipple and pinch it until she screams for him. Shifting his weight, his hand abandons her chest. It drags down her sweater before diving inside her leggings and the warmth between her legs. His fingers are running along the elastic of her underwear when her body tenses.

"Don't pretend you don't like it."

Her response bends him. A burning electricity shoots up until it overwhelms the beat of his heart, liquifying the thoughts in his head until all that is left is pain, filling every recess of his body. Through the agony still burning a hole in his chest, and fire in his lower abdomen, he is loosely aware of Ellie shoving and wiggling beside him until all that's left is the sharp edges of steps digging into his waist and chest. Through a veil of tears, he watches her socks scramble up the stairs, abandoning him to his fetal position, hands cupped around his balls as he rocks himself through waves of pain. One more humiliation she'll have to pay for.

Amid the darkness, there is nothing else to do but breathe through the pain until the tide recedes and he's able to form coherent thoughts once again. Bitch. Picking up the knife, Steven peels himself off the ground and limps up the stairs. Slowly. Each step wakes the latent ache that has stayed behind. He commits it to the ledger of his grievances against her, uses it to revive all the ideas of what he will do when he catches up with her.

Upon reaching the landing, he stops. What if she has the car keys already? Had them all along, and that's the reason why he can't find them. She could sneak back down while he wastes his time searching for her upstairs. What if she gets to the car first? She's trapped him, but he can't let her leave. Everything she will put into motion once she drives away without him . . . all that knowledge comes back, scaring him into the unthinkable. He knows what he needs to do.

58. Steven

Outside, an eerie silence greets him, and the light of the moon behind a thin veil of cloud taints the night with a purplish-blue glow. The worst of the storm has moved on, but the sense of danger lingers amid lashing gusts of wind. The only noise the crunch of his footsteps as his shoes compact the snow beneath them.

Insulated inside a layer of Gore-Tex, phone raised up in the air, he tramps around staring at the screen, praying for those two bars he had in the car two days ago to return, even one would be enough. A failed endeavor: wherever he stands, whatever angle he holds the phone at, there is no signal. No car keys. No hope of escape, and a deranged girl upstairs hell-bent on destroying his reputation and career or, even worse, forcing him... He sticks the phone in the air once more, wiggles it around. A low growl gathers in his throat and erupts out of him as he hurls his phone through the air. The rash gesture makes him feel good for a second or two until he regains his common sense.

Shit. He half-trudges, half-runs over to where the black rectangle has sunk in the snow. He retrieves it before wiping it with his sweater—the last thing he needs is for his only connection with the outside world to die. Once the sun is up, he'll walk to the main road, find a spot with cell reception or hail a passing car, get the cops, the sheriff, whatever, the fucking cavalry and put an end to this madness. In the meantime, he has one option left.

The freezing air burns his nose and throat with every

breath he takes, it pricks his cheeks. *I wonder how long someone could survive in this kind of weather without proper clothing.* Those had been her words when they lay on the floor of the living room tangled up in plaid, back in a different life. A manufactured one. The answer is, he won't last long. Slipping the phone in his pocket, he feels the comforting shape of the front door key and he gets on with what needs to be done.

At no time does he turn back to look at the house, half expecting to catch a figure at one of the upstairs windows, the wrong silhouette, the impossible silhouette, one that should be resting six feet below on the opposite side of the country. But the reflection in the kitchen window, the unmistakable cascading curls...He shrugs off the ridiculous thought. He doesn't believe in an afterlife: when you're dead that's it, so make the most of it while you're here. What he thinks he saw was just a subconscious projection, his mind processing all those revelations Ellie dumped on him laced with the dregs of whatever drugs she fed him. Content with his rationalization, he doesn't look back. In front of him, the forest sprawls fathomless and inscrutable. He is desperate for a light to tell him that help is nearby. Nothing. He's completely alone. His shoulders slump with a shiver, and he resumes tramping over to the garage.

He fights to open the door against the piled-up snow. It barely moves an inch. The muscles in his arm burn. It gives an inch. He turns around, expecting Ellie to come at him, but there's no one there. He searches the windows for her silhouette, a clue. Come on, he's wasting time. He wedges his shoulder in the gap. Putting all his weight and anger against the wood, he pushes it open enough to slip in. The curves of the Lexus stand out against the darkness, the faint glint of the pearlescent gray catching whatever phantom light exists in this place. His gloved fingers run over the arch of the driver's side's fender. A car is an unnecessary extravagance in Manhattan, with the terrible traffic downtown and the convenience of the subway system, but he couldn't resist when he first saw the SUV standing in the center of the dealership's window. He stares at the beige leather seats haunted by the ghost of his relationship with Ellie. The car parked outside her apartment building, making out like teenagers in the front seat, when she made him feel ten years younger. But he has to face the reality that all his memories of her and their relationship are lies. Instead, he imagines her in the driver's seat, pulling away, her bag, filled with his downfall, in the passenger seat.

His gaze snags on something on the dashboard. The origami crane she made out of his gas receipt taunts him. All the signs he didn't see or even worse ignored. Like how he should have known she'd been here before. *The master bedroom is upstairs to the right.* She didn't hesitate: she knew the front lock needed a jiggle, where the mugs or napkins were. But then, he'd had no reason to doubt her.

If only he knew how to hotwire a car, but he doesn't. So the knife sinks into the rubber of the front tire over and over again. Under the hiss of escaping air, he does the same to the left one. He has just sabotaged his only means of escape, but he has stopped Ellie's chances of turning her threats into a reality too. She's as stranded as he is now. It is done—for better, for worse, till… He doesn't allow himself to finish that sentence. He only has one place to go now.

To his surprise, his gaze lingers toward the dark mouth of the private path. Before he has the time to think, he finds himself trampling the snow away from the house. The pull of the main road and its possible traffic, a chance he cannot resist. After a couple of minutes—along with the searing cold—a profound sense of abandonment crawls under the layers of clothes until it reaches the innermost parts of him. Surrounded by darkness, he hasn't felt this alone since he was six.

His parents had taken him to Disneyland in California, giving in after months of relentless campaigning on his part. His mother had agreed quite quickly; it took longer for his father to cave and begrudgingly indulge him, a feeling that didn't leave his father the entire time they were in this godforsaken place called Los Angeles. Steven had been conflicted between wanting to please his father and his desire to see the magical place his friend Joseph had talked about nonstop for months during recess at school. But his struggle vanished the moment he set foot on Main Street, tugging his mother along. He had spent weeks studying the park's map in preparation, learning the path to every kingdom. First stop was Frontierland. Somewhere by the penny arcade, his mother's pace stopped matching his excitement, and his hand slipped out of hers.

He doesn't remember what he turned to ask her, only that, just like that, his mother was gone. An overwhelming panic rose inside him as he found himself surrounded by legs. Legs everywhere crowding him, a forest of legs whirling around, bare ones that disappeared under Bermuda shorts or skirts, others clad in front-pressed linen trousers. Head tilted back, he spun around for the familiar features of his mother, but all the faces were bleached or shadowed by the California sun. The joyous laughter and festive music twisted into a pandemonium which swallowed his cries for his mother. The atmosphere of the park suddenly crushing him.

The same feeling accompanies him now as he struggles down this sunken path, splitting the forest until his foot catches on the edge of a stone or a broken branch. He tumbles forward, his hands breaking his fall, sinking deep into the snow, the freezing wet seeping under the exposed skin between his gloves and his jacket. The weather and the woods have conspired to thwart his attempt to flee this place and put as much space as possible between him and her. Ahead, the dark mouth of the path, impenetrable, keeping the main road out of his reach. He stares at it through eyes watery from the wind slapping his face, while his hope of escape disappears behind a wall of tears. He clambers to his feet. The freezing cold has worked its way through every extremity, through his mind, until all he can think of is how cold it is. Once his teeth start chattering against his will, he's forced to turn around.

59. Steven

In the unlit lobby, the rope and its noose welcome him back to hell. But now that he's free, the possibilities of whose neck might slip inside this loop have expanded. He starts with the lobby, switching the light on, repelling the darkness and shadows where she could possibly hide. A quick look in the kitchen reveals no trace of her presence. He peers through the double doors in case she's waiting for him in the recess of the bookcase with a knife of her own. Fear tastes metallic, like pennies on his tongue. The space is empty of danger. In the main room, the wheelchair still stands vacant, the tapes that had restricted him for hours dangling from the arm and footrests. The chair topples on to its side as he kicks it out of the way. It skids across before colliding with the window. Grabbing the bottle of bourbon from the cart, he washes the taste of metal out of his mouth. She isn't here either.

Leaving the ground floor behind, he heads upstairs, his back to the banister. Once on the landing, he announces his progress and presence by bringing light to the darkness. First is the office. The door swings wide open until it hits the wall. The low thud of the handle hitting the plaster speaks to him; it says she's not behind it, waiting with a knife, a vase or a statue, some blunt instrument to fracture his skull with, mat his hair with blood. The metallic taste floods back into his mouth. The space behind doors, under furniture, the folds of curtains, have become untrustworthy places, as if the house has sided with Ellie, shielding her from him.

The guest bedroom lies ahead, a virgin territory of

pristine, untouched sheets in soft beige and camel tones, but still a land devoid of Ellie. Her absence does nothing for his blood pressure. With every room cleared, the possibilities of where she's hiding are dwindling. The main bathroom floods with light under his touch, a floor-to-ceiling oasis of whiteness, towels included but spoiled by the smell of stale tobacco. Still she eludes him; she's not cowering in the oversized tub.

He only has one place left to look. He enters the time capsule of the master bedroom. The smell of vanilla and jasmine hasn't pursued him here. The air instead is thick with the lighter flowery notes of Ellie's perfume and body lotion. On the made-up bed, her pajamas lie half-folded, taunting him. He feels so cheated for having gone to the trouble to get those made for someone intent on deceiving him from the start. Propped against the headboard, the pillow where—only last night—she sighed his name, her face glowing under a mist of perspiration while he moved above her. She's always been at her most striking during those moments of abandonment, eyelids fluttering or those few seconds where her eyes were unfocused in pleasure. That night now belongs to another life, another reality, where he made love to a girl who never really existed. Her face, her open arms, even her orgasms were all threads in the web she had crafted to entangle him. The girl he met tonight hates him. For something he didn't even do. He didn't kill Wendy. He had nothing to do with it.

Hitting the light, he assures himself that the ensuite is empty. As he moves deeper into the master bedroom, something catches his eye that eluded him before, something out of place, but he's not quite sure what, like in a "spot the difference" game in a newspaper. He can't figure it out for a while, and then it hits him all at once. The walk-in closet. He stares at the door standing ajar. Did he leave it like that before he headed down for dinner? Is this the clue that he has trapped himself in the room with the person who wants him dead?

Creeping to the door, he slowly pulls it open, trying to picture which side the light switch is. He stays put, peering inside the darkness, but he can't see past the outline of the first few rows of hangers and their clothes, the main bedroom light dimly reflecting on the plastic of the garment bags left in there by the owners. Beyond that, the contents of the closet melt into an impenetrable void, black enough to conceal the body of a psychotic girlfriend—a blank canvas his imagination fills with all sorts of wild scenarios that all end with him bleeding on the cream carpet. Her weekender bag sits on the closet floor, unzipped mouth gaping open, the lacy end of bra sticking out. Her messiness, her bags always bulging from the plethora of junk she carries. The next thought hits him like a taser. What if she has a gun? He's being stupid: if she had a gun, she would have used it to intimidate him when he was strapped to that wheelchair. *Unless.* Unless she has been withholding it, as a Jack-in-a-box surprise. No, that's ridiculous. Fear is robbing him of his common sense, and he hates her for doing that to him too.

Out of the corner of his eye, he spots the switch and hits it, the way you crush a mosquito in the summer. The light stutters to life, offering him snapshots of the inside of the closet. Empty. As he moves in, Ellie's clothes hang on the right like bodies waiting to be filled. The flat flannel shirt, the limp pink cardigan taunting him as a reminder that she's not there. Her scent trapped in the fabrics all around, overwhelming him. She's a ghost looking to turn him into one too. The knife flies down in a swift move, tearing the shirt fabric, sending buttons flying. He stabs over and over again, shredding her belongings. Dropping to his knees, he strikes her bag on the floor.

Under the blows, the memories of everything that has happened in the last twelve hours take hold of him and weld him to this spot on the carpet, driving his arm down as they unfold in his stomach, climb over his organs, pile up in his throat and the narrow wedge between his shoulder blades. They drag him under a flood of emotions: the moment she wheeled him out, revealing the noose for the first time, the ice chilling his veins, the discovery that the woman he thought loved him turns out to be the person who possesses so much hatred she wants him dead.

A ripple escapes his core, traveling outward until it reaches the surface in an explosion of tears. Utterly alone, he lets the tears soak his cheeks as he continues shredding her bag. She has forced him for the first time to feel the edges of his mortality. It tastes salty on his lips. It's only nervous energy. He doesn't want to die, not just tonight, ever. He cannot fathom the perpetual void: to just cease to exist terrifies him. Like during surgery, the vacuum of anesthesia and the complete annihilation of passing time. In the privacy of the walk-in closet, his chest heaves with sobs, snot hems his upper lip. He lets go without shame holding him back.

The wave finally recedes, leaving him wiped out. His arm is sore, his neck stiff. He needs to collect himself and clear his mind, get the drugs she fed him out of his system, then he will figure everything out—Ellie, how to escape this place, get his life back, stop her from ruining his reputation.

Before he does anything else, he drags the chair to the door and jams it under the handle, barricading himself in.

Keeping the knife with him, he drags his bones over to the bed. Even though his safety is precarious—oak and upholstery wedged under the handle—he feels soothed by the knowledge he's alone in here and that Ellie/Verity is as much trapped in this house as he is.

Day Three

The prudent carries a revolver,
He bolts the door,
O'erlooking a superior spectre
More near.

Emily Dickinson

60. Steven

Hands on either side of the sink, the icy water bites his submerged face. The chill punches through the chemical fog in his mind and dispels the tiredness knotted in his neck. This will do for now. His body craves the restorative power of a shower, but he can't bear the idea of putting himself in another vulnerable position inside this house.

Once he had sealed himself inside the master bedroom, the adrenaline receded, and exhaustion claimed his body, although he couldn't really call what he did sleep. His eyes were closed, but he didn't rest. Ellie's voice had stayed in his ear, where it continued to whisper her pernicious litany. Along with that soundtrack, he saw them behind his closed lids—the faces looking at him in horror and disgust: Schumacher, students' parents, his colleagues, but the clearest of all, his father's face contorted in a sneer of disappointment and loathing. With every toss and turn, he repeated to himself that he was being ridiculous, nobody would believe her, his reputation and spotless career spoke for themselves. But doubts crept back every time with the words "but, what if...," overpowering him like a wave of nausea. Even though it had been a few hours, he woke up more exhausted and heavier, as if her words had solidified inside him.

He plunges his head in the water again, drowning the noxious thoughts she's planted in his mind. With a wet washcloth, he scrubs the tape residue off his wrists until the skin is red. He's settling back into his own skin. He remembers who he is—someone in charge of his life who can reclaim his future. Decisive and taking charge. He won't yield to her, even if she talks: it will be her words against his. A.'s photos don't prove anything. The one of W. a badly photoshopped attempt to smear him. He possesses the reputation and the trust of the academic community; she's a mere NYC student, a disgruntled girlfriend out to get him. He has the words and the skills to shape them into a compelling narrative. They will believe *him*.

Hair dripping, he stands by the window, clutching a towel, the fabric soft under his fingers. The glass presents him with a reflection of himself up on his feet. He remembers who he is. These are the fingers that have graded thousands of papers, typed critically acclaimed essays. These are the hands that shook the hand of the dean of Columbia, the hands that cupped the face of his perfect girlfriend, the hands that cradled success. In this house, he nearly lost it all. She ground his future into sand which ran through his fingers, but she didn't count on their grip, his refusal to let it go. She had to drug and imprison him to have dominion over him, but he's free of her restraints. As he dries his face, the fabric catches in his stubble. Sitting in the club chair facing the door, he waits, palming his chin; the bristle grates his fingertips, the sound an echo of the crackling fire downstairs. He wonders if it's died already.

Wendy. The name enters his mind with his next breath. All of this because of her, because of a transgression he made almost eight years ago—the flap of butterfly wings that almost ripped apart his life during these last twenty-four hours. He had no inkling she would turn out to be that sort of a girl, that her adoration would slip into desperation as he pulled away. He had imagined her a Jane Eyre of strong will, but she revealed herself to be weak-minded. When he was trapped in that damn wheelchair, Ellie had asked him the question.

Did you go? Did you meet her as she asked you to?

He remembers. He remembers them all.

The envelope was waiting for him on the hallway floor. He would have missed it if it hadn't been for the crunch of paper under his foot instead of the soft bounce of carpet pile. The cursive handwriting and double underlining under his name told him he would need a drink before he read whatever was written on the heavy craft paper. Armed with a double measure of bourbon, he dropped onto the sofa, taking a swig before tearing open the envelope.

He read the words, listened to her voice deliver them in his head. The drama of emotions, the whirlwind of affected speech, the demands, the requests, the pleading—he found it all quite tiresome and swallowed the last dregs of his drink before getting up to pour another one. Why do they always hang on once the moment has passed? Their whole life ahead of them yet they tangle themselves with the past. All they do is sour the good memories. Like a great paragraph in a novel ruined by the author's inability to know when to stop, that one sentence too much that spoils the preceding beauty. A quick look at his watch told him Sloane would be there in less than an hour. Just the sound of her name in his mind was enough to slow the rhythm of his heart. Her name possessed the sophistication girls like Wendy lacked. Sloane offered the opportunity to share a bottle of wine as they held insightful discussions about art and current affairs, go to restaurants and exhibitions.

She had told him about a potential position at an exclusive prep school that her younger brother attended. Now might be the time to head back east. His absence always made it easier for them to let go.

He hated himself for standing on this cliff, because she'd begged him to. He didn't plan to come at first, but her words had kept him tossing and turning at night. Three bourbons had been required to dull her voice and allow him to sleep. He might be able to bring her some closure, impart some wisdom to help her move on—and leave him alone.

"Steven." His name in her voice lifted like a joyful promise. He shouldn't have come.

"Hello." He kept his tone even, and his hands clasped behind his back, calculating every move, choice of words and intonation to decrease the chances of giving her the wrong impression about his intentions.

"I wasn't sure you would come. I hoped but..." She moved, closing the distance between them, but Steven took a step back.

"Wendy," he said her name slowly, using it to erect a barrier between them. The last syllable dragged out of him, telling her he was tired and they couldn't go on like this.

Her bare shoulders dropped in response. A gust of ocean breeze caught in the slinky fabric of her top and flattened it against the curves of her breasts. Their afternoons and weekends in bed came back to him with the shiver of her skin. His fingers rolling those straps over the cliff of her shoulders, exposing her breast ready for his lips. He suspected she wore that top on purpose, but when he looked at her face, the look of adoration he had been accustomed to had been replaced with one of desperation that made him shudder. The prickle in his back told him he should leave, walk over to his car and not come back.

"I don't understand. It was going so well. Did I do

something wrong?" The tears gathering in her eyes were another signal that he should flee.

He scanned their surroundings and, taking a calculated risk, he rubbed her arms until a weak smile flitted on her lips.

"We shared a beautiful moment together, it lasted as long as it should. Instead of being sad it's finished you should be happy it happened." He gave her the words he had rehearsed in the car, the ones he hoped she would listen to.

"But why does it have to end?"

"Everything does."

"I think you've forgotten," she said so softly he wasn't certain if her words had been intended for him.

He didn't say anything in return. That close, he started to lose himself in the familiarity of her perfume, a mix of jasmine and vanilla that until recently was still trapped in the folds of his sheets.

"When you were away at Christmas. You've forgotten how good we are together, how we make each other happy…" Her fingers closed on the fabric of his shirt as she pulled him to her. Resistance failed him once her lips were on his, parting them gently as he tasted her tongue. Weakness grew hard in him as her kiss pried open the door he had closed. As their mouths gathered momentum, the act rearranged itself into something different. Her lips turned thin and tense against his, her fingers clung stiffly to the fabric of his shirt, their pressure on him spreading a chill that stifled any desire.

Grabbing her wrists, he extricated himself from the tangle of her embrace. "Stop it. Please."

"I just need to remind you…"

The hand reaching out for his face repulsed him, the chipped nail polish, the long bony fingers like the bars of a prison, ready to snatch him. Her sniveling grated on him. Had she always been so insipid?

"For God's sake, Wendy, just stop." He sidestepped her, walking toward the parking area, his car, tomorrow.

"Steven…" His name faltered on her lips, the rhythm broken by her hiccupping sobs. Above them, the shrieks of gulls competed with the roar of waves breaking on the rocks down below. Surrounded on all sides by a pandemonium of noises, the most irritating being Wendy's cries chipping away at his composure.

"You need to get it through your thick skull, it's over," he said, letting go of the little restraint he had left.

He watched how his anger twisted her face, how the cruelty of the words he used pulled at the thread of her confidence, unraveling her. He should have stopped there but he couldn't, even though he was acutely aware of the devastating effect they would have on her, that the damage he was inflicting would last a lifetime and shape any future relationships.

"Have you got no self-esteem? If I had known this was going to be just another childish plea, some kind of emotional blackmail, I wouldn't have come."

She backed away from the brutality of the truth he hit her with, but he wasn't ready to let her go that easily. She was the reason for his frustration and anger, and she had to suffer the consequences of it all, she had only herself to blame. She should have let him go. Another step forward by him sent her another step back, taking her closer to the edge, the green grass hemming the rocks giving way to the blue of the ocean thirty feet below.

"You and I were a mistake." He delivered this last truth towering over her, his shadow shrouding her.

She flinched, the blow too hard for her soft body. Her foot slid back, taking the rest of her away.

"Jesus, be careful, you're gonna fall," he said, yanking her back.

She just stood there, puffy red eyes, wet cheeks, the motion of her teeth below her skin, gnawing her inner cheek. The girl he had liked was completely erased. His darling Jane was gone. He was done here.

"I'm moving at the end of term anyway," he announced, letting go of her arm.

"What?"

"Moving to New York, so until then please remember I'm your teacher."

"Steven…"

"Please. It's Mr. Harding."

Those were the last words he ever said to her. He isn't to blame for Wendy's death. He caught her when she slipped. Whatever happened afterward was not his fault. Her death was just a tragic accident, something no one could have seen coming. He couldn't be held responsible for her actions.

But her actions that day had been a catalyst for his change. When he got back to his apartment, he swore he was done. He called Sloane to cancel their dinner before crawling into the shower. After that he spent the rest of the evening home with a bottle of bourbon. He stayed away from girls like Wendy, refocusing his energy on his career. He dated women his friends introduced to him, women he met at bars, or exhibitions, but it never lasted more than a few weeks. Things remained that way for a year until T. landed in his class with her thick bangs above those pleading eyes. She broke down the defenses he had put up and swept him away.

He could explain this to Ellie. In his mind, he entertains fantasies where he finds her and drags her kicking and screaming to that damn wheelchair in the living room, restraining her like she had him, and forces her to listen. He could make her understand. He had to give her credit: the scent of jasmine and vanilla she sprayed around was a clever touch, enough to drive him crazy.

A loud growl rising from deep inside him interrupts his thoughts. Massaging his stomach, he tries to remember when he last ate. The scene comes back to him like the film of someone else's life. Him and Ellie, sitting at the table, enjoying stuffed eggplant with some fine wine, discussing a trip to Italy he wanted to take her on. She played the part, knowing there would be no vacations away, feeding him lies stuffed in that soft smile of hers. His stomach moans again, and there'll be no soothing the beast until it's fed. Despite it all, he still can't think of her as any name other than Ellie. The alarm clock on the bedside table tells him it's just past three a.m.; he hasn't eaten in over twenty-four hours; no wonder his stomach is wailing like a noisy brat. Acknowledging the time only sharpens his hunger.

This might turn out to be a terrible idea, but he needs his full strength. With one hand tightly wrapped around the knife's handle, he moves the chair and opens the door.

61. Steven

At the threshold, he listens to the silence for a clue to Ellie's whereabouts. The little freshening-up he's managed has swept away the last tendrils of drugs that tangled his mind and washed them down the drain. He feels alive again, more alert. His senses may be too heightened: every creak or change in air pressure makes his muscles tense.

All the lights he's switched on hours before are still shining bright, the house left untouched after his earlier sweep. Strangely, he feels alone. His view—unobstructed to the top of the stairs—reveals no presence or shadows to conceal one. He rocks on the balls of his feet until he has gathered the courage to let go of the sanctuary of the bedroom. Once in motion, he doesn't stop until he reaches the bottom of the staircase. In his rush, his foot catches on something on the stairs. A white blur flies across until it catches the side of the door frame to the main room. The mug Ellie desecrated earlier when she used it as an ashtray lies split in two. He stares at the broken shell leaking foul water, somehow this mug the first casualty in the war they are now waging against one another. No, the second casualty. He forgot for a moment about the car and its slashed tires.

Dry-mouthed, he creeps forward, running his tongue over the ridge of this teeth. Every step could be his last. Worst-case scenarios crowd his mind: Ellie lunging at him from some secret place, jamming a needle into his neck, catching his feet and sending him tumbling down. He's scurrying across the lobby when a sharp hissing somewhere behind him sends a shudder down his spine. *Shit.* Just the wind howling down the chimney. The same noise he chastised Ellie over earlier on when she jumped and cut herself on the mug.

Peering into the main room, he's confronted by more silence and everything in the exact same position, including the wheelchair still lying on its side like the metal carcass of a wounded animal. Gone is the earlier scent of vanilla and jasmine; all that lingers in the air is the aroma of smoky wood mixed with the pungent smell of her cigarettes.

In the kitchen, every large cupboard is a potential hideout. Ellie's body bent inside one of them, ready to leap on him when he least expects. Or she could tease open the cupboard door as he walks past and slash his Achilles tendons, his body collapsing to the ground like a marionette with its strings cut. It's all there behind his eyes: him dragging the dead weight of his body across the floor, leaving a trail of blood smearing the tiles, her above him ready to strike again.

Back against the island, he crab-walks to the fridge at the other end, throwing glances in every direction while hating himself for being so dramatic. He snatches a block of cheese, the plate of leftover bacon and a tub of butter. Once he has the bread, he doesn't hang around. Balancing his supplies in his arms, he heads back for an impromptu picnic on the floor. During the entire round trip, his eyes avert from the rope and its noose dangling from the banister.

Back in the bedroom, he devours cheese and bacon sandwiches until the soft bread jams in his throat. In the ensuite he gulps water from the tap to push the sludge of mashed food down his throat until it drops inside his stomach. As he wipes his mouth with the back of his hand, the porcelain carcass of the mug spilling its innards on the lobby tiles comes back to him, the tar-colored liquid, and he wonders if the same filth runs in her veins. Though he's alone, she's everywhere around him: her toothbrush shares the tumbler with his, her cream, soap and make-up bag clutter up the space around the washbasin. Next to his hand, her brush, full of tangles of her hair caught in the bristles. She has become inescapable.

Once full, he is drawn to the bedroom window. Outside, morning still belongs to the night, the sun not even an idea edging on the horizon. The ground is a uniform blanket of white; it must have snowed again after he fell asleep; the latest fall has erased his previous footsteps, as if he had never escaped outside. It looks deep even from up there, about calf deep. Trudging in this earlier had been a struggle, his feet sinking until they were entombed by snow, and the fight to extricate himself from its icy grasp as if it had latched on to him and refused to let go. Beyond, the woods are still a hostile mesh of knotted trees that doesn't offer any insight as to what might lie beyond, or how far away the next cabin might be. If only he had paid more attention when he drove down here.

The outside has no answers for him, but maybe some are hiding here. The open door of the walk-in closet calls to him. He needs to find out what else she might have brought here to confront him with.

He drops her bag on the bed. The canvas bears the marks of his anger toward her. Each nick of the knife a testament to how she's driven him crazy. Hands disappearing inside, he guts the bag of its contents. He tears through the shredded sweaters, blouses and lingerie, expecting to find a recording device, a USB key, more pictures. Something. The remains of her wardrobe litter the bed, but there's nothing incriminating. He needs to find something, anything that can define the breadth of her knowledge. Instead, he holds in his hand the

317

black and pink lace bra she wore when she danced in front of the fire, which only reminds him of the depth of her treachery. She's got that damning picture of him and Wendy, Ashley's photos and that bloody diary. She has her body too—the split lip, the bruises on her wrists and thighs and whatever new ones he gave her on the stairs. Broken capillaries damaged under his touch, the blood slowly pooling under Ellie's skin. With the right context he knows the kind of story these hematomas would narrate.

There must be something. Throwing the bra, he rushes to the bathroom and upends her toiletry bag into the sink. He wades through bottles, lotions, lipsticks and compacts. Still nothing, so he ransacks the cabinet, hoping that she's hidden something there. Bottles rain down into the sink, clanking against the porcelain. Nothing.

Frustrated, he rushes back to the main room. Sliding to the ground, he searches the narrow space under the bed, almost expecting to find Ellie staring back at him, but she isn't there, he has no idea where the hell she is and he can't find any evidence of what she's got on him. Abandoning the underside of the bed, he spins about the room looking for another place to search. He needs to find a piece of evidence, something tangible he can burn, rip, step on. Frustration and bile rise in his throat, and he dashes back to the ensuite, just in time to throw up sludges of mashed-up bread and cheese in the toilet.

After rinsing his mouth, he lies on the bed, working to settle his breathing. He looks on the white expanse of the ceiling for answers to the multitude of questions bumping around in his head—what he should do next—when a muted rattle spreads above. He squints at the ceiling. Damn rats . . . as if dealing with one type of vermin were not enough. Then the scuffle starts again. This time, the scratching is more pronounced; an image forms in his mind that jolts him upright.

"Bitch." The word leaves him as he grabs the knife on the nightstand. The chair wedged under the handle flies across the room as he storms out. He didn't know where to look until now. He even considered that she might have been holed up in some outbuilding in the woods he didn't know about.

Why didn't he think of it earlier? The one obvious place he completely overlooked when searching the whole house, because she told him in passing it was locked, because she told him there was no key, because he had no reason at the time not to believe her, because he liked the security of a locked door, because she dulled his mind with drugs, because when he heard it yesterday after he showered he had blamed rodents for the noise.

By the time he reaches the attic door at the end of the hallway, anger bellows inside his chest. He focuses his rage in his right foot as he drives it into the wood just below the lock. On the third kick, the wood whines, on the fifth it splinters. By the seventh kick it's Open fucking Sesame.

62. Ellie

My mind hovers in the hazy twilight where sleep and consciousness blur. A space which smells of jasmine and vanilla. She waits for me there along with my first memory of her. Half-dream, half-recollection, turning our first meeting into a myth or an origin story. The encounter which shaped who we would become.

Monterey was a nice town. I liked the air there, warm but dry and scented with the wild vegetation and flowers that hemmed the coastline, nothing like the humidity of Orlando, air loaded with moisture which weighed you down as soon as you stepped outside. Still, no matter how nice the air was, it didn't change my status of being the new girl. Again. The perpetual new kid. Sucking in a deep breath, I climbed out of the car and into an environment of close-knitted friendships refined over years where there was no place for me to fit in. Hands clasped over the strap of my backpack, I loitered by the steps, already feeling eyes prying, knowing I didn't belong. *Fake it 'til you make it, Bug,* Dad would have said. Fifth grade, here I come.

Under the sprawling shade of a cedar tree, a brigade of ponytailed girls clad in varying shades of pink formed a semicircle around a girl sitting cross-legged on the ground. Even at a distance I could see the mirror of tears in the girl's eyes. Sound or commentary unnecessary, the malice curling their mouths, the pack surrounding its prey, shoulder to shoulder, isolating it from the rest of the herd: it was a universal story, one that took place in every elementary or high school. The way they were picking on that girl angered me, even though I didn't know her. My status as the new kid already made me the lowest form of life in this ecosystem; I had nothing to lose.

"... You are such a loser. Who does that?" Mean-girl-in-chief delivered her venomous words framed with a pernicious smile.

"Leave her alone." I planted my feet apart ready to stand my ground.

"Who are you?" she sneered, giving me a once-over. "Look, weirdo, you've got a fan."

"Hey, I'm not a weirdo," the girl on the floor shouted.

"Is your ponytail too tight or you're just too slow to understand?" I said. "Leave her alone." This time, the smile slid off her face as her little posse stifled rising giggles.

"You two deserve each other." She walked away, giving us a contemptuous flick of hair, the others trailing off behind her.

"You OK?" I sat in front of her. Bowed head, the masses of her curls obscuring her face, her gaze fixed on her cupped hands, where a tip of yellow paper peeked through. "What's that?"

The pod of her hands opened to reveal a tiny bird made of folded paper; the intricacy of the shape created was mesmerizing.

"Wow, that's really cool. Did you make it?"

Her smile bunched the constellations of freckles on her cheeks. "It's origami," she said. "I'm Wendy."

"Verity, but you can call me Vee."

In my vow to avenge her death, I became one of her origami creations. Like her paper crane, I folded myself into a shape which would appeal to Steven. Creating lines where there were none, I made myself pliable, concealed the hinges. The memories drum in my head like a heartbeat.

The next bang jolts me to my feet. He's found me. My heart rate spikes with every kick, while my eyes roam the room, searching for a place to hide, but the space houses only a few boxes—too small for my body to fit in—the few things I brought up here as backup, and a square of dim light cut on the bare floor. The light. Pushing hard, I shove a heavy box into position and slip my boots on.

The sound is still bouncing off the walls of the staircase by the time I flip the handle of the rooflight. I push, and nothing happens. The window won't budge. Another bang, louder this time. Panic spreads between my shoulder blades. I rattle the handle, but still no movement. Downstairs, Steven kicks the door with all the resentment he has been amassing since I drugged him. I remember his breath on my cheek when he had me pinned on the stairs, the way his hand molested my breast, the plan he had for my body before my knee rammed into his balls. The possibility of what he might do if he catches me again kickstarts my survival instinct. I slam my shoulder into the glass. On the second attempt, my effort is rewarded with a faint cracking from the ice sealing the window shut. The frost breaking and Steven's efforts are all the motivation I require.

A loud crash, and I know he has burst through the door. Already his footsteps stomp up the stairs. He'll be here in seconds. I gather all the rage, the will and energy I have and concentrate it in my arm. With a low growl I ram my body into the glass. The window bursts open with a loud crack and a whoosh of freezing air, leaving half of me hanging onto the slope of the roof.

"You bitch." Before I can haul myself through the window, his hands close around my calves. As he yanks me back, I scream into the night. The ledge digs into my chest. I cling onto the roof with stiff crooked fingers, nails clawing at the rough surface below the snow. Anything to stop him getting his way.

No matter how hard I hang on, I feel myself being reeled back into the attic. Freedom finally slips away when the last inches of the roof escape from my fingers. Steven's body breaks my fall, but that involuntary kindness is the only one he has for me. His fingers knot in my hair, pulling it back until my eyes water.

Panic and bile sour the back of my throat. I struggle against the cage his body has become. With every move his restraints on me tighten. Come on, Vee, think. Use your head. Yes, use your head. Pulling forward, gathering momentum, I crash backward, my skull connecting with facial bones with a crunch. Pain explodes inside my cranium, but his hold around my body slackens, and I wrench myself away. I stagger up onto the box, my hand gripping the ledge of the window for stability, and then to haul myself out. I'm dangling half out when Steven gets hold of me again.

If he drags me back in, I'm dead. My legs buck and kick; every inch gained adds to my lifespan. My free foot finally hits something hard, a clavicle or a sternum, the blow strong enough for him to loosen his grip. With one last effort, I hoist myself out of the window and slide down to the edge of the roof. Making myself as small as possible, I jump off, bracing for the impact. As the air slaps my face, I externalize a scream and internalize a prayer before my body burrows into the snow. The intense cold hits me like a defibrillator. I emerge with a gasp and all bones intact and accounted for, melting flakes stinging my skin. No time to dwell on my good fortune, Steven isn't done now that he knows where to find me.

Calf-deep in snow, I stumble across the open space separating me from the garage, leaving a trail behind, making it impossible to conceal where I'm going. But Steven isn't my only worry. The snow burns my skin, numbs my fingers raw and red. An icy wetness seeps in under my clothes, under my skin, burrows past my flesh. It fills my veins and spreads through my system, climbs the ladder of my spine to my brain. A shivering cold.

When I slide through the gap in the garage door, my hands have curled into claws under an icy arthritis. With slow breaths, I unfurl them painfully. With trembling fingers, I get my phone out of the pack around my waist. The light splits the darkness, revealing snapshots of the garage. A slice of shelf with old paint pots, a garden hose. A tremor rocks my arm, and the phone clatters to the ground. As I pick it up, the light sweeps across the back tire—a deflated ring of rubber slumped on the floor. Same for the front tire. The sight liquifies my insides, fear sloshing about the hollow space in the pit of my stomach. *Crap*. Even if I find the keys, I won't be going anywhere now. I looked in all the usual places but they weren't there. Steven made it painfully clear when he attacked me on the stairs that he didn't have the keys and didn't know where they were; the bruises on my back and arms are a testament to that. I should have made a spare of them, but he has serious trust issues when it comes to a woman driving his precious car. He never let me get anywhere closer than the passenger seat. Now he has made sure I wasn't getting anywhere too.

This changes everything.

"Ellie." My name trails out of Steven's mouth with an up-and-down pitch. He elongates the syllables as if trying to eviscerate it. "There's nowhere for you to go."

I kill the light. Terror has turned into nausea flooding

the back of my mouth, but I swallow it back. Now is not the time. Staying low, I tiptoe to the back of the car when my boot kicks something hard on the ground. My fingers blindly probe the floor until they find a long, narrow shape. I pick it up. It'll do. Something which will allow me to gain some time to gather myself and think about what to do next.

"There's no hiding. Come on out. Let's talk." His arrogance—as always—is an unwilling ally, his need to assert his dominance out loud letting me know where he is.

Quickly exiting the garage, I run in a circle around it before I sprint to the line of trees as fast as my sinking feet allow me. Hiding behind a wide trunk, I wait. With every wintry gust of wind, my cold damp clothes feed on my heat, leaving me with increasing shivers. I'm worried my teeth chattering will betray my location. If Steven doesn't get me, winter will. Without a coat I won't last long out here.

I listen to the crescendo of his footsteps squeaking in the snow before his silhouette finally cuts against the charcoal morning sky. He waddles toward the garage, his body hidden under the bulk of his padded jacket, his scarf coiled around his neck. I envy his layers. In his gloved hand shines the long blade of a knife. He pauses by the door, scanning the edge of the forest. Ducking behind the trunk, I breathe into my sleeve, waiting until the moment I hear his footsteps again.

While he rummages inside, I sneak around the perimeter of the garage and position myself by the entrance, arm raised ready to strike. His footsteps get closer to the door, and a mix of anticipation and apprehension flutter in my chest and tighten my grip around the smooth steel, knowing that what happens will determine the shape and length of my future.

63. Ellie

He emerges from the garage, unsuspecting of the danger hiding behind him as he offers me the back of his skull. The tire iron falls down, but the whoosh of air betrays my presence. Steven whips around, arm up, barring my attack. He staggers back. I throw my weight forward. What follows is a jumble of arms milling about to get to the other in a violent adult version of "tag you're it."

He aims high, slicing the air with his knife. I go low, and the iron catches his ribs. The blow folds his body. His arm flails about, catching me on the side of the head. The blow knocks me off balance. A low growl rumbles out of him. He lunges forward, and I ram into him head first. The blow is enough for him to lose his footing, falling back into the snow. I flounder away from him. But not far enough. He latches on to the back of my jumper, tugging me toward him. We stumble and then race to be the first one up. He's still kneeling when I swing my weapon down. His arm flies up in response. A reflex drives me to shield myself, when a searing pain burns my forearm, spreading upward until it explodes in my chest. In a jerking reaction, my hand swings the tire iron around. Without aiming, it connects with the side of Steven's head.

He collapses on the snow. Arm up, I'm prepared to hit him again if he moves. After a few seconds, his body is still, apart from the slight rise and fall of his shoulders. Towering over him, I am tempted: just a couple more blows to the head. But he doesn't deserve an easy death he won't see coming. He doesn't deserve that kindness.

Move, Verity, move. Every moment he lies unconscious is precious time I can't waste. I hobble to the house, falling into the snow, legs stiff, the rhythm of my breathing fractured by the cold. When I crash through the front door, the central heating is so deliriously warm I could cry. The rising temperature dissipates the numbness of limbs, wakes up toes and nerve endings. Multiple pains pull me apart, each demanding my attention, from the agonizing burn of my fingers to the acute throbbing pain radiating down my left arm. With caution, I examine the laceration across my sleeve. As I take in the trickle of blood running down my hand, the floor sways unexpectedly under my feet, and I lean against the door frame for support. The deep gash runs along the inside of my forearm, the blood dripping onto the checkered tiles into Rorschach shapes, next to the remains of a broken mug. From the wound rises an overpowering stench of rust spoiling the air, and a surge of fear and nausea soils my mouth. As I swallow it back, the wound seems to ignite, as if acknowledging its existence has magnified the pain. It's all I can think about, all that exists, all I'm reduced to, that unbearable pain. The intensity reaches such a level I feel woozy; my legs buckle under the weight of how much this hurts.

Cradling my arm, I rock myself and breathe through the pain and the tears. Low grunts escape through my clenched teeth until my body grows accustomed to the pain. I can't stay here. Back on my feet again, I stagger across the living room to the bar cart. My shaky hand grabs the gin, leaving smeared blood on every surface; I snatch a couple of things from my bag before heading to the kitchen.

I drop the bottle and my bag on the counter before retrieving the roll of duct tape. The painstaking task of pushing the sleeve up to my elbow draws a series of hisses out of me. The sight of the parted flesh and the iron smell of blood tightens my stomach, and bile rises in my throat again. Folding over, I throw up into the sink. Once my stomach is empty, I gargle some water before spitting it out along with the sour taste. I can do this. I repeat the words as a mantra until I believe them. A swig of the gin steadies my nerves before I drench the wound in alcohol. The burn unleashes an unrestrained scream out of me. Tears sting my eyes. Cleaning it again, I bite into the neck of my sweater, grinding the pain into the wool. A clean dishcloth serves as a makeshift gauze secured in place with the help of duct tape. Another long gulp of gin spreads its warmth down my throat, grateful for its analgesic properties. Fishing out the cigarettes from my bag, I pull one out with my teeth. I fill my lungs with smoke and exhale it all with a grateful sigh.

Steven is free. Unconscious for the moment, but free. The car is out. Somehow the words don't ring true, even though the deflated tires are undeniable. The leaves of the giant ficus glow a waxy green; Steven has switched on all the lights like a child afraid of the dark. I snatch a leaf, rolling it between my fingers. He's sabotaged his only means of escape just to stop me getting to it first. The man can still surprise me. After what I've put him through, what I've promised him, he's a man unhinged. God only knows how far he's prepared to go if he gets his hands on me again. I remember the staircase, his weight and his anger smothering me. Tears well up in my eyes.

Fear tingles in my fingertips, it soars up my arm, shudders rippling all through my back. I try to shake it off, but it clings to my flesh. It scares my breath away.

Z, Y, X…W, V…

Ears full of the deafening thumping of my blood.

U, T…S, R.

Mouth gaping, I inhale in short gasps, with no result. Concentrate on the letters.

Q, P, O...O...

Slowly. In. And. Out.

The calming rhythm of "in" and "out" guides me until my lungs remember how they work. The oxygen lulls my racing heart and mind enough for me to become conscious of myself again, the burning in my fingers, the throbbing sting in my arm. Those pains tether me back to the present, to the living room.

Around me the house is a silent spectator waiting for what will happen next, until the silence is invaded by a pernicious ticking: the antique clock, sitting in one of the alcoves of the bookshelf, its existence irrelevant until now. It's all I can hear, a doomsday clock counting down to the inevitable catastrophe waiting ahead. I need a new plan. Quick. Outside the floodlight is still out. Time hasn't run out. Yet.

Turning my cigarette into ash, I play with the leaf in my hand. Its smooth surface folds and folds again, a crude version of Wendy's delicate origamis.

The abandoned wheelchair lays tipped on its side by the window. The broken symbol of how far I was willing to go, the monument of how much Steven hates me right now. Maybe he'll use the noose on me. I close my eyes, and the faces of those I love float behind my lids. Connor. Oh God, Connor. I can't do that to him after all he's done, what he means to me. His existence is what keeps me tethered a lot of the time; it reminds me good men exist. Steven killing me would crush him but if it helps show who Steven is, if it saves one girl...At least Dad won't have to go through this, or Kate. For all he's done, Steven can't get away with it, so many men like him already do. Wendy, those girls, the wheelchair, the noose, my arm...gathering the pieces in my head, I stitch them together until a new picture emerges showing me a way through, a way out of this.

I smile at the other me reflected in the window, the one with the damp hair, the ragged sweater, and a dishrag taped to her wounded arm. And she is there with me in that reflection: her fiery curls I used to twist my finger around, the girl who stole cigarettes for us, who knew all my secrets, like that I cried at *Jurassic Park* or how I really broke my big toe that summer. She's a hallucination conjured up by the blood loss, mild hypothermia, and possibly a little concussion, but the illusion of her brings me peace and comforts me in my decision. I smile and nod to her. I have a plan.

The duct tape unpeels slowly from the chair. It crumples into a ball inside my fist before it is melted into oblivion by the smoldering ashes in the fire. I wrap fresh pieces on the arm and leg rests. I sit in the wheelchair. I put my arms where Steven's have been restrained for hours. I pull the new strips of cut tapes over my wrists, watch the adhesive tug on my skin and hair before letting go, catching specks of me along with threads of red and blue wool, leaving a sticky residue behind on my skin and clothes. My blood leaves dark stains on the leather. I repeat the ritual with the tapes around my ankles, catching black fluff from my leggings. Out of nowhere, dizziness grabs hold of me. Darkness creeps in at the edge of my sight. My hands grip the armrests, the light in the room dims, I slowly disconnect, edging toward fainting, until a switch flips somewhere inside my brain, bringing me back online. Light powers back through my vision, and brightness floods the living room once again. I shake my head for the feeling to let go of me. I can falter but not yet, there are still things that lie ahead.

As I slowly unfurl from the chair, pins and needles travel down the knobs of my spine. The room sways for an instant before the earth solidifies into an unmovable surface once again. In the kitchen, the maple syrup waits on the shelf. Head thrown back, and the thick golden ribbon fills my mouth, the rush of sugar hitting my tongue. I need to hurry.

The banister bears most of my weight as I climb the stairs toward the attic. The varnished wood pulsates under my fingers—the heart of the house beating for me. Maybe I am the ghost, the house has known it all along, sheltering me until I haunt its walls. If we carry our ghosts with us, I hope Wendy will haunt this place with me. An eternity here with her wouldn't be such a terrible end. Sometimes the end is just a new name for beginning.

Goose bumps bloom on my skin. Despite the heating in the house and the warmth left behind by the dying fire, my clothes are still wet and stop my body from warming up. Battered and shivering, I take comfort in the notion that soon this will all be over, but I have no idea which one of us will make it.

The brightness in the foyer intensifies under the new light spilling in from the other side of the windows.

He's awake.

64. Steven

The forest swims in and out of focus. Long figures cloaked in black dance toward him—the mob finally coming to carry him to the rope and stick his head through the noose. Will they burn Ellie at the stake once they're done with him or will they throw her into the sea like the puritans used to? But the figures stop moving, his sight sharpens, and they congeal back into the lanky shapes of trees.

The left side of his face feels like it's on fire. He groans as he rolls onto his back. Every blink reveals snapshots of a sparkling sky, but he cannot work out if the pinpricks of light are up above or in his eyes. He lies there while the cold climbs into his lungs and the snow soaks his hair. Numbness has taken hold everywhere on his body apart from his left shoulder and the fold where it connects with his neck: that spot is dominated by a throbbing pain. He can't stay here. He peels himself from the wet blanket of snow his body is encased in, and the movement wakes up the floodlight tucked under the edge of the roof, which blinds and disorients him for a moment.

He trudges back to the front of the house but doesn't go in. The wood and glass building looms over him, presiding over the surrounding darkness. It hasn't struck him until now. The privacy windows don't allow him a peek inside. The house stands silent, holding its secret like he would a breath. It is cold and unwelcoming, not a place of romance but a modern mausoleum lost amid nature and the elements. Somewhere behind him, the wind slithers through dead branches with a hiss, warning him not to go in. As if the house has been conspiring with her, shielding her from him.

He decides against the hostility of the front door, and the tableau waiting on the other side. Instead, he sneaks in through the kitchen, where his boots leave puddles on the tiles, but nothing compared to the blood splashed and pooling on the counter, sink, and part of the floor. Around him, the house smells wounded.

What happened before he lost consciousness filters back to him in flashing images, blurs of colors: the glistening black of a tire iron, the ambush at the garage door, the multicolored wings of her sweater flapping like a vicious bird, his milling arms fending off her attacks, the bite of the iron on his flesh, red and orange pain exploding in his head.

His fingers probe cautiously the tenderness at the back of his neck. The applied pressure shoots a savage pain down his arm that leaves him wincing. Cautiously, he rotates his shoulder, rolls the head of his humerus inside the scapula, painful but bearable, no bones seem broken. But she's hurt. The revelation brings a smile to his face. At some stage the knife connected with a part of Ellie. The knife abandoned now beside the imprint left by his body, like a twisted attempt at a snow angel.

Across the counter, the gin bottle winks at him, but the heavy smear of blood on the glass sickens him. Retrieving a dishrag from one of the drawers, he moves to the living room, where the bourbon waits for him. He swigs straight from the bottle; the sweet and smoky flavor smooths down his throat and warms his body. He chucks a couple of logs in the hearth, stuffs some newspaper balls underneath and lights a fire to stave off the cold still spreading under his skin. Tentative flames curl the paper into ash but fail to latch on to the wood. Speeding up the process with a lick of bourbon, he watches the explosion of flames leap high, the drunken fire feeding on the alcohol, the aroma of burning wood dissipating the stale stench of Ellie's presence.

Hope she hurts like hell, he thinks, collapsing on the sofa, and ruffles his hair dry with the kitchen rag using his good arm. She breathes somewhere upstairs. In his mind, she is curled up like a wounded animal that has learned its lesson. The status quo has shifted in his favor. Without drugs or restraints to impair him, she is no match, the gazelle against the lion. He has smelled her fear in the kitchen, seen it painted red on the worktop. Morning will cast a light on all this, shine on the craziness of the situation; this sham won't survive sunrise, like all other evil it can only thrive in darkness.

Once the sun is up, he'll run to the end of the private path and onto the main road, where he'll be able to get a signal, flag down a car. Back within the arms of civilization, he will tell the story of his disturbed girlfriend and the paranoid and jealous tendencies she hid for months, until she lured him to an isolated location, where she drugged and tied him up—undeniable proofs of her instability and mania.

That's all he needs to escape this messed-up house and its messed-up inhabitant—sunlight. He takes a celebratory swig from the bottle, and the bourbon dulls the ache swimming behind his forehead. The nightmare cannot persist past the resurgence of the sun. His mother used to tell him that when he was a young boy who screamed at the monster at the window, rattling its skeletal fingers against the glass, ready to snatch him from his room. She sat on his bed, her weight pinching the covers tighter across his body. Scary things are not that scary when you look at them in the light, she said as she switched on the bedside lamp. The monster of rattling bones' true identity revealed—just branches from the oak tree swaying under a strong wind. See, she said, her hands smoothing his hair and his fears, now you know there's no monster even if I switch the light off again. She smelled of lavender back then and when she smiled it always reached her eyes. The time before his father snuffed that life out of her with his indifference and indiscretions. Some monsters do not change in the light.

Heat and the crackles from the fire lull him to the place where consciousness and sleep co-exist. He cannot drop his guard. If he wants to win, his mind needs to stay sharp. Jumping off the sofa, he paces in front of the fireplace. It would be easy to give in, lie down on one of the plump pillows, but no matter how enticing this is, he cannot. Coffee. Coffee is the rational answer. A strong coffee would be a welcome drink, one to sharpen his senses and carry him to morning. He really should stay off the alcohol. In his mind, he's already enjoying the aroma of the strong brew awaiting in his near future when the overpowering scent of jasmine and vanilla brings him back to the present of the living room.

The scent stops him in his tracks. He scrutinizes the open space, fully alert. *How does she do that*, he wonders, *manage to get that smell in the air without a sound?* He scours the perimeter of the room, searching for an air freshener plugged into one of the electrical sockets. His search turns out to be fruitless—they are all barren or connected to lamps. The leaves of the ficus tree swish as he pushes the branches aside, looking for a device somewhere inside the pot.

He spins around, the living room speeding past until a faint reflection stops him cold, reaching inside him and strangling his heart. There, in the swath of glass, the outline of a body standing behind his reflection clothed in the delicate camisole she wore on the cliff that day, and a head crowned with those unmistakable copper curls.

"What do you want from me?" he screams at her.

Her lips part, mouth forming intangible words, trapped in the same glass where she lives.

"I'm sorry. Is that what you want me to say? I told you it was over. Why did you reach out? It all happened so fast. I didn't mean to...God damn it. Why did you have to grab my sleeve that way?"

Her listless arm rises, fingers stretching like they did almost eight years ago on that cliff—before he ran to his car—when a shiver of air brushes at the back of his neck. He flips around to confront the space where she should be standing but finds it empty. When he checks the window again, she's gone.

"I don't deserve to die for this," he says, pummeling the glass. "I don't...I'm sorry. Is that what you want to hear?"

He throws agitated looks around but there is no way out to escape the anxiety building inside him. Once in motion, his eyes can't find a place to rest, afraid of what might or might not be there if he looks. Fingers knotted in his hair, fear tickling the back of his throat. He feels exposed with no real place left to hide.

65. Steven

Somehow Ellie's driving him insane. She has to be the one pulling this stunt because the alternative is inconceivable to his pragmatic mind. *The bottle.* He grips its neck tighter and stares at it with horror—what if she's drugged him again, slipped something in the bourbon, or maybe she's spiked all of them. Nose to the mouth of the bottle, he cannot detect any abnormal smell, or a hint of powder, or the remains of a pill dissolving amid the amber liquid.

Still not convinced, he runs to the kitchen. Bending over the sink, he probes the back of his throat with two of his fingers until the contents of his stomach respond to his taunt, splattering the white porcelain, his sick mingling with Ellie's blood before being washed away by the onslaught of water gushing from the tap. He has always been able to rely on himself, trust his own judgment, but now she has taken that away from him too. His anger toward her deepens, until it graduates into full-blown rage. A wave of brutal energy sweeps through his body, turning his knuckles white as they grip the edge of the counter. The bottle of gin stands next to him, defiant and smeared with her blood like some sort of tribal war paint. Just the fact it exists so close to him exacerbates the storm within. His hand is swift, the gesture precise—the broken body of the bottle lies in the sink. Tendrils of blood dilute in the alcohol, slowly unfurling and edging toward the drain. He glares at them while red and black thoughts explode in his head, where he shoves Ellie down the stairs, the hard wood smacking her head, spine, and limbs with every tumble until the crunch of a vital bone.

His image in the kitchen window shows a disheveled, unraveling version of himself that shocks him. Unlike Ellie, he does not experience a pandemonium of emotions that dictates his every action. He just needs to occupy his mind.

Heading to the bookcase in the main room, he peruses the titles on the shelves, deciding against *In Cold Blood*, despite his love for Capote's mellifluous prose. Each title slows those destructive tendencies along with his pulse until they are buried once again deep within his flesh. The tremor in his hand is barely noticeable by the time it settles on a leather-bound copy of *For Esmé—with Love and Squalor and Other Stories*. Nothing like a classic American author to keep him company until sunrise and help him take back control of his intellect, rise above the primal instinct she has awoken in him. Or maybe it's this place, or rather nature closing in on him.

He's turning around when he sees it, peeking from under the sofa—the handle of Ellie's bag. Among the deluge of everything that's happened he has forgotten about it. The book slips from his fingers as he crouches down. A couple of tugs and the bag comes out from under its hiding place. Something else comes along with it. His car keys catch the light from the fire and wink at him. Because he didn't find them, he assumed she had them all along, and she didn't deny having them when he confronted her on the stairs, and now he's really trapped, but by his own making. After she had tricked him with the way she danced, he was too eager, chucking his clothes at the sofa. The keys must have fallen from his trouser pocket. He can't do anything about the car now. But there's something else he can do.

Without another second's delay, he upends the bag over

the fire. The contents crash onto the burning logs before the bag drops on top of them. Sheets of paper curl under the lick of flames, the words on them turning black. Ellie's narrative disintegrates into ashes, her precious evidence she won't be able to use against him. The corners of his mouth curl upward at the sight.

But he won't be here for very much longer now. Soon he will be reunited with civilization, with its penal codes and fully functioning cell signals. He pats his pockets at the thought but is surprised to feel them empty. His hands dive in, probing their emptiness further.

"Left it in your coat again?"

His shoulders tense at the sound of her voice, like teeth biting a fork. She stands at the threshold of the living room and the lobby, a smirk on her face and his phone in her hand, her left arm crisscrossed with the silver of duct tape. Staring at his cell and the slender wrist below, he sees it for the first time, the clue that has always been right in front of him and yet eluded him until now, the infinite symbol with the loops not quite connecting at the top—an elongated "W," branding herself with the initial of her vendetta.

She stands in front of him, rebellious, but the bruised skin underneath her eyes betrays an exhaustion brought by lack of sleep and possibly blood loss. Still her haggard appearance doesn't arouse one shred of sympathy in him. On the contrary, one look at her is enough to trigger his rage, burning bright red behind his eyes. She has taken so much from him already; she will not take this away too.

"You'd better give it back," he warns her, jaw clenched so tight his teeth could shatter.

"Or what?"

"I've burned your precious diary and everything else in that bag of yours."

His revelation doesn't change the lines of her face. "Do you think I'd have brought the originals along?"

She has an answer for everything. Every time he feels like he is breaking through she pushes him right back under the surface. This nightmare won't ever stop as long as she's around, it just won't stop. She has taken his phone hostage, but she can't have it. He will hang on to this one piece of himself.

"Give me my phone back." The words roll out like thunder.

"If you want it so much, just come and get it, professor." The belittling way she flings his title at him one more time infuriates him.

Before he can reply, she breaks into a run but instead of heading for the stairs she goes the opposite way. The front door bangs open. Without a thought, he chases after her.

66. Steven

Using the tracks they left earlier, Ellie flits ahead of him toward the edge of the forest, before the darkness stitched between the trees swallows her body. Losing sight of her sends an electric shock down his legs that pushes him harder. He kicks against the snow, increasing his pace.

Inside the sanctuary of skeletal trees and silence, the squeak of her footsteps echoes from all directions.

"Do you give up already?"

He smiles. For once he appreciates her cockiness for giving her away. His animosity and resentment focus into a single point that propels him forward. He hunts her down. The outline of her body emerges from the blackness ahead. Picking up speed, he has almost closed the distance between them when a dark shape detaches itself from the darkness. The collision inevitable, the mass hits his shins, and he loses balance.

"Shit." The word escapes him as he tumbles headfirst into the snow.

Untangling himself, he sits spitting up ice, before spitting out blood. The culprit responsible turns out to be an old slumped armchair. What the hell is it doing here in the middle of the woods? Scrambling to his feet, he kicks the rotten frame, which has already collapsed onto itself, taking out his frustration on this useless forgotten piece of furniture, haunting the woods. He continues until he loses his footing and crashes back on his ass.

"Are you finished yet, old man?" She leans against a

nearby tree within lunging distance, a smile slicing her face that he wants to slap off her.

He springs back up on his feet, and the chase resumes. She darts between trees until she breaks her straight line and bolts to the right. The cold stings his cheeks, and tears well up in his eyes. He doesn't slow down. The hunt invigorates him, he feels more alive and connected than he's ever been before.

They break through the barrier of trees and its claustrophobic darkness into the open space of the beach. She runs ahead of him, her hair flapping into the wind, the light over the ocean diluting the black into a bruised indigo. The sun is advancing and so is he, gaining on her, revenge tingling in his fingertips ready to snatch the flag of her hair. Win the game. Until she lengthens her strides, leaving him behind. Oxygen burns in his chest, blood turning into lead in his legs.

"Want your phone?" she shouts as she turns around and jogs backward.

Before he answers, she lobs his phone like a hand grenade; the perfect arc it makes flying through the air stops him in his tracks. The resounding dunk when it's swallowed by the ocean snaps something in him. A last restraint, the last shard of humanity that he was holding on to, shatters with the impact of his cell hitting the water. She has just drowned his last hope. She'll never stop taking things away from him. This has to end.

"Don't worry, I've saved all the texts and photos."

A low growl rises from his chest, entirely fueled by hatred. He sprints toward her slanted body, gathering speed. Before she turns around, he catches a glimpse of fear on her face. "If and when" drop from his vocabulary: he will catch up to her. He will make her sorry. Her back is a target made of bones that will break under his hands and feet. What she knows will never leave this place.

They have gone full circle, and the outline of the house detaches itself from the part of the sky that still belongs to the night. As they grow near, a shard of light hits the huge windows of the living room and ignites the glass, the inside of the house shrouded behind such a glare he has to squint. The house keeps its secrets, bricks and mortar so much better at keeping confidences than people. Whatever happens within its walls is shielded from the outside, not truly existing. He will end it where she started it all.

67. Steven

Edging closer, he hears her labored breathing, the exertion of her body trying to sustain her frenzied pace. He jumps after her over the porch steps, his arm extended, and for a second his fingertips graze the ends of her hair. Flying through the front door, she swings it at him. He avoids it without slowing down. The sound of the solid oak hitting the frame thunders through the air like a warning shot. She rushes straight up the stairs, climbing them two at a time. Running herself into a corner just for him.

As she steps onto the landing, he lunges at her. His arms close around her legs, and he tackles her to the ground. A whimper follows the thump of her body hitting the carpet and the hardwood beneath. He claws his way up until her warm breath hits his cheek. Hand knotted in her hair, he yanks it down and draws a whimper out of her. The cut on her lip hidden behind a crust is bleeding again. Under his weight and the pain he's inflicting, her body bucks and struggles, but each thrash fails. He lies on top of her as he has done dozens of times before, back when her body moved in rhythm with his, arching to meet him and not get away. As she continues fighting, he feels himself grow hard against her. The sheer horror widening her eyes tells him she feels it too. Behind those eyes all the knowledge she has on him. He could shatter her skull against the hardwood floor and watch all that information seep from her skull and soak the carpet.

"Get off me, you sick bastard." She spits the words at him,

fists against his chest and the bulging eyes of an unhinged woman glaring at him.

"Admit it, you've lost," he shouts.

She pummels his shoulders, slaps the tender spot on his neck, until her nails find his cheek, plowing deep burning furrows. The pain drives his hand across her face, leaving its imprint on her cheek. Before she retaliates, he shackles her hands with his, cuffing her wrists and pinning them to the ground. That close, he smells the rustiness underneath the alcohol and the improvised bandage—dried blood rotting, death already spreading from the wound on her forearm.

"Fuck you." The vulgarity of her words foams at her mouth and reeks of nicotine, her face twisting into an ugly mask. The insult sickens him—how could he have ever been with someone so vulgar? Deceit ran deep in her, but no more. He can see clearly now. Soon he will bury her foul language under the pile of her broken bones. The blood from her cut lip has pooled at the corner of her mouth.

She lifts her head, her face inches from his. "Get off, you...rapist—"

"Stop it."

"I'm going to tell all of them everything about you. How you prey on little girls—"

"Didn't you hear me?" Thighs on either side of her chest, testing the flexibility of her ribs. She replies to the pain with a rebellious scoff.

"How you groom them, so they'll follow you blindly into your bed. Like the—"

Letting go of her wrist, he covers her lies with his hand, her breath clammy against his palm until her teeth sink into his flesh. The pain is immediate and excruciating and maddens him.

"Bitch."

Teaching her who's in charge, his fist hits the wound on her arm. The howl that escapes her throat resembles the cries of a dying animal.

Free from his gag, she heaves before spewing her venom again. "Like the Pied Piper of Hamelin, following you all the way off a cliff—"

"Shut up."

"Like you drove Wendy off a cliff."

"It was an accident!"

His heart drops.

"I knew it. You were there. You pushed her, didn't you? And then you ran like a coward. You killed my best friend. She was just a kid. I'll tell them. I'll tell them all."

"She lost her footing. It was an accident." His voice has lost the edge of confidence it has always had. This is her doing. All of this is her fault.

"I will rent a billboard on fucking Madison Square Garden to let them all know. Imagine your father's shame, the utter disgrace his son will become—"

"Just shut up. Shut up."

Her taunts saturate his ears. Her eyes hold all of his secrets, she'll take them with her wherever she goes. Her hissing. An army of rattlesnakes. It has to stop. He needs to make it stop. Make her stop. That deafening static. A nuisance driving him crazy, killing his ability to think. Until there is nothing left other than the need to shut her up. It pounds in his ears. He kneels astride her, teeth bared, drenched in sweat, his skin on fire. His hands leave her wrists and cup the soft lines of her neck. He looks at them pressing on her throat as if they belong to someone else. She can only blame herself for her own death, she's pushed him to take such drastic actions. She's making him do this.

He sees it all happening in his head. Her lifeless body

weighted with rocks stuffed in her jacket pockets, in the space between her chest and the padded down. Like the early settlers used to toss witches overboard into the bay to stop storms, she'll sink into the depths of the Atlantic Ocean, her hair swaying under the surface like seaweed. Her white face will recede before she disappears from his life and the surface of the earth forever. She'll become one of those statistics on the missing persons database, someone who went out for a walk and never came back. Fish and crabs can feast on her, pluck at her gray flesh and glassy eyes.

Under his weight she frets and scratches his hands, tries to prize them open. Pleas, prayers or insults gargle inside the cave of her mouth. He doesn't care until he catches the shape of a word amid the sludges of syllables. One that he wasn't expecting, one that relaxes his grip on her.

"Police're coming," she stutters in a hoarse tone. Her chest spasms as she props herself on her elbows.

"Bullshit. There's no signal." Her lips move again but her voice is too broken for him to make out what she says. "What?" he asks.

"Cell phone jammer."

With three words, she's unleashed an earthquake ripping through all hopes that this ludicrous shamble was almost over. His hands abandon her neck, his fingers instead knotting into his hair.

"When . . ."

"Called them before I ran outside." She coughs the words as she heaves to take deep breaths in.

"Liar," he screams, hands flying back on her neck, choking her again but without the same conviction.

"If you kill me now, you won't have time to hide my body. You'll be a murderer." The jumbled death sentence she's handing him strains to get past the garrote of his fingers.

She's lying. The desperate lies of a desperate girl. She has to be lying. It's a ploy to scare him into letting her go. He will reclaim his life, pry it from her cold dead hands. She's lying. She must be lying. Like a witch, she reads his mind and shoots him a steely glare. Her bloodshot eyes seem to belong to the devil, entirely green, the blue completely gone.

"Tick, tock, professor... What's it going to be?" Her face gives nothing away. "I'm ready to die." With those words, she tilts her head back, offering him her throat, arms limp by her side. Her life right there, presented to him for the reaping.

Does he believe her? Should he believe her? The rest of his life and his reputation hinges on it. Did he just hear the whisper of a siren, or is fear tricking his mind? He leans forward, the soft cartilage beneath his hands so breakable. The wind hisses, and the noise bends into the wail of a siren again. Sharper. Closer.

He sees Ellie, blood running down her chin from her split lip.

He sees his father's face.

He sees Wendy standing on that cliff, reaching out for him.

He knows. He knows what needs to be done.

68. Ellie

The house will tell them what happened. Everything here tells a story. The truth will set you free, they say. They're wrong.

It begins with the silent heartbeat of blue lights pulsing through the windows, before the outside world invades the space with thuds and footsteps. Through the open front door, cold sneaks in and rushes up the stairs like a nosy neighbor. The house shudders and comes to life.

It spreads with voices, which shatter the silence further. Gradually, a few words rise above the pandemonium of noises—*victim, unresponsive, Jesus Christ*. They belong to a police officer with a Burt Reynolds mustache. A shiny badge reads "Deputy Wilcox"—black letters etched on brass, the O almost scratched into another C. His eyes are full of questions as he tries to take in what happened here. He smells of coffee, the foam of it hemming the bristles of his mustache. Yellow teeth in need of cleaning peek from under his chapped lips.

That is how I survive. Concentrate on the details.

Palming his chin, he takes in a scene rarely witnessed in those quiet parts of the county. A car wreck, maybe, the odd wood-chopping accident. But this? This is what animals do to each other—and in the bowels of the forest, not in some fancy house. What's happened here stains the carpet and the walls with red and reeks. More words—*leave, hospital*—but still missing too many connectors to make sentences and sense of all of this. The weight of a blanket and the scratchy warmth of wool settles on my shoulders. Moving awakes the stench living in the folds of my skin, in the gash on my arm. Words jam in my throat like barbed wire. They don't need them. The house will tell them what happened.

Standing up now, and with Deputy Wilcox's help maneuvering down the stairs. Look at the steps, he says. Look at the steps. On the third step lies a discarded heart on a broken chain. A present to a girl who no longer exists. One of Deputy Wilcox's colleagues collects it before dropping it into a little plastic bag, where the romantic token merely becomes another clue to the gruesome events that unfolded here. Once sealed, the bag joins others, mostly pregnant with what looks like shredded clothing; one of them holds the broken pieces of a mug. Another detail of Steven's violence against me.

On the first floor, more officers dotted around, more eyes asking questions, more chaos. An explosion of camera flashes; the static fuzz from police radios; the smack of latex gloves. The smell is worse down here. A rustiness mixed with something acrid, almost sulfurous. I dry heave but I have nothing left in me. Blood streaks the door frames and walls; the kitchen counter is smeared with it—a narrative staining plaster and wood, written in cast-offs and spatters left to be deciphered. Everywhere the vestiges of Steven's anger toward me.

The house will tell them what happened.

In the living room, the wheelchair is toppled on its side where Steven restrained me when he confronted me about what I'd found out, while the charred remains of my bag smolder in the fireplace.

Ahead, Deputy Wilcox ushers me toward the gaping mouth of the front door. Behind us, the lobby's high walls and ceiling showcase the rope Steven was going to use to kill me once he realized I knew too much.

Standing outside, the sharp bite of cold air stings, and I pull the blanket tighter around my shoulders. Sunlight stains the horizon with pale yellow and orange, leading the way for a new day which might have never existed. No more overbearing clouds stretching across, blue has reclaimed the sky, where seagulls scream at the intruders disturbing the peace and quiet of the coast.

The snow out front is peppered with a trail of blood; at the end of it a gloved hand excavates from its icy tomb the knife Steven used to attack me after I escaped. In the distance, the double doors of the garage yawn open where another officer on his haunches inspects the deep gashes in the front tire—Steven's desperate attempts to keep me trapped and unable to go looking for help.

Everything here tells a story.

Amid the askew police cars, there's an ambulance waiting. Behind its bulky shape and flashing lights, the woods have stopped being an ominous presence: trees have disentangled themselves from the darkness. Everything is different under the light of day. But even if the snow is shimmering now with beauty, beneath it the ground is still dead.

Two paramedics jump from the back of the ambulance and help me inside. The comfort of the heavy blanket is replaced by the fluttering lightness of survival foil. The air around is flavored with the strong smell of the ammonia used to scrub away diseases and death from shiny surfaces. The mattress on the stretcher is thin and squeaks with my every move. They look at me, and all they see is what Steven's done.

"Where to, guys?" asks Deputy Wilcox.

"Mercy General Hospital," replies the medic with blond hair in a low ponytail. He looks too young to be responsible for someone's life.

After the ambulance's doors slam shut, one word hangs in the air, acrid like sulfur from a lit match, one word that doesn't belong in this place.

Mercy.

69. Ellie

My mind first stirs with the whir of engines, so deliriously welcoming I almost burst into tears. Then, sometime after we arrive, the mayhem of hospital noises and the strong, sanitized smell wake me up completely, and thoughts fill my head once again, and with them comes the rest of civilization—an unchoreographed ballet of people filling the space around me. Only two days, and I have forgotten how much noise people make.

I'm undressed by two nurses who carefully fold my clothes inside bags under the supervision of Deputy Wilcox. Unaffected by the expanse of skin only covered by underwear, he photographs my body, every blotch of red and purple, the cut dividing my lower lip, the gash on my arm. His left eyebrow rises, and the mask of immutability slides off only when he notices the piece of paper peeking from the line of my bra. I fish out the picture, paper warm from my skin, and carefully unfold it, the deep groove running through the middle threatening to permanently separate Wendy and me. He examines the image of the two teenagers, their grin and embrace—the evidence of the close relationship trapped forever by chemicals on photosensitive paper.

"Can I keep it? Please?"

Reading on my face that this is not just a trinket, but a rock to which my sanity is tethered, he agrees with a nod. The photo nests back against my breast, before we resume the cataloging of my injuries. He asks me to tilt my head and hold back my hair when he aims the camera at my neck.

His expression shifts again at the purple shadows of fingers extending across it, his mind most likely stitching a thread that connects one injury to the next until the patchwork of a story emerges. Am I still a whole person for him or am I just the sum of my injuries? Next, he scrapes my fingernails, dropping whatever is trapped under them into little plastic bags.

When he's finished, I slip inside the hospital gown held by one of the nurses, an older lady with pinned curls and a worn badge on her chest identifying her as Nurse Chandlers. Her hair is shorter in the picture, and the expression on her face is caught in the tension of that first day at work.

Deputy Wilcox stores the samples he has of me in a protective case. "Is there someone we can call for you?"

My mind goes straight to Connor. The hours he spent listening to me over fries and milkshakes when I visited when I was nineteen and after moving to the city to attend NYU. Connor, whom I still haven't called back since he left me a message three days ago. *Hey cuz, listen, Joao and I've been talking about going to Vermont with some friends for a weekend. Do you want to tag along? You can even bring your mystery man I know nothing about, if you want! Anyway, call me back.* Easygoing Connor, in the Brooklyn apartment he shares with his boyfriend, his life split between his job in publishing, cycling around Prospect Park and friends' parties on rooftops decorated with fairy lights. When I first arrived in the city, he waited for me at La Guardia even though I didn't ask him to—*Welcome wagon*, he said as he relieved me of my bag and handed me a pretzel. What is it with you and food, I laughed. Just the memories of him are enough to melt the frost deep in my marrow. That frost is keeping me numb, it's what's holding me together. If I call him now, he will abandon everything and be here in a matter of hours. He will be there for me, whatever I need. But he doesn't know about Ellie. And right now, Ellie is all that matters.

"No, there's no one," I reply.

My perspective shifts—from the scuffed linoleum to the stippled ceiling tiles. Deputy Wilcox has gone, out of the room, the hospital maybe. The speculum is cold inside me. It burrows deep, looking for the evidence of him. His name is still jammed in the back of my throat and the back of my mind; I can't even say it inside the privacy of my own head—the weight of it might just shatter me. The speculum burrows deeper and nips at me, but a different pain hits me—the hard edge of a dining-room table bruising my diaphragm as he pushes up my dress. My fingers clench the thin mattress, palms tearing the paper cover. I wish I'd asked Nurse Chandlers to stay when she offered.

"I'm sorry, it won't be long now," a disembodied voice offers as a Pavlovian response to the new tension in my body.

I wonder how many times she has said those words to a woman lying here, how many eyes have stared at the exact same ceiling tiles, the left one with a slight chip in the corner, how many hands have ripped the paper covering while shrapnel of memories rips their minds apart, while they try to ignore the piece of metal shoved inside their vagina, another unwanted intrusion but a necessary one. Another pain to go through, hoping that justice will wait on the other side of it. The speculum burrows deeper, and a tear burrows into the hairline at my temple.

The syringe glistens under the artificial light. The needle disappears under the skin of my hand with a pinch.

"What's that?" I rasp. Each word burns my raw throat.

"Something to help with the cold burns."

Sitting on the edge of the examination table I concentrate

359

on the posters about flu vaccinations and the symptoms of shingles taped to the wall. Anything to keep my mind anchored in the present. Anything not to be dragged back. A shiver rockets through my body, leaving a field of goose bumps on my arms in its wake.

"Poor child," says Nurse Chandlers in a Southern drawl, before disappearing behind the pulled curtain, the illusion of privacy between here and the rest of the ward. I guess she is old enough for me to be a child in her eyes.

From behind the accordion of blue fabric, I spy on ghostly conversations, getting reacquainted with the clutter of life.

When she comes back, she has a robe and a pair of wooly socks, folded on a wheelchair. My heart quickens at the sight.

"You've gone so white. You must be freezing. Here you go." She fusses over me, pulling the socks up my feet, easing my arms into the robe's sleeves. All the while my eyes stay fixed on the wheelchair, an overwhelming presence in the center of the space, silently accusing me, a secret only we share, even though I know it's not the one from the house.

Once she's finished dressing me, she brings the chair closer.

"Nurse Chandlers..." I stop, wheezing for some air.

"Please call me Shelley." Her voice is warm like a sunny day out on Bourbon Street. Being close to her warms me up, helps me feel like a human being and not just the shell of one.

"Can't I just walk?"

"Sorry, darling, hospital policy, we can't let you walk until we're sure you're not concussed. See it this way: you get your own private chauffeur." She smiles at me, and I try to return the gesture, but I can feel mine is off.

The first stop takes us to a small cubicle, where a young doctor, with peach fuzz and freckles on his face, cleans and stitches the gash on my arm. Every new face I collect is a bead in a thread distancing me further from the house. Twelve stitches later, Shelley drives me to my next appointment, the X-ray department, where they check that I don't suffer from something called pulmonary edema, then another X-ray, this time of my throat, to rule out soft tissue damage.

A new doctor displays the ghost of me caught on film, illuminating the negative space of my body, as if the darkness of the forest and the last two days had stained my insides in blacks and grays. She stares at the hollow shell of my bones, with the intensity of someone deciphering a secret language, translating the meaning of lines and curves. I wonder how much of my recent history she can read on there.

"Looks all good here." She smiles as if I have won some sort of competition. "No vertebral fracturing, no broken hyoid. Just some swelling and bruising." I don't feel as confident as she does; there are some breaks that don't show up on medical equipment.

Back in the chair again, I'm wheeled to the next stop on this circuit, the next battery of tests. As I sit, spine straight, fear slimes down my back. I don't dare to turn round, worried I will see him push me. In the hallway, we pass Deputy Wilcox, nursing a steaming cup of coffee, his presence a surprise. I thought he had gone back to the station or maybe the house.

"Where are you off to now?" he asks Shelley.

"Taking her for an MRI." She stops next to the plastic chair where he has taken up residence. It looks uncomfortable. Still, I would gladly switch with him.

"My head's fine," I say in a hoarse voice. Of the two, my throat, not my head, is the one hurting like hell.

"You got your head bashed on the floor, darling. We need to make sure there is no concussion or TBI." Her Southern drawl rises on the word "darling."

"TBI?"

"Traumatic brain injury." She smiles. "Nothing to worry about, it's all routine. All routine."

"You ladies gonna be much longer?" the deputy asks before taking a sip from his Styrofoam cup. I didn't know they still made those—it's all cardboard cups in the city.

"Look at her, Joe, she's exhausted. She needs to rest after this." He opens his mouth to reply, but she's not finished. "Your statement can wait. I'll call you the minute she wakes up after she's had a good rest."

The MRI machine is a narrow space, a plastic coffin where I'm asked to lie very still—play dead. The empty room and the low humming of the machine force my mind to wander, thinking of other confined spaces, of dead things, until a thought chills my blood. Is he here? Is he lying in his own confined space, somewhere in the basement of the building? I wonder how many layers of plaster and concrete separate us and how easy it could have been for me to be the one to end up in the sub-level floor of the hospital.

"Please, you need to stay very still," a disembodied voice reminds me. There is no reproach, just a matter-of-fact tone with a metallic edge to it.

How can I explain to them that lying motionless only reminds me how close I've come for the stillness to be permanent; that the heaving chest, the burning lungs and throat are necessary reminders of my existence?

Parked in my chair afterward, I wait for a new doctor to update me on the latest status of my anatomy.

"All good," he confirms, with the excitement of a coach who has been waiting for me at the end of a grueling decathlon of medical tests. "No concussion, but we want to keep you in for observation, just overnight."

This time I don't ask questions. I just accept their decision, unsure what those observations will be or how they will be made but resigned to whatever's coming next. Shelley takes back the command of my wheelchair, pushing me toward my next appointment. A place where they will stick electrodes on me, the gel cold on my skin, connect me to a machine; maybe there will be a physician or two behind a glass window, monitoring jagged lines and beeps from machines translating what's happening inside, turning me into scribbled lines of data.

"This is the observation room?" I ask Shelley as she wheels me into a regular hospital room.

"Of course, darling. What did you expect, that we'd put you in the middle of a room surrounded by medical students?" She laughs while she helps me out of the chair and into the bed. I stay silent, unwilling to admit my exhausted brain actually imagined something even more elaborate than the scenario she's come up with.

Once I'm in bed, she folds the covers over me. "You just rest now. If you need anything you can press the call button, otherwise we'll check on your every few hours."

Before she leaves, she drops two oval pills in the palm of my hand. "What are those?" I ask.

"Something to help you manage your pain. Bottoms up," she adds as she hands me a glass of water. I gladly welcome any chemically induced oblivion, even though the road to a medical Shangri-La involves swallowing a gulp of water that goes down my trachea like a barbed-wire ball which leaves me with a coughing and spluttering fit.

"Are you sure there ain't anybody we can call for you?" Nurse Chandlers asks, pausing in the doorway.

I smile and shake my head. "No, that's OK, Nur—Shelley."

"All right then. Sleep well, darling."

"Shelley?"

"Yes?"

"Do you mind leaving the light on?"

She doesn't ask why, just removes her finger from the switch. "If you need me, push the call button," she says again before she closes the door behind her.

I shimmy into the depth of the cotton sheet until I have completely disappeared. Under the warmth of the heavy blanket and a fresh scent of laundry detergent, the meds kick in. My mind takes me back to the house, thoughts of visiting it again—after all this is finished—bloom in my head. I'm part of it now. My blood lives in the pipes, has seeped through the pile of the carpet and stained the wood below, forever linked to the building. A ghostly presence none of the future guests staying within its walls will know about. Clinging to the idea, I dissolve into nothingness as the adrenaline melts away.

70. Verity

Propped on pillows, I sit in bed while Deputy Wilcox occupies a hospital armchair which looks anything other than comfortable. He balances on the hard, wooden edge, worried that, if he sits back, his ass will sink into the quicksand of the soft cushion. Behind him, a young officer shifts from one foot to the other. They watch my fingers fold and press the piece of paper in my hands, creating shapes where before there were none. It's coming back to me, even though I haven't attempted this particular design in a few years.

Those two uniformed men watch me, and I see the victim I am reflected in their faces, in the pity that pinches their mouths, but I see something else too, the question written on the lines that crease their brows, the one they shouldn't think about, but they can't help themselves—what did she do to provoke him?

"Sorry, we don't have a female officer," Deputy Wilcox explains.

Between us, there's the strong scent of fresh pine and that chemical hospital smell, like chlorine or old people.

"Are you feeling all right?" I'm unsure if it's a general question about my physical health, the official start of our interview, or whether he is referring to the new length of my hair.

After emerging from the last bout of unrestful sleep, I took a labored walk to the bathroom. Under a sputtering yellow light, I met myself in the mirror, this girl with dark circles under her eyes, the cracked lip, wearing the purple choker of his fingers on my throat, a gaunt face framed by limp strands of hair falling over my chest.

Shelley brought me the pair of scissors I asked for. She was reluctant at first—it took me a few seconds to understand why. I told her she could stay and watch if it made her feel better. She did.

"Do you want me to do this for you, darling?"

I shook my head.

One by one I took sections between my fingers and cut just above my shoulders, feeling the weight falling off and pooling on the floor around me. I reinstated the blunt bangs of my teenage years, resuming the life interrupted for the time necessary to avenge Wendy. Once the task was completed, I stared at this new me in the mirror until she became the old me again—Vee sleeping under the skin, now stirring, slipping into the gloves of my hands, stretching and clenching fingers, expanding my lungs, getting reacquainted with her body. I left the bathroom and Ellie in the mirror; the reflection of someone I had to be for a while who wasn't needed anymore.

But I was wrong.

Before Deputy Wilcox can speak another word, a soft knock disturbs the silence. Shelley walks in with two cups of coffee. She settles one on the nightstand and hands the other to the deputy.

"Thanks, Shelley. You're the best." He grins at her, and she rolls her eyes in response before she smiles back. Their inconspicuous moment lowers my gaze, feeling I have been trespassing on an intimate exchange.

Taking the compliment with her, she leaves behind a renewed silence, which settles at the foot of my bed, as if the officers and I need her as some kind of interpreter. I trade the origami for my drink. I wrap my hands around my mug, and the hot porcelain burns my fingertips as I gather the necessary courage to answer the policeman's upcoming questions. My mind wanders back over the last two days, earlier this morning, over the details that populate the tale.

"Did you sleep all right?" Wilcox says in an attempt at small talk.

He gives me a smile which tells me everything will be fine. He'll guide me on this road to recovery and hold my hand when I stumble over a painful moment or detail, he'll stand by me when my own words undo me, he will allow me all the time I need to put myself back together to continue. I see what I look like in his eyes—a frail girl who has lived through a terrible ordeal and hasn't escaped unscathed.

I lie with a nod. Despite the drugs, I hardly slept. Every time my mind sank inside the deep silence of sleep, the same sound brought me back to the surface—it wasn't the one I had prepared myself for, there was no snap of the rope, no tension under the pull of a body. Instead, I heard the crack of bones, an echo from that afternoon when we stumbled on the trapped seagull on the beach, only magnified, the crunch from a body being twisted at an impossible angle, the shock from hitting marble floor fifteen feet below. Even at the end he had to regain some control, shunning the rope I had laid out for him to choose his own death. Every time I close my eyes that noise rings in my head as clear and sharp as the first time I heard it last night.

Back at the house, it had dawned on me then. *It was over.* Over. I exhaled deeply. As the air left my lungs and burned its way through my throat, I realized I had been holding that breath for a long time, since that day at the New York Public Library when his fingers had disappeared under the pleats of a school uniform skirt. I expelled it all. The tension tightly packed inside over the last few days came gushing out. It ran down my face and dampened the collar of my jumper. I made my body small against the wall, my arms wrapped around my chest, tight, fingertips resting on my back, despite the pain in my arm. I disappeared inside my own embrace, even though it was other arms I craved. Feelings and aches poured out in heavy sobs, which cleansed, which swept all the darkness, pushed it out. When Deputy Wilcox had found me, he waited until the crying subsided and my body stopped shaking to tell me that I was OK, that it was all going to be OK. I wanted to tell him I knew, but I couldn't.

"Miss...Miss Masterson, are you all right?" Deputy Wilcox's question and slight edge of panic bring me back to the present. His ass hovers over the cushion on his chair while his younger acolyte stares at me with the eyes of a bewildered animal.

I want to tell them Steven visited me last night, stood by the chair Wilcox is currently sitting in. The sun seeped in between the slats of the blinds, leaving striations of light leading from my bed to him. Someone had switched off the light when I wasn't looking. I stared, but the rhythm of my heart stayed steady. We carry our own ghosts, so he was bound to appear to me at some stage. Arms crossed, he looked at me with sunken eyes, head cocked to the side, until it dawned on me his bent neck and tilted head were the result of his snapped spine protruding at the side below the skin. He didn't scare me. He was like Ellie, a ghost of my past I had to say my goodbye to. He was guilty. Whether it was his words or his hands that pushed Wendy over the cliff that day at Cypress Point didn't matter. He was responsible all the same.

I motion for the deputy to sit back down. Wiping the tears with the back of my hand, I curl my mouth into a smile— the proof I'm fine—before taking a sip of my coffee.

"Miss Masterson?"

"Please, call me Ellie."

I still need her. Because after leaving Ellie on the bathroom floor, I settled back in bed, sipping on a glass of water. My mind wandered past the walls of the hospital, back to the city where my apartment waits to be packed, to the call I will make explaining the situation to the NYU administration and why I have to drop out, take time to heal. I wondered how many newspapers will report the death of Steven Harding, son of renowned author Professor Stewart Harding, and the systematic abuse that went on during most of his teaching career. The truth finally exposed, they will rise. In my mind they all wear her face and her name—Wendy—an army of Lost Girls, the ones who escaped with shattered lives, but still alive, finally telling their stories, each one a layer to bury Steven deeper. The thought spread a new warmth through my body. That's when I heard it, the voices drifting through the open door, background conversation until all too familiar words sliced through my daydreaming.

"Horrific, just horrific. Barely fifteen. Can you believe that? You should have seen her."

"What happened?"

"She can't remember. Intoxicated, possibly drugged. Just waiting on blood test results. Once they'd finished with her, they dumped her on the outside lawn."

"My God." In my mind, the nurse crossed herself in the quick pause that followed.

Steven's gone but nothing's changed. *They* are still around, waiting to sink their hooks into young girls, yanking them out of their childhood, tossing them to the side when *they're* finished, getting away with it.

Ellie isn't done.

"I'm ready," I tell him in a hoarse whisper, the rhythm

and tone of my voice still fractured by the swelling of my vocal cords.

"Maybe we should get a written statement. What do you think, Joe?" It's the first time the younger deputy speaks— his rugged voice at odds with his lanky shape, as if his body is possessed with the ghost of someone who has smoked for forty years.

Every muscle in my shoulders tightens at his suggestion. Before Deputy Wilcox can respond, I shake my head, furiously ignoring the shooting pains in my neck. Now is not the time for a written account, the words need to get out of me, physically. They need to fill the air before they darken pages.

Back in his chair, Deputy Wilcox assesses me and my request, debating, I imagine, whether I'm strong enough. We all wait for his decision.

"In your own words, tell us what happened. Take all the time you need," he adds but I don't need more time. Not any more.

Eyes closed, I take in a deep breath. In my head, I see it all. Lying on the floor of the mezzanine, sirens rising in the distance, air rushing into my lungs, each mouthful burning my throat.

Do you promise? Steven asked. His final words.

My throat was raw, each word a needle jammed into the soft flesh. A simple nod in agreement sealed our deal before he backtracked to the banister, and gravity claimed him.

Do you promise? But three more words come to me.

Nobody but us.

I open my eyes.

"I guess it all started when I found some compromising emails and disturbing pictures on my boyfriend's computer."

*

After today, New York will know my name, my story, but our old house in Monterey offers me a home and anonymity. A place where I can put the pieces of me back together, but which me am I now? Even though the house is empty, someone waits for me there. I can go and visit her, finally tell her it's done. On the bedside table, the origami lotus flower stands in perfect folds. Wendy. Her name pinches my heart. Maybe all of this will make her rest a little better, but it won't for me. Not when there are so many more Stevens around. Same man, just different faces. I know what to look for now, what they like, where to find them, and how to deal with them. When I prepared for Steven I did my research. Men have disguised their crimes under narratives so twisted they are bent out of shape into something else. *She said no but her eyes said yes. She got that black eye walking into a cupboard door. Look what you made me do. She came on to me.* But I can disguise myself too. I can get close, slip into their lives and into their beds, all to spare one more Wendy falling off a cliff.

The coffee tastes bitter. Ellie. Verity. Co-existing out of necessity, and maybe something else. Maybe, after everything, I like having her around.

I take another sip, and smile.

Author's Note

The day #MeToo swept through Twitter is etched on my memory. That day, not one of my female friends didn't have at least one story to share. Their testimonies appeared on my feed; traumatic experiences, often born in isolation, now united by those two words: Me Too. Suddenly, we weren't alone anymore. The solidarity and bravery that day helped me share my story, too.

This novel is partly inspired by my experience, and the experiences of other women who have been victims of sexual assault. Like Wendy, I was flattered by the attention of an older man when I was a teenager. Luckily for me, things didn't go as far, but like Wendy I felt deeply ashamed and, when it was over, was convinced that I had done something wrong or led him on in some way. It took me twenty-five years to tell my mother—not because I was worried she wouldn't believe me, but because I was trapped inside my shame. It was important for me to tell Wendy's story—to remind myself, and other women, that we are not alone, and that it's not our fault.

I couldn't end this novel without sharing a few resources. If you have been affected by the issues raised in this story, you can reach out to the organizations below:

- RAINN (Rape, Abuse & Incest National Network) is the nation's largest anti-sexual violence organization. They operate the National Sexual Assault Hotline

(1-800-656-HOPE), and work in partnership with more than 1,000 local sexual assault service providers across the country: https://www.rainn.org

- The National Sexual Violence Resource Center (NSVRC) has a directory of organizations that lists state and territory sexual assault coalitions, and victim/survivor support organizations: https://www .nsvrc.org/find-help
- RALIANCE partners with a wide range of organizations to improve their cultures and create environments free from sexual harassment, misconduct, and abuse. You can also find a rape crisis center or sexual assault program near you by searching their directory of local programs: https://www .raliance.org/rape-crisis-centers/

If you want to help, you can donate to the above organizations. But more importantly, you can help by creating a safe environment in which women can come forward and report their sexual assault or rape. You can do that by believing women when they tell their stories, and by never blaming victims for their assault. To men asking what they can do to help: don't stay silent. Call out other men you see catcalling women, or who make unsolicited comments which visibly make women uncomfortable. We are all responsible for improving the society we live in.

Acknowledgments

I love book acknowledgments. As an aspiring author I must have written mine in my head over the years about a hundred times, never truly believing that one day I would get to write them for a published book. And here we are.

First of all, these acknowledgments wouldn't exist without my amazing agent, Juliet Mushens. Juliet, you plucked my submission from your slush pile and essentially turned my dream into a reality. Your passion, energy, and support have been incredible and unwavering since the first time we met. I now live by the rule, "if Juliet is not worried, then I'm not worried." Thank you as well for validating my love of leopard print. My thanks as well to Jenny Bent at The Bent Agency for her help and support.

I couldn't be happier for *Nobody But Us* to have found a home at Grand Central Publishing; my biggest gratitude to the entire team who have worked on this book. To my editor, Wes Miller, thank you for your focus and dedication. A cliché maybe, but the devil is in the detail, and you've helped get all those little details right for an authentic US setting—your knowledge of New York and the US education system has proved invaluable too.

To my UK editor, Clio Cornish, you have been a dream to work with. You have understood this book and its characters from day one. Thank you for your help shaping Ellie and Steven's story into what it is today.

I've been lucky that countless people have supported my writing along the way. A special thank you to Philippa East for being a wonderful critique partner over the years: for your insight, enthusiasm, and talking me off the proverbial ledge so many times when doubts crept in. Thank you to Joanna Barnard for your thoughtful critiques and for being so generous with your time. Not forgetting my early readers as well: Anna, Kathryn, and Danielle. Thank you for your feedback and helping shape the early version of this story.

My gratitude to my Ink Academy tutor, Marina Kemp. Thank you for your guidance and support (and thank you for alerting me to my overfondness for zeugmas and making me discover Edward St Aubyn's Patrick Melrose series).

I stand on the shoulders of the women writers who came before me. Their stories showed me female protagonists could be dark and flawed, and still deserved to be the heroine of their own stories—Emily Brontë, Sylvia Plath, Sarah Waters, Emily Dickinson, and especially Gillian Flynn. Thank you for your stories and being a never-ending source of aspiration and inspiration.

I wouldn't be where I am without my mother. Mum, you gave me my first book without any pictures (*Les Malheurs de Sophie* by La Comtesse de Ségur) and ignited my love of reading and storytelling. You have believed I could be a published author since I was eight years old (sorry it took so long). You believed in my writing long before I did.

My gratitude to the wonderful writing community for its support—fellow authors, 2022 debut comrades, and the book bloggers and reviewers. Thank you for your love of books and taking the time to read and comment on mine.

Finally, to the readers, thank you for picking this book, and for those of you who—like me—always read the acknowledgments first, I hope you enjoy the story.

Nobody but Us
03/28/2022